TIME DESERTERS

Until he had met Hunter, Lucas had not been aware of the existence of a temporal underground, a network of deserters from the Temporal Corps. Most of them had chosen to defect to the time periods in which they had deserted, but a few, like Hunter, possessed stolen chronoplates whose tracer functions had been bypassed. These people had achieved the ultimate freedom. All of time was at their beck and call.

Lucas wondered how many people in the past were actually from the future. It was frightening to realize how fragile the time-stream had become!

2 *TIMEWARS*
THE TIMEKEEPER CONSPIRACY

BY
SIMON HAWKE

ACE SCIENCE FICTION BOOKS
NEW YORK

THE TIMEKEEPER CONSPIRACY

An Ace Science Fiction Book / published by arrangement with
the author

PRINTING HISTORY
Ace Original / April 1984

ISBN: 0-441-81136-1

Ace Science Fiction Books are published by
The Berkley Publishing Group,
200 Madison Avenue, New York, New York 10016.
PRINTED IN THE UNITED STATES OF AMERICA

THE
TIMEKEEPER
CONSPIRACY

PROLOGUE ═══════════

Garvin's life was leaking out of him in a dozen different places. He didn't think that it was possible to lose so much blood and still be alive. He knew that he had only moments left to live, probably less.

Lodged beside a nerve behind his right ear was a microcircuit that, when activated, sent out a coded signal to the agency. They would find him by homing in on his implant signal, but they wouldn't be in time. He would be dead in moments, at which point another signal would be sent. It would be the termination signal and it would let them know that agent Richard Garvin, code name: Ferret, had bought the farm.

He had made a mess of it. Garvin had no idea how they had caught on to him. He would never learn how his cover had been blown, but that was of no consequence. He didn't matter anymore. What mattered was that they hadn't finished the job.

They had left him for dead, but he wasn't dead yet. He had to hang on just a little while longer, just long enough to transmit his information. If he could do that, then it wouldn't be in vain. He would have died for something, something that mattered. And he'd be able to get back at them, even from the grave.

He no longer felt any pain. All he felt was a deep and numbing cold. His breath came in burbling gasps and he was shivering, even though it was a warm spring day. Springtime in Paris, he thought. A lovely time to die. He chuckled and started coughing up blood.

He reached behind his left ear, only to discover that that side of his face was nothing but raw meat. So much for the transmitter. The subcutaneous implants were very fragile. They had known just where to cut. They hadn't bothered with his cerebral implant. They knew his fellow agents would never get to him in time. And time was running out. He had to let them know, he had to leave a message.

He dragged himself slowly across the floor, leaving a wide trail of blood behind him. With each movement, more of his intestines tumbled out onto the floor. He didn't bother trying to push them back in. What was the point? It didn't matter. He was a dead man. Nothing mattered except what he had learned.

After what seemed like an eternity, he had dragged himself over to lean against the chalky white wall of the tiny apartment on the Rue de Seine. Time. If only there would be enough time. . . . His vision was blurred. He felt very dizzy.

He had never thought that it would be like this. He had always known that he could die and that his death could be unpleasant. It was something every agent knew and lived with. But he had never thought that the end would be so damned undignified. They would find him vivisected in a puddle on the floor, his entrails torn out as though he had been the victim of an augury. Read my entrails, tell the future. Or, in this case, the past.

He dipped his finger in his own blood. There was a plentiful supply. Please, God, he thought, just let me live a little longer. Just long enough to write my epitaph.

He closed his eyes and took a deep, shuddering breath. It brought on another coughing spasm. Fighting the encroaching blackness, Garvin used every ounce of will and strength that he could muster to keep his finger from shaking. He began to write his last words in his own blood.

Time. In the last analysis, it always came down to time. And Garvin's time had run out. They found him slumped against the wall, his eyes wide open in an unseeing stare.

Outside, it was morning and the birds were singing songs of spring.

1

What goes around, comes around, thought Lucas Priest. Life was turning into a series of repetitive experiences. Floating on a cushion of air, the ground shuttle threaded its way across the plaza that formed the center of the giant atrium that was the Departure Station at Pendleton Base. Lucas bummed a smoke from the driver. He rubbed the cigarette against the side of the pack, igniting it, then breathed in a deep lungful of smoke and leaned back against the padded seat. The administration buildings towered overhead, surrounding the plaza on all sides. Skycabs and cargo ferries filled the air above him as they followed the traffic patterns, barely avoiding the numerous pedestrian crossways that connected the buildings.

They passed groups of soldiers who snapped to attention and saluted as the shuttle went by. Lucas was fairly certain that it wasn't he they were saluting, as much as the staff shuttle. He saw men and women dressed in the silver uniforms of Belt Commandos gathered before banks of vending machines. They were loading up on snacks, cigarettes, and coffee. Soldiers of J.E.B. Stuart's Confederate cavalry conversed in animated tones with Persian Immortals about to clock out to fight under the command of Xerxes. Knights in the armor of Crusaders sat cross-legged on the floor by their equipment, a position that would have been impossible for them had not their armor been constructed out of flexible nysteel, an ad-

vantage the real Crusaders never had. He saw Spartans in
bronze chest armor and red cloaks playing cards with the
black-garbed members of a German Panzer unit. A mixed
group of British redcoats, World War I doughboys, and Japanese samurai compared war stories as they passed a bottle
back and forth and listened to the computer-generated voice
announcing departure codes and grid designations over the
public address system. One Departure Station looked much
like any other and the ride across the plaza reminded Lucas of
Quantico, where it all began.

Things had been different then. He hadn't known what to
expect. He had quit his job at Westerly Antiagathics to enlist
in the Temporal Corps because he had been bored. He had
fallen for the recruiter's pitch and he had joined up with grand
visions of adventure and romance filling him with delightful
anticipation. That first day, that first sight of a Temporal
Departure Station, had been much like this. The only difference was that now his heart wasn't pumping at what seemed
like twice the normal rate and his breath didn't catch at the
sight of soldiers dressed in period, waiting to clock out to their
assignments. It was a familiar sight now. He had been here
before.

He remembered, with a sense of wry amusement, that the
fascination with his new career had been incredibly short-
lived. It had worn off on his very first mission, when he had
learned for the first time in his life what it meant to be afraid.

He had learned the hard way that the past was nowhere near
being as glamorous and romantic as he had supposed. He had
gone on forced marches with Scipio's Roman legions. He had
gone on mounted raids with Attila and his Huns and he
had flown aerial sorties with the "flying circus" of Baron
Manfred von Richthofen. He had seen squalor, disease, death,
and devastation. He had learned that life in the Temporal
Corps was far more violent and primitive than he could ever
have imagined. Far more ephemeral, too. He had lived for
only one thing then—to beat the odds and to survive, to complete his tour of duty and get out. He had, but along the way,
something inside of him had changed.

He had returned to civilian life, to a laboratory job where he
worked in pleasant, sterile, safe surroundings. Nothing had

changed. At least, it had seemed so at first. On the surface, it felt as though he had never left, as though his experiences in the service had been a part of some particularly vivid dream. Yet, it was a dream that wouldn't quite let go. Like the disorientating traces of a nightmare that linger on into the morning, the memories of bygone battles clung to him, leaving their mark. It had not taken him long to discover a hard truth about the soldiers of the time wars. They leave pieces of themselves scattered throughout all of time. They can't go home again.

He had fallen victim to the restlessness, the boredom, the feeling out of place. He had continued fighting deep inside, even though the battles had been left behind. He had become a dog of war, unsuited to a life of domesticity.

He felt uncomfortable with the way civilians reacted when they learned that he was a veteran of the time wars. They wanted to know what it was like, but somehow, he couldn't tell them. He would try, but the answers he gave were never those which they expected. What he tried to tell them, they didn't really want to hear. He was not a soldier anymore, but *they* were still *civilians*.

The decision to re-enlist had not been an easy one to make. It had been like standing on a very high diving board over a pool filled with ice cold water. It was difficult to summon up the courage to dive in, but once he had committed himself, all the tension simply went away. Things had come full circle, only now it felt a little different.

It all felt pleasingly familiar. He had always thought that he hated army life and it came as something of a shock to him when he discovered just how comfortable it felt to be back in.

He had re-enlisted with the rank of captain. The promotion had come as a result of his last assignment, an historical adjustment in 12th-century England. When it was all over, he had vowed that he would never go through anything like that again.

An adjustment was nothing like a standard mission. It wasn't like being infiltrated into the ranks of soldiers of the past, fighting side by side with them to help determine the outcome of a war being fought on paper in the 27th century. In an adjustment, temporal continuity had been disturbed. What Dr. Albrecht Mensinger had referred to as a "ripple" had been set into motion and there was a threat of serious temporal contamination. The timeflow was endangered and the timestream could be split. That, the greatest of all possible temporal disasters, had to be prevented at all costs.

The timestream split, Mensinger's solution to the grandfather paradox, had been the focus of the Temporal SALT talks of 2515, when the treaty that governed the fighting of the time wars had been hammered out and all power given to the extranational Referee Corps, who acted as the managers and final arbiters of all temporal conflicts.

The past was absolute. It had happened, it had been experienced, it could not be changed. Prior to the treaty, it had been believed that the inertia of the timeflow would prevent all but the most limited and insignificant temporal disruptions. Dr. Mensinger had proved otherwise, using the grandfather paradox for his model.

The riddle posed the question of what would happen if a man were to travel back into the past, to a point in time before his grandfather procreated a son. If that time traveler then killed his own grandfather, then his father would not be born, which meant that he would not be born. Hence, the grandfather paradox. If the time traveler had never been born, then how could he have traveled back through time to kill his grandfather?

Mensinger had shown how the inertia of the timeflow would compensate for such a paradox. At the instant of the grandfather's demise, the timestream would be split, creating two timelines running parallel to one another. In one timeline, the absolute past of the time traveler would be preserved. In the other, his action would be taken into account. Since there had to be an absolute past for the time traveler in which he had not yet interfered with the continuity of time, he would find himself in that second timeline, which he had created by his action.

The split would result in a universal duplication of matter. Everything that had existed in the past, prior to the split, would now exist in that second timeline, as well. Events in that timeline would proceed, affected by the action taken by the time traveler. Mensinger had stated that it might be possible to deal with a split timestream by sending someone back into the past to a point in time prior to the split. Then, theoretically, the time traveler could be prevented from murdering his grandfather. However, in the event of such a split, the split would have had to have occurred before it could be prevented from occurring. Anyone going back in time to prevent the time traveler from murdering his grandfather could be coming from a future in which that grandfather had already been murdered by his grandson.

Mensinger had discovered, to his chagrin, that split time-lines would eventually rejoin. If the timelines had already rejoined at the point that those going back into the past to prevent the murder of the grandfather departed, then their actions in preventing the split would not, in fact, be preventative. Rather, they would be in the nature of *changing* something which had already occurred *before* it occurred. This raised the possibility of yet another split. If not, then it meant the eradication of an entire timeline, which raised equally frightening possibilities. It would mean the genocide of everyone who existed in that timeline created by the murder of the grandfather. Not only would this be mass murder on an un-imaginable scale, it would also mean dire consequences for the future, the events of which could have been dictated by actions taken in that second timeline.

Mensinger had been awarded the coveted Benford Prize for his research, but he had frightened himself so badly that he had discontinued his experiments. He had called for an immediate cessation of temporal warfare and for the strictest moni-toring of time travel. He claimed that the dubious advantages of waging war within the conflicts of the past in order to spare the present from the grim realities of warfare were far out-weighed by the dangers inherent in the system. No one had dis-agreed with him, yet the time wars continued. In order for temporal warfare to become a thing of the past, someone would have to stop it *first*. And not one nation had been will-ing to refrain from time travel out of fear that other nations would continue the practice, using time as a weapon against them.

The adjustment to which Lucas Priest had been assigned had represented the closest potential for a timestream split in the history of the time wars. The mission had been successfully completed and the continuity of time had been preserved, but it had cost the lives of half of Priest's unit. Only Lucas Priest and Finn Delaney had returned alive, and not even they would have survived had it not been for the intervention of a Temporal Corps deserter by the name of Reese Hunter.

Lucas had often thought about Reese Hunter since then. Until he had met Hunter, he had not been aware of the existence of a temporal underground, a loosely organized network of deserters from the Temporal Corps. These were men and women whose cerebral implants had either been damaged or removed, so that they could not be traced. Most of them had chosen to defect to the time periods in which they had deserted, but a few, like Hunter, possessed stolen chronoplates whose tracer functions had been bypassed. These people had achieved the ultimate in freedom. All of time was at their beck and call.

There was but one limitation placed upon the existence of the members of the underground. A split or even a minor disruption in the timeflow could affect their very existence, so in that respect, even though they were deserters, they were still bound by the General Orders that defined what actions a soldier of the Temporal Corps could take in Minus Time.

Lucas often wondered how many people in the past were actually people from the future. It was frightening to realize just how delicate and fragile the timestream had become. If the ordinary citizen had any idea how precarious the balance was and how easily it could be tipped, he would become a raving paranoid. It was within this system that Lucas had to function. It was to this system that he had returned, by choice.

It made him wonder about his own stability. It also made him wonder if there had really been a choice for him at all.

They had, predictably, assigned him to the Time Commandos as a result of that last mission. His commission was in Major Forrester's First Division, an elite unit assembled for the express purpose of dealing with threats to temporal continuity. Being an officer in the First Division entitled him to certain perks, such as free transportation anywhere in Plus Time and luxurious billeting in the bachelor officer's quarters at TAC-HQ. But hand in hand with special privileges went special risks. Though he was in a higher pay scale now, the

odds of his not living to collect his pay had gone up corres-
pondingly. Standard missions had scared him half to death
before and now his assignments would almost certainly all be
adjustments. It was a far more lethal proposition now.

"So how come I'm not shaking like a leaf?" Lucas mumbled.

"Sir?" The driver turned around briefly.

"Nothing, Corporal. Just thinking out loud." Lucas finished his cigarette and threw the butt away. Leaning back
against the seat again, he sighed and closed his eyes. Oh, well,
he thought, at least I won't be bored.

The shuttle dropped him off in front of the headquarters
building of the Temporal Army Command. As he rode the lift
tube up to TAC-HQ, he watched the bustle of activity in the
plaza far below. He carried no luggage, nothing in the way of
personal possessions. The few material possessions he had ac-
cumulated during his brief return to civilian life had all been
left behind in his conapt, a bequest to some future tenant.
From now on, his life would once again consist of necessities
picked up in the PX, issued field kits, and following orders.
Paradoxically, he felt marvelously free.

It felt strange to be saluted in the corridors. As a noncom,
Lucas had never insisted on military protocol, or as most
soldiers called it, "mickey mouse." It was an age-old expression and no one seemed to know where it had come from.
Lucas had once queried the data banks on it, only to discover
that the information was classified.

The First Division lounge was a small bar and it was almost
empty, so Lucas spotted Delaney at once. He was sitting all
alone at a table by a window, hunched over his drink. He had
lost some weight and the thick red hair had been shaved, but
as Lucas approached the table, he saw that at least one thing
hadn't changed. Delaney still could not hold onto a promotion.

"Well, that commission didn't last long, did it?" Lucas
said, eying Finn's armband, emblazoned with the single chev-
ron of a Pfc.

"Priest! Good God!"

Lucas grinned. "That's *Captain* Priest to you, Mister."

Delaney got to his feet and they shook hands warmly, then

hugged, clapping each other on the back. Finn held him at arm's length, his beefy hands squeezing Lucas's biceps.

"You look good, kid," he said. "But I thought you'd mustered out."

"I did. I re-enlisted."

"Whatever happened to that burning desire for the easy civilian life?" said Finn.

Lucas shrugged. "It burned out, I guess."

Finn chuckled. "I might've known you'd screw up on the outside."

"At least *I've* managed to hang onto my bars," said Lucas, glancing at the silver insignia on his armband. "You seem to have misplaced yours."

"Hell, you may be an officer now," said Finn, "but you'll always be a grunt at heart. That's how it is when you come up the hard way. I'm damned glad to see you, Lucas. Welcome back."

"I'm glad to see you, too, Finn. What're you drinking?"

"What else?"

"Irish whiskey? Good, I'm buying. I see you've already got a sizable head start. Look, I'm not due to report in until 0600. If you've got nothing better to do than sit and drink, what say we have a few and then go out on the town?"

Finn grimaced. "I'd love to, kid, but I can't. I'm under house arrest."

"*What?* What for?"

"Striking a superior officer," said Finn.

"*Again?* How many times does that make, four?"

"Six," said Finn, wryly. "The ref made a point of reminding me."

"They brought you up before a referee for *that*?" said Lucas. "Who'd you hit, a general?"

"A light colonel," said Finn.

"I'm almost afraid to ask, but why?"

"Because he was a pompous military asshole, that's why," said Finn. "I had my blouse unbuttoned in the officer's club. And this runt of an administration desk jockey starts chewing me out about it. I told him to fuck off, so he sticks his face about two inches from my nose and starts screaming, spraying me with spit. So I just popped him one."

"And they dragged you up before a referee?"

"Well, no. Not exactly. That happened after the fracas with the M.P.s."

"*What* fracas?"

"Oh, you know, the standard bullshit. Resisting arrest, direct disobedience to a specific order, striking officers in the performance of their duty, damaging government property, and a few other things that they tacked on that I can't remember."

"Oh."

"Yeah. So I'm confined to quarters until further notice. The old man's been nice enough to give me some slack there, which is why I'm here, but I can't so much as go near the lift tubes. I've been cooling my heels for the better part of a week, waiting for the review board to meet. Been spending most of my time right here in the lounge, trying to drink up my back pay. It's kind of funny, actually. Remember the old days, when we scarcely had a moment to ourselves between assignments? Now that we're here in this 'elite' unit, it's nothing but hurry up and wait."

"You said the ref put you down for a review board," Lucas said. "What was the ref's recommendation?"

Finn grunted. "She was a real hard-assed bitch. Read me the riot act about all the 'previous irregularities' in my record. I think her exact words were, 'Perhaps you'd be better off in a nontemporal unit. Someplace where your flamboyant tendencies won't be quite so much of a disruptive influence.' You know what that means, don't you?"

"The Belt Command?"

"I'll lay you eight to one," said Finn. "If I could get my hands on a plate, so help me, I'd skip out to the underground."

"Not so loud, friend," Lucas said. "Somebody might hear you."

"Who gives a shit? I don't see how I could possibly be in any deeper than I am now."

"You can *always* get yourself in deeper," Lucas said. "It's the getting out that's not so easy. Maybe something can be done."

"Like what?"

"I don't know. But at least they haven't reassigned you yet."

Finn scratched his head. "Hell. I had to go and hit that asshole. They've probably fixed his jaw by now and he's back pushing papers, while I'm going to get stuck out in the Asteroid Belt, keeping those crazy miners from killing each other. You know, I might've expected just about anything, but somehow I never thought I'd wind up as a policeman."

He looked out through the giant window that was the outside wall of the First Division lounge. It was dark outside and all the buildings were lit up, bathing the plaza far below in a garish glow. The skycabs threading through the maze of buildings made the night a sea of red and amber running lights. The window shut out all the noise, rendering the scene outside into a silent ballet of light and steel.

"Doesn't look real somehow, does it?" Finn said as he continued gazing out the window. "I really hate it here, you know that? I was born into this time and yet I don't belong to it."

Lucas smiled. "You're a romantic, Finn."

Finn snorted. "I'm a soldier, kid, that's all."

"Look, nothing's settled yet, right? The board still makes the final disposition."

"When's the last time you heard of a review board going against a ref's recommendation?" Finn said.

"There's always a first time."

"Don't hold your breath."

"Well, if they send you out to the Belt, I'll go along and keep you company. I can put in for a transfer."

"Don't be an ass."

"Why not? How bad can it be? The duty's less hazardous and it would sure beat hell out of the lab job I left behind to re-enlist. Besides, we go back a long way together. All the way to 1194, to be exact."

Finn smiled, recalling the adjustment in 12th-century England. He nodded. "Yeah, that was a hell of a mission, wasn't it? We almost didn't make it back."

"We did make it back, though," Lucas said. "And we were in a worse fix than you're in now."

"Maybe. Hooker never made it back, though. And Johnson bought it, too." He tossed back his whiskey. "Hell, I must be getting old. I'm turning into a maudlin drunk.''

Lucas pushed back his chair and stood up. Finn glanced at him, then turned to see Major Forrester approaching their table. He wasn't required to stand to attention in the presence of a superior officer in the lounge, but he made a determined effort, anyway. He was slightly more than halfway out of his chair when Forrester said, "At ease, gentlemen. As you were.''

Lucas sat back down.

"Sorry, sir,'' said Finn. "I gave it my best shot, but I can't seem to feel my legs too good.''

"I've got half a mind to cut 'em off for you, Delaney," Forrester said.

The old man hadn't changed. Antiagathic drugs made it difficult to accurately guess a person's age, but Forrester looked as old as Methuselah. Even his wrinkles had wrinkles. Yet Forrester stood ramrod straight and he was in better shape than most men under his command who were one-sixth his age. He had been their training officer in the field and Lucas knew only too well just how "old" the old man really was. He glanced at Lucas.

"You just get in, Priest?''

"Only just, sir. I was going to report to you in the morning.''

Forrester nodded. "I knew you'd be back. There's nothing on the outside for a soldier." He sat down and ordered a drink. Both Finn and Lucas were glad that they had already started on their Irish whiskey. It meant that they had an excuse not to join the old man in his favorite libation. For some unfathomable reason, Forrester had picked up a taste for Red Eye. Of all the swill that he had downed during his temporal travels, Lucas hated that old west rotgut the most. Those oldtime gunfighters either had iron constitutions or a deathwish. The stuff could make a man go blind.

"I hope you haven't gone soft on me, Priest," said Forrester. "I just got a hot one dumped into my lap and I need to put a team together in a hurry, so I hope you haven't lost your edge.''

"I'm ready, sir,'' said Lucas. "But what about Delaney? He's filled me in on the situation and if you don't mind my saying so, sending someone with his experience to the Belt would be a waste.''

"Thanks, kid," said Delaney, "but you don't have to—"

"I agree with you," said Forrester. Finn's eyes widened in surprise. "He's insubordinate, but he's a hell of a good soldier."

"Thank you, sir," said Finn, taken aback by the compliment.

"Don't thank me, Mister. I'm just stating a simple fact. You're a good man in the field, but when you're between assignments, you've got the emotional stability of a ten-year-old. I'm all too well acquainted with your record. Well, you're under my command now and I'll only tolerate so much before *I* lose my temper. You've got a yardbird's temperament, Delaney, and if you get back from this mission, I'll beat it out of you if I have to."

Finn stared at him. "You mean—"

"I mean you've got a temporary reprieve," said Forrester. "You two have pulled off tough ones in the past. I don't like to break up a good team. You'll still have to get past that review board, assuming you'll make it back, but I've been talking to the officers who will be sitting on that board and I've been given to understand that if you do well on this one, they'll take that fact into consideration. So it's up to you to pull your own fat out of the fire. But if you screw up on me again, I'll personally drag your ass down to a plate and clock you out to the Paleolithic Age. You should fit right in. You'll be able to brawl to heart's content with all the other Neanderthals."

"You've made your point, sir," said Delaney. "And thanks."

"Just get the job done, Delaney. That'll be thanks enough for me."

"Any idea what it is, sir?" Lucas said.

"None whatsoever," Forrester said. "But this one's got full priority. I can't say that I like the arrangements, though. You'll be loaned out to the agency for this one."

"The TIA?" said Lucas. "That's a bit unusual, isn't it, sir? They don't normally use outsiders."

"No, they don't," said Forrester. "That's why I know that

it's a hot one. If Temporal Intelligence figures they need help, it's got to be a bad one."

"I'm not crazy about working under some spook," said Finn. "Those guys are a bunch of psychos, if you ask me."

"I didn't ask you," said Forrester. "And for your information, you've got those psychos to thank for saving your bacon. They specifically requested the team that pulled off the 1194 adjustment. Or what's left of it, anyway. And that's you two."

"I suppose we should be flattered," Finn said. He raised his glass and toasted Lucas. "Welcome back to active duty, kid. Looks like you've got perfect timing."

"While we're on that subject," Forrester said, "I wouldn't make it a late one if I were you. The mission briefing is at 0700, so get some rest. You're clocking out tomorrow." He pushed his chair back and stood up. "Enjoy your drinks, gentlemen."

Lucas grimaced. "Hey, Finn," he said, "what was that you said about 'hurry up and wait'?"

Delaney poured himself another shot. "I don't know," he said. "What was it you said about 'You can always get in deeper'?"

Lucas tilted his glass toward Finn. "Cheers."

Finn raised his own glass. "Confusion to the French."

2 ─────────────────────

The briefing took place in a secured area on the sixty-second
level of the TAC-HQ building. Normally, this was a floor occupied by the administrative personnel working directly under
the local office of the Referee Corps, but this morning they
had all been assigned to other office space, on other floors.
There was no one allowed on the sixty-second level who had
not been cleared and checked through by the TIA. They had
taken over the floor the previous night and even while Finn
and Lucas sat drinking in the lounge, agents had been securing
the area, failsafing it against surveillance.

Finn and Lucas walked together down the empty corridor,
having been checked through by the agents at the lift tube.

"These people give me the creeps," said Finn.

"You might as well get used to it," said Lucas. "This is
going to be their ballgame."

"Oh, I'll get used to it," said Finn, "but I won't like it."

They came to the briefing room and were checked through
again, their papers verified and their retinal patterns scanned
for positive identification.

"Bunch of paranoid assholes," mumbled Finn.

Forrester was waiting for them in the briefing room, along
with a referee, one other man, and a woman seated at a desk
terminal.

"Gentlemen, please be seated," said the referee. He waited

until they had taken chairs and until one of the agents outside
brought them coffee.

"That was thoughtful," said Lucas.

"I'll wait until you taste it first," said Finn.

"All right," said the referee. "Let's begin, shall we?"

"Sir?" said Lucas.

"Captain?"

"Aren't we missing some people? Like, the rest of the
team?"

"No, Captain, we're not."

"You mean, we're it?"

"Not exactly, Captain. I don't know how much Major Forrester told you, but this is a TIA affair. You'll be on loan to
the agency for the duration. We have an adjustment on our
hands, or a potential one, at any rate. It's a unique situation,
one in which the functions of the TIA and those of the corps
overlap. Frankly, they're more qualified to handle this one,
but as the case could develop into an adjustment, they've requested commandos to supplement their effort. Your role in
this mission will be defined as you go along, but it will be
defined by the agency. Therefore, I am turning this briefing
over to Mr. Darrow, of the TIA."

The ref turned to the agency man and nodded. Darrow was
a slender man whose hair was graying. He was dressed in a
nondescript clingsuit. He was of average height and average
weight. A man who would not stand out in a crowd.

"I'll bet it's not even his real name," said Finn, softly.

"No, it isn't," said the man called Darrow. He stretched his
lips into a mirthless smile. "I have excellent hearing, Mr.
Delaney. And there's nothing wrong with your coffee, by the
way. You can drink it safely. If you have any other pertinent
comments, I'd like to hear them now, so we may proceed."

Finn cleared his throat uneasily and shook his head. Lucas
grinned.

"Very well, then," Darrow said. "Are you gentlemen
familiar with a group calling itself the Timekeepers?"

"Terrorist organization," said Lucas.

"Correct, Captain. Specifically, they are the terrorist fac-
tion of the Temporal Preservation League."

"Mensinger's group?" Finn frowned. "I had no idea they were in any way connected."

"Supposedly, they're not," said Darrow. "The league has formally disassociated itself from the Timekeepers, condemning their actions and branding them fanatics. A case of the pot calling the kettle black, but be that as it may. We believe that the league is still funneling funds and providing other means of support to the Timekeepers."

"I can't see that as being consistent with Mensinger's aims," said Finn.

"Yes, well, he's dead, isn't he?" said Darrow. "And politics, especially the politics of fanaticism, makes for strange bedfellows. But not so strange, perhaps. The league functions openly, lobbying and agitating, all perfectly legal and aboveboard. The Timekeepers prefer a rather more extreme means of persuasion, but their goals are still the same. Cessation of temporal warfare and the cessation of time travel. That last is a somewhat more extreme position than the late Dr. Mensinger's, but it's still roughly consistent with his ideas, wouldn't you say, Mr. Delaney? You're the expert."

"All right, so you know I studied Mensinger's research," said Finn. "You probably also know when I spoke out of turn as a kid and when I wiped my ass for the first time. Mensinger was still far from a fanatic. Get to the point."

"Delaney, shut your mouth!" said Forrester.

"That's quite all right, Major," Darrow said. "I'm well aware of the fact that Private Delaney has a rather low opinion of the agency. That's of no consequence, unless it were to interfere with his performance on this mission."

"It won't," said Finn.

"Yes, I know," said Darrow, giving him his mirthless smile. "Your record is particularly impressive. I'm not especially interested in your disciplinary problems. Some of our finest operatives have spent time in military prisons, a singular distinction which you have been spared. So far. But you wanted me to get to the point.

"We had succeeded in infiltrating the league some years ago. However, it wasn't until recently that we were able to infiltrate the Timekeepers. They've been escalating their terrorist campaigns lately and we had a feeling that they were building up to something big. In point of fact, we underestimated them.

"They're more clever than we thought. They managed to penetrate our agent's cover and eliminate him. However, he managed to leave behind a message. He didn't live long enough to complete it, unfortunately. Pity. As a result, we don't know the full extent of their plans. What we do know doesn't make us very happy.

"Our agent had reported earlier that the Timekeepers had made contact with someone in the underground. One of your old people gone bad. The logical assumption was that, since they made this contact in Plus Time, this deserter was obviously one of those having access to a stolen chronoplate." He glanced at the referee briefly. "It's bothersome to us how those things have a habit of walking away from time to time. At any rate, we assumed that the connection had been made in order to allow them to escape to Minus Time to avoid detection following their terrorist acts, but they evidently have something much more ambitious in mind.

"Terrorists are not the most logical of people. They see their goal as being to tear down an established system and they often don't think much past that point. To date, their activities have been limited to the more traditional methods. Bombing, kidnapping, assassination, etc. They're especially fond of taking hostages to use as leverage for their demands. Well, this time, they've outdone themselves. They've taken time itself hostage.

"They now have a chronoplate in their possession and they're using it to blackmail the Referee Corps. Their demands are that the apparatus for fighting the time wars be dismantled, that the Referee and Observer Corps be disbanded, along with our agency, and that time travel cease. Otherwise, they will create a timestream split."

"They're bluffing," said Delaney. "The threat of a timestream split is the sole reason why the league came into being. What you're saying is that they're threatening to create the very thing that their whole aim is to prevent!"

"Mr. Delaney, if there's one thing that we've learned in our efforts to break the Timekeepers, it's that they never bluff. I told you, they're fanatics. Fanatics are not rational human beings. They have no reason to bluff; they're holding a hell of a hand. Look at your history. There have been terrorist organizations in the past who have had peace as their goal, and yet they didn't hesitate to use violence in its pursuit. There is no logic to terrorism, there's only the very unpleasant reality of its existence."

"Jesus, it's just like the last time," Finn said. "It's going to be hell trying to stop someone with a chronoplate."

"Not necessarily," said Darrow. "Remember, they don't know that our agent had a chance to communicate their plans to us. They will be proceeding on the assumption that we won't know where they'll be in time nor what they'll try to do to effect the split in the event we refuse to meet their demands. And, obviously, meeting their demands is unthinkable. Well, we don't know exactly what they're going to do or how they'll do it, but we do know where they'll be. And unless something occurs to change their plans at the last minute, we've got a chance to stop them.

"We know that they have selected as their operating time the month of April in the year 1625. We know that they'll be operating out of Paris, France. And we know that was a particularly volatile time period. Can we have a brief readout on that, please?"

The woman seated at the desk terminal began to speak in a monotone.

"France in the period 1610 to 1643, reign of King Louis XIII, regency of his mother, Marie de' Medici, 1573 to 1642. The king was declared of age in the year 1614, the year of the Summons of the States-General. The queen mother was banished to Blois in the year 1617, with the king under the influence of the Duke of Luynes. 1619, Armand Jean du Plessis, Cardinal-Duke of Richelieu, mediated a treaty between the queen mother and the Duke of Luynes. Civil war. Marie de' Medici and Richelieu in control following death of Luynes in 1621. 1624 to 1642, administration of Cardinal Richelieu, who became the man behind the throne in France. 1625, the Huguenot Revolt under the Dukes of Rohan and Soubise. Siege of La Rochelle in 1627 to 1628. England dispatched three fleets to the aid of the Huguenots, but the city sur-

rendered on October 28, 1628 after a fourteen-month-long
resistance. War in Italy with Spain, Richelieu in command of
army. Treaty of Cherasco in 1631, beginning of French participation in the Thirty Years' War. Foundation of the
Académie Française in—''

"Thank you," Darrow said, "that will do. As you can see,
gentlemen, it was a violent time, full of intrigues, conspiracies,
wars, and alliances. They couldn't have picked a better milieu
within which to function. Nor, we believe, could they have
picked a more difficult time period in which to effect an adjustment, if it came to that."

"So you believe their target to be Richelieu?" said Lucas.

"We don't know for certain, Captain. Our agent died
before he could complete his message. But we're assuming
that Cardinal Richelieu will be involved, either directly or in-
directly. He was without a doubt the most influential man in
France at the time and he's a pivotal character in history.
However, our research department has brought out yet another factor which we find extremely significant.

"The month of April in 1625 was when a young man named
D'Artagnan arrived in Paris."

The last time she had been in France had been almost five hundred years earlier. Her name had not been Andre de la Croix
then. It was not her real name, but her real name no longer
mattered to her. That had been another time, another life.

She had not belonged in 12th-century England any more
than she belonged in 17th-century France. She had been born
in the western Pyrenees, Basque country, but she often felt
that she did not belong in any time or place at all. The feeling
of being different, of not fitting in, went back almost as far as
she could remember.

It had started when her parents died, leaving her to take care
of her little brother. She had been just a child herself. It had
not taken her very long at all to find out just how vulnerable a
young girl could be, so she had learned to act the part of a
young boy. That deception had constituted the first major
change in her young life.

She had continued the masquerade into adulthood, having

learned that being a man offered far greater opportunities than being a woman. Her breasts were small and easily, if uncomfortably, concealed and the hard life she had led as a "young boy" had given her a body that was lean and strong. After years spent as itinerant thieves and beggars, she and her brother had been taken in as squires by an aging knight-errant whose brain had been befuddled by one too many injuries. The old knight had never learned her secret and he had trained her in the martial arts of chivalry. That had been the second major change in her life.

She had known that living free in a time when freedom was a commodity in scarce supply meant becoming strong and self-reliant. She worked hard, developing her body into an efficient fighting machine. She was taller than most women of her time, broad-shouldered, and long of limb. Her drive and physical characteristics combined to give her a body and a degree of fitness that would be unknown to women for several hundred years. She became the physical equal of most men in strength and the superior of most in endurance and reflexes. After the death of her mentor, she took her own brother as her squire and became a mercenary knight, a "free companion" with the fictitious name of Andre de la Croix. She chose for her device a fleury cross of white on red. Guarding her secret with her life, for that was what exposure as a woman would have cost her, she entered into the service of Prince John of Anjou. Shortly thereafter, she met a man she took to be a sorcerer and he had brought her to the third and greatest change in her young life.

His name was Reese Hunter and he, too, did not fit into his own time. On the day she met him, his time would not yet come for another fourteen hundred years. He was a deserter from the Temporal Corps and he possessed a device he called a chronoplate, a machine for traveling through time.

He had told her that he was not a sorcerer, yet what he called "science" seemed nothing less than magic. Though he had learned her secret, he was the only man she had ever met who did not treat women as inferiors, as possessions. He had told her that there would come a time when she would not have to resort to her deception to live life on her terms. That

time would not come for many hundreds of years, but he
could take her there. He had told her of the life he led, the
times and places he had been to, and she had been both awed
and frightened. She would not have believed him, would have
thought him mad, had he not demonstrated the power of his
science. He said that he saw in her a kindred spirit, a person
out of time. He had offered her an equal partnership, on her
own terms.

She had lost her brother to a traitor's sword and Hunter had
helped her to avenge his death. Once that was done, there had
no longer been a reason for her to remain in England or in the
year 1194. She had joined Hunter and left England and her
time behind. She became part of the underground.

Antoinette de la Croix was not her real name, either. She
felt less comfortable with it than with her masculine alias.
They had only just arrived in the 17th century and it had taken
Hunter some time to purchase what he called "necessities."
These included their clothes, their horses, their carriage, and
the services of liveried footmen. They were on their way to
Paris and they had stopped for the night at a small roadhouse.

Andre had undressed to her undergarments. She didn't like
them, but at least they were more comfortable worn alone
than with her outer clothing. The silks and ruffles, the lace
and the dainty shoes were all impractical and, worse, uncomfortable. She recalled that armor had never been comfortable to wear, but at least it had a function. She could see
no purpose to her ornate apparel and she had remarked to
Hunter that in this time, at least, the role of women seemed
not to have changed at all. They were still dressed as dolls for
men to play with, only now they had to dress up more. She
had gone along with the clothing, but she had refused to have
her hair "arranged." Instead, she had worn a wig that Hunter
had bought for her, a wig of tight blonde curls whose color
matched her own somewhat shorter, straighter hair. She had
ripped it off upon entering their rooms and now she paced
back and forth like a caged animal, scratching her head ir-
ritably. She much preferred the apparel of the men, though
even that seemed senselessly foppish to her.

She thought that Hunter looked amusing in his scarlet
doublet, ornately worked baldrick, and long cloak of dark

burgundy velvet. Somehow, she thought he looked more natural in the magician's robe he had been wearing when they met, back in Sherwood Forest. His high boots seemed practical for horseback riding, but the lace collar, cuffs and boot tops seemed out of place, as did the wide black sash he wore around his waist. What puzzled her the most was Hunter's rapier.

He had laid it down upon the bed when they came into the room and now she picked it up, hefting it experimentally.

"*This* is a sword?" she said, dubiously. She had been curious about it all that day, but she had not wanted to overburden Hunter with too many questions.

"It's called a rapier," Hunter said, "and yes, it is a sword."

She swung it once or twice, holding it awkwardly, as though uncertain of its sturdiness.

"There is no weight to it," she said. "And the blade is far too narrow. It would never penetrate armor and a single stroke with a good sword would break it in an instant." She threw it back down onto the bed disdainfully.

Hunter picked it up. "To begin with, it isn't meant for use against an armored knight. And no one uses broadswords here. In this period, things are done a little differently. I suppose you'd say that this was a more genteel weapon."

He made a few passes with the rapier, showing her the wrist action, a beat and riposte against an imaginary opponent, and a lunge.

"It's used primarily for thrusting, but you can also slash," said Hunter. "It's called fencing."

She frowned. "So is the enclosure used to keep in goats. I see no connection."

"There isn't one."

"So why is it called fencing?"

"I don't *know* why it's called fencing. It just is, that's all."

"It's foolish. These clothes are foolish. This is a foolish time. I do not like it. This is nothing like what you told me."

"Give it a chance, Andre. You've only been here for one day."

"I see no reason why we have to wear these foolish clothes. I saw other people on the road who did not dress this way."

"They were peasants," Hunter said. "This is how people

who are reasonably well off dress in this time period. We're going to have to stay here for a while, until I can contact my friend in the underground. I explained all that to you. If we're going to travel to the time I spoke of, you're going to need an implant and not just any implant, but one that can't be traced. It's the only way for you to learn things that would otherwise take you a lifetime of education. You're going to need that knowledge in order to survive. It's a very complicated procedure."

"Why can we not go directly to the time you came from to get this implant?"

"Because it would be too dangerous. Besides, it has to be surgically implanted and—"

"It has to be what?"

"Implanted. The implant must be implanted."

"I do not understand. I thought it was a device."

"It *is* a device."

"Then what does 'implanted' mean?"

"It's an action. You must implant an implant."

"How can it be a device and an action at the same time? And what does this word *surgically* mean?"

"It's too difficult to explain right now," said Hunter. He knew only too well how her 12th-century mind would react to the idea of minor brain surgery. "What matters is that I have to get in touch with a certain person who has the skills to accomplish this and that person chooses to reside in Paris, in this time period. Our mission will go easier for us if we assume the character of people of a certain social class."

"Why can I not wear man's clothing?" she said. "It certainly appears to be more comfortable than this dress and these absurd undergarments."

"It probably is," said Hunter, "but that's not the point. The point is that you're a woman and you've never had a chance to learn to act like one. You never know, the knack might come in handy someday."

"I see no advantage in learning how to flirt and simper and use my sex to advance myself."

"I think there's a little more to being a woman than that," said Hunter.

"If there is, then I have not observed it."

"Well, even if there wasn't," Hunter said, "the simple fact is that using your sex to advance yourself, as you put it, works on occasion, and I believe that one should use anything that works."

"Then why use that child's plaything of a sword?"

"Child's plaything, is it?" Hunter tossed her his rapier, then unwrapped a spare one from its cloth covering. He tossed both cloth covering and scabbard onto the bed. "Let's see just how much of a plaything this is," he said. "Attack me."

She swung the sword, awkwardly. Hunter parried easily, using the Florentine style—rapier in one hand, dagger in the other. He had little difficulty in blocking her crude strokes. The weapon was strange to her and she was uncomfortable with it.

"It's not a broadsword," Hunter said. "It's meant for speed. Watch."

This time he went on the offensive and she redoubled her efforts, taking her cue from him but still parrying clumsily. In seconds, he had disarmed her of the rapier, tapping her wrist lightly with the flat of the blade after hooking her sword, showing how a slash there would have caused her to drop her weapon and sustain a wound at the same time.

She looked down at the floor, then picked up the rapier he had disarmed her of so easily. She stood silently for a moment, studying it.

"I have misjudged this weapon," she said. "That was unwise of me. Clearly, there is a skill to using it correctly. I will learn it."

"Fencing isn't exactly something one picks up overnight," said Hunter. "You're not exactly a beginner, but—"

"No, I am far from a beginner. I have lived by the sword most of my life," she said. "This is a different blade, but it is still a sword. It will not take me long to learn. Teach me."

"There's really not much point to it," said Hunter.

"Why?"

"Because women in Paris don't carry rapiers," he said. "Sometimes they carry daggers, but mostly they carry fans and handkerchiefs." He grinned.

"Truly potent weapons," she said, sarcastically.

"It all depends on how you use them. Well, all right. I'll

teach you. It may not take you very long to learn, at that. You're already a demon with a broadsword. You're strong and you've got terrific reflexes. You just lack the correct technique. I think it will probably be tougher to teach you how to use a fan.''

''I see. You imply that you are qualified to teach me how to be a woman, is that it?'' she said.

''Not me,'' said Hunter. ''You're already more woman than any man I know can handle. The trick is not to let men know that. That shouldn't be too hard. Most of us aren't very smart when it comes to women.''

''And you are one of the smart ones, I suppose.''

''No, unfortunately, I'm one of the stupid ones,'' said Hunter. ''But I've learned a lot because of that.''

''Very well,'' said Andre. ''I owe you much. I will learn to act the part of a fine lady if you think it will prove helpful.''

''Just call me Professor Higgins.''

''Who is Professor Higgins?''

''He was another stupid man,'' said Hunter. ''But never mind. For a start, let's see what we can do about that walk of yours. You can dress the part of a woman, but you still swagger like a soldier. Now, take this book. . . .''

3

Charlotte Backson, the Countess de la Fère, Milady de Winter, had seduced more men than she could count. She had never before met a man who could resist her. Now she had. The man called Taylor was totally immune.

"You can turn it off, Milady," he had said, the first time she tried to work her charm on him. "You've got nothing that I want."

"Are you quite certain?" she had said, trying a different tack. She put just the right amount of throaty submissiveness into her voice. "After all, I am your prisoner. Your men have taken me against my will. You've killed my coachman and my footmen, brought me here with my eyes blindfolded, there must be something that you wanted from me. I assume it's ransom that you're after. Rest assured, you will be paid. But I do fear for my own safety. I am entirely in your power. I would do anything if it would insure my survival through this ordeal." She paused for just a second, her gaze meeting his directly. "Anything," she said softly.

The man called Taylor had laughed. "I'm afraid you're wasting your time, Milady. I'll be quite blunt. I'm not interested in women. You understand?"

"Oh. Yes, I'm afraid I do."

"You see, someone who doesn't share my sexual preferences would doubtless be extremely susceptible to you, which is why I'll be the only one to come into contact with you during your stay with us." Taylor had smiled. "Your reputation precedes you, Milady. We're fully aware of the kind of person that you are."

"I'm afraid you have the advantage of me, sir," she had said, stiffening slightly. "I do not know what you mean when you speak of my reputation. Doubtless, you have heard some malicious gossip from—"

"Don't be coy," said Taylor. "Here's what I mean." He reached out quickly and ripped her dress away from her shoulder with a suddenness that caught her unprepared. Quickly, she clapped her hand to her shoulder.

"There's no use in hiding it," said Taylor. "If you ask me, it's your best feature. The brand of the harlot. The fleur-de-lis. I've known women like you all my life. You're a slut, my dear."

"Who are you?" she said, angrily. "What is it you want from me?"

"Why, just your companionship, Milady. Nothing more."

"What is the ransom for my safe return? How much do you want to release me?"

Taylor raised his eyebrows. "Why, we're not asking anything for you, Milady. All we want is the privilege of entertaining you for a short while. A week, perhaps, no more."

"And then?"

"And then you won't be seeing us again," said Taylor.

Now a week had passed. It had been a maddening week. Each day, the man called Taylor came to her. He brought her all her meals and he would stay a while to talk with her. They would talk about the most meaningless of things, the weather, what fashions were popular at court, what her favorite foods were, what she liked, what she disliked, whom she had had affairs with. . . .

Taylor seemed to know almost as much about her as she knew herself. That frightened her. How could he know such intimate details of her private life? How could he know that she had once been a nun and that she had seduced a priest at the convent of the Benedictines of Templemar? How had he known about the fleur-de-lis, with which the executioner of

Lille had branded her? Who was this man, who seemed to know her almost as well as she knew herself?

She could get nothing out of him. On several occasions, he had come with a slightly older man, another stranger to her. This man would gaze at her strangely, then approach her. He would study her intently. Sometimes, he would touch her face, running his hands along her jawbone, touching her nose, the corners of her eyes, her lips. Once, when he had done so, she had softly kissed his finger, licking it lightly with her tongue. His hands shook slightly after that.

"Think you can do it, Doctor?" Taylor had said at one such time.

"I—I can do it."

"You'd damn well better be sure," said Taylor.

"I won't let you down, Adrian."

"It's not just me, Doc. You know what's riding on this."

"Yes, I know," said the one called Doc. "I know only too well." He had sounded frightened.

She had no idea what any of it meant. Sooner or later, she knew, they would have to make their purpose clear. She would bide her time and wait.

A week and two days had passed when she received yet another visitor. This one was a lady. The door to her room opened and the man called Doc entered, along with the lady and two other men. The lady hid her face behind a fan. Milady was certain that now she would find out the reason for her abduction, the purpose behind all this intrigue. She stood up, giving her jailors a haughty look.

"Well," she said. "It appears that at last I will—"

The words caught in her throat as the lady dropped her fan, revealing her face. It was the Countess's own face. Milady stared at her living reflection, struck speechless at the sight.

"You see," said the woman, in Milady's own voice, "I told you that we would only keep you for a week or so."

Milady backed away from the woman who was her twin in every way. She had her face, she had her voice, she had her manner. . . .

"Who—*who are you?*" she whispered.

Her double laughed and it was her own laugh, exactly. Then

she spoke in a completely different voice. A voice Milady had come to know only too well. "Why, Milady, don't you recognize me?"

"*Taylor!* In God's name, how is this possible? How—"

"Why don't you ask Him when you see Him?" Taylor said. He pointed a slim tubelike instrument at her. A bright, pencil-thin light stabbed out from it as Taylor quickly flicked his wrist.

Milady's head, severed by the laser, fell upon the floor and rolled grotesquely into a corner of the room.

The man called Doc turned his head away and made a whimpering sound.

"Jesus, Taylor!" He leaned against the door jamb for support.

"Weak stomach, Doc?"

"You didn't have to kill her," Doc said, his voice quivering.

"Oh, I did, indeed. We're playing for high stakes, my friend. It wouldn't do to have *two* Milady de Winters running around now, would it? Besides, I did her a favor. I spared her from the headsman's axe."

"By beheading her yourself," said Doc. "You didn't tell me you were going to kill her."

"She would have done the same to me, Doc, or to you or any one of us. This was one very nasty lady. Besides, if you want to salve your conscience, think of all the lives that will be saved when we bring the time wars to a halt."

"I agree that the time wars should be stopped," said Doc, "but I can't believe that your end justifies your means."

"You went into this with your eyes wide open, Doc," said Taylor. "It's a bit late for second thoughts now, don't you think?"

"Yes, I'm afraid it is." He took a deep breath, refusing to look at the headless body on the floor. "Well, I've done all that you asked. You don't need me anymore. Am I free to go, or am I going to end up like her?"

"Why, Doc," said Taylor, gently placing his hand along-side the man's cheek, "what makes you say a thing like that?" His voice was a perfect mimicry of de Winter's voice. Doc jerked away.

"Let him go," said Taylor.

The man was led away.

"You think he's going to be a problem?" said one of the others.

"I doubt it," Taylor said. "We've got his chronoplate. What harm can he do? Still, I don't suppose that it would hurt to keep an eye on him." He walked up to the mirror in the room and examined his reflection. He smiled de Winter's smile. "He did a hell of a good job, wouldn't you say? Amazing what just a little cosmetic surgery can do. Damn, look at me. I'm beautiful."

The other man cleared his throat uneasily.

Taylor grinned. "Sort of gets to you, doesn't it? What do you think, Jimmy? You think Richelieu will know the difference?"

Taylor threw back his head and gave a startlingly feminine laugh. Jimmy left the room.

Their instructions were to proceed to the tavern in Meung, and from there to make their way to Paris. Somewhere along the way, they would be contacted by an agent code-named "Mongoose."

"Are they all named after animals?" Finn had asked Darrow.

"Yes, why do you ask?"

"Oh, I was just wondering if there was an agent Jackass or an agent Baboon, you know. Just curious."

Darrow had not appreciated Finn's sense of humor.

"What is it you've got against these people, anyway?" Lucas asked him as they rode their horses at a walk on the road to Meung.

"They're sly," said Finn. "I don't like people who are sly. They're always sneaking around like weasels—wonder if there's an agent Weasel?—and they're totally untrustworthy. I prefer to work with people I can depend on. I wouldn't turn my back on a TIA agent for one second."

"You don't really think *we* have anything to worry about, do you?" Lucas said.

"Who knows, kid? Who knows what this mission *really* is?

They say it's the Timekeepers, but it could be the Daughters of the American Revolution for all I know. They don't even tell each other everything.''

They conversed in French, a language they spoke as easily as English, thanks to their implant programming. Anyone seeing them upon the road would have taken them for nothing more than what they appeared to be, cavaliers, soldiers of fortune, comrades in arms. Finn's normally red hair was now an auburn shade, Lucas's was a chestnut brown. Both men wore their hair down to their shoulders, in the style of gallants of the time. Lucas wore a waxed moustache, Finn wore a moustache and a goatee, a style that would one day be known as a Van Dyke. Both men wore high boots and leather baldricks, both carried daggers and rapiers. Their apparel did not lend an air of wealth or fashion to them. Both their cloaks were brown and well worn. Finn's doublet was yellow, cut from inexpensive cloth; Lucas's was brown. Neither man wore lace anywhere about his person; both wore simple sashes of green silk and white shirts that were in need of laundering. Their hats were plumed, but the feathers had seen better days.

"I hate this cloak-and-dagger stuff," said Finn, then chuckled at the thought that both of them actually had real cloaks and daggers. "I don't like the idea of not even knowing what our contact is supposed to look like. I'm not even sure what we're supposed to do."

"My impression was that we were to act as a sort of back-up team to the TIA boys," Lucas said. "Look, it might not be so bad. They might not even need us. This mission could turn into a Minus Time vacation."

"You wouldn't want to place a little bet on that, would you?" said Finn.

"Actually, no. Not really."

"I didn't think so."

"What do you think about this idea of someone in the underground going in with these Timekeepers?" Lucas said.

"I don't know. Why, you thinking about Hunter?"

"How'd you guess?"

"Wasn't too hard."

"I just can't see it, somehow. I couldn't see someone like Hunter going along with that kind of insanity. No one appreciates the potential dangers of a split more than a soldier, even a deserter. Why would someone who has gone to all the trouble of going over the hill and stealing a plate place himself at the disposal of a bunch of terrorists? It just doesn't make sense. What could they possibly have that he would want?''

"They wouldn't have anything that Hunter would want," said Finn, "but not all deserters are like Hunter. Think about all the things that would make a man desert. This character is probably someone who couldn't take it anymore or some maladjusted individual who just couldn't make it in Plus Time. Maybe it's some fanatic who joined the service with some idea of subverting it from within, who knows? Whoever he is, he's got to be just as crazy as the Timekeepers. No one in their right mind would set out to cause a split.''

"I can't believe anyone would really go that far," said Lucas.

"Darrow may have a point on that one," Finn said. "They may hope that they won't have to, but if they get pushed, if their bluff gets called, they'll have no choice. Nobody knows what sort of an effect a split will have. Maybe they think that that's what it will take to bring the war machine to a grinding halt. It might at that. But I'd just as soon not have to find out just what a split would do. Just researching it made Mensinger a nervous wreck. And the whole idea of this mission isn't doing my nerves any good.''

They reached the inn at Meung without being contacted by anyone. They took a room and ordered dinner in the tavern. The wine was passable and it felt pleasant after their journey. The innkeeper, although he had been somewhat wary of their well-traveled and rough appearance at the beginning, had warmed up considerably at the prospect of entertaining two customers who paid as they were served. He had been stiffed so many times by gallant cavaliers that he fussed over Finn and Lucas like a mother hen, ever solicitous of their satisfaction and trotting out from the kitchen constantly to see if they were enjoying their meal. Finn was on his second roasted chicken and Lucas was enjoying the innkeeper's best wine, a pleasant Bordeaux, when a young man almost completely covered with dust entered the establishment. Once inside the door, he began pounding at his clothing, so that within seconds he became almost completely obscured by a dust cloud.

"Some more wine, Monsieur?" said the innkeeper, bringing yet another bottle to their table.

"With pleasure," Finn said. "And pour a glass for young Lochinvar over there, he looks as though he could do with some refreshment."

At this, the young man looked up. He was scarcely more than a boy, perhaps eighteen years of age. He had a thick shock of disheveled blond hair and his clothes looked like hand-me-downs.

"I beg your pardon, sir," he said, "were you speaking of me?"

"Do you see anyone else in here besides ourselves?" said Finn, smiling.

"I fear you have taken me for someone else, sir," the young man said. "My name is not Lochinvar."

Finn chuckled. "It was just a figure of speech, lad. Lochinvar was the hero in a tale I heard once."

The young man frowned. "You seek to mock me, sir?"

"Don't get your feathers ruffled, son," said Finn. "I'm only offering you a drink. You look like you could do with some refreshment."

"And what, may I ask, is there in my appearance that leads you to believe I am in need of charity?" the young man said.

"Look, let's try this again," said Finn. "We've been traveling a long way ourselves, my friend and I. You came in, looking all dusty and bedraggled and I thought—"

The young man stiffened. "My clothing may not be quite so fine as your own, Monsieur, but nevertheless, it is not good manners for a gentleman to remark upon the difference."

"Leave him alone, Finn," Lucas said.

"Forget it, kid," said Finn. "Buy your own damn wine." He went back to eating his chicken, shaking his head in resignation. "Try to be a nice guy," he told Lucas.

"Monsieur," said the young man.

"Yes, what is it now?"

"I am not in the habit of being dismissed so cavalierly."

Finn raised his eyebrows. "Excuse me," he said. "I was not aware that I was dismissing a cavalier."

"Finn—" Lucas said.

The innkeeper backed away from the table.

"Then I will make you aware of whom you are dealing with, Monsieur. D'Artagnan suffers slights from no one." He drew his rapier. " 'Guarde, Monsieur!"

"Oh, Christ," said Finn. The innkeeper dove under a table.

"Monsieur D'Artagnan," Lucas began, "allow me to—"

"I will deal with you presently, sir," D'Artagnan said, "after I have done with your unruly friend. That is, unless you wish to increase the odds against me. I will not shrink from crossing swords with both of you at once." He swished his rapier back and forth a couple of times.

"Put that thing away," said Finn. "It's almost as big as you are."

"Nevertheless, its size will not impede my use of it," D'Artagnan said. "Now, 'guarde!"

"Oh, sit down," said Finn.

"You will stand, Monsieur, and draw your sword!"

"I will sit, my friend, and finish my dinner. And you would be wise to do the same."

D'Artagnan's sword stabbed out and lanced Finn's chicken off his plate. With a flick of the wrist, he sent the bird flying into a corner of the room.

"You appear to have finished your dinner, Monsieur."

"That does it," Finn said. "I'm going to take that pig-sticker away from you and spank you with it." He started to stand.

Lucas took hold of his arm. "*Finn, sit down. Don't be an idiot.*"

Delaney stood. "Look," he said to D'Artagnan, "can't we just forget the whole thing? I'm willing to overlook the chicken, but—"

"But I am not willing to overlook your insults, sir," D'Artagnan said.

"*What* insults?"

"Your sword, Monsieur!"

"No."

"You refuse to draw your sword?"

"That's right, I refuse."

"Then you are a base coward and no gentleman!"

"Listen here, you—"

"Finn . . ." said Lucas.

Delaney took a deep breath. "All right. I am a base coward and I'm not a gentleman. Does that satisfy you?"

D'Artagnan looked disappointed. "Well, then, in that case, I must demand an apology."

"For what?"

"Finn, will you for Christ's sake apologize and have done with it?" said Lucas.

"Well now what the hell should I apologize for?"

"It doesn't matter, just apologize, if it will make him happy."

"Sir, I will not be condescended to," D'Artagnan said.

"Just stay out of this," said Lucas. "Finn, say you're sorry, all right?"

"All right, I'm sorry. I apologize."

"I do not think you are sincere in your apology," D'Artagnan said.

"Please accept his apology, Monsieur," said Lucas. "It will bring this entire affair to a close and do wonders for my digestion."

"This is most perplexing," said D'Artagnan. "Your friend clearly does not wish to apologize, yet he apologizes. And although he is not sincere in his apology, he will do as you wish to spare himself from dueling with me. It appears that there is no way I can gain satisfaction in this affair. You place me in a most disadvantageous situation, Monsieur."

"I only wish to avoid unnecessary bloodshed," Lucas said. "It was all a misunderstanding, nothing more. No offense was meant."

"And yet offense was given. And I cannot attack a man who will not draw his rapier. It would be unseemly and dishonorable. Yet honor must be satisfied."

The innkeeper peeked out from beneath the table.

"Would honor be satisfied if we were to fight with our fists?" said Finn.

"It would be most irregular," said D'Artagnan, "but I can think of no other way out of this predicament."

"Then it's settled," Finn said. "We duel with fists."

"Done," said D'Artagnan. He started to remove his baldrick and Finn walloped him right between the eyes.

The blow knocked him back several feet and he sat down hard upon the floor. The innkeeper ducked back beneath the table. D'Artagnan shook his head, stunned.

"For such a little squirt, he takes a punch pretty good," said Finn. "I've laid out guys twice his size with that shot."

"That was most unsporting of you, sir," D'Artagnan said, getting to his feet.

"Fighting's not a sport, son," Finn said. "At least not where I come from. You either win or you lose and I prefer to win."

"Yes, clearly you are not a gentleman," D'Artagnan said. "In Gascony, we do not hit a man when he isn't looking."

"Well, I'm looking now," said Finn. "Take your best shot."

"Prepare yourself, my friend. Though you be twice my size, I'm going to teach you manners."

"Are you going to talk or fight?" said Finn.

Lucas rolled his eyes. "You know, Forrester was right," he said. "You *are* a ten-year-old."

D'Artagnan swung at Finn wildly. Finn easily ducked beneath his swing and gave him a hard uppercut to the jaw. D'Artagnan went down again.

"And that's that," said Finn.

D'Artagnan started to get up. His mouth was bloody.

"I thought you said that was that," said Lucas.

"Stubborn little bastard, isn't he?" said Finn.

D'Artagnan came at him again. Finn blocked his punch and gave him a right cross. D'Artagnan fell again.

"That ought to satisfy his honor," Finn said.

Slowly, D'Artagnan rose to his feet.

"I think you're losing your touch," said Lucas. "He keeps getting up."

"We'll fix that," said Finn.

D'Artagnan swung again, only this time it was a feint and he caught Finn off guard. As a result, Finn caught a left hook and fell back into a table.

"You fixed that real good," said Lucas.

"All right, enough's enough," said Finn. This time, when D'Artagnan came at him, Finn used karate. He stopped him cold with a front kick to the chest, then dropped him with a side kick and a roundhouse to the temple, both delivered off the same foot with lightning speed.

"That wasn't really fair," said Lucas.

"Screw fairness. This kid's built like an ox." He sat down and poured himself a glass of wine. "Hits well, too." He rubbed his jaw.

Lucas tapped him on the shoulder and pointed. D'Artagnan was getting up again.

"I seem to recall that we agreed upon fists, not feet," he said. His words were slurred and he was unsteady on his feet.

"He's got a point," said Lucas.

The innkeeper had ventured forth from beneath the table and he now watched with interest.

Finn got up again. "Feel free to use whatever works," he said. He put his fists up. D'Artagnan, moving faster than he looked able to, hit Finn with a chair. The chair broke and Finn fell to the floor, unconscious.

"That worked very well," D'Artagnan said. He turned to Lucas. "Now, Monsieur, it is your turn."

Lucas raised his hands. "Not I. We have no quarrel, Monsieur. If honor has been satisfied, will you allow me to share our wine with you while my friend gets some much-needed rest?"

D'Artagnan pondered this invitation for a moment. "Honor is satisfied," he said, "though I do not think that this is what my father meant when he urged me to fight duels. Besides, I welcome the chance to rest myself. Your friend has the strength of ten." He sat down at Lucas's table.

Lucas poured him a glass of wine, which he drank quickly.

"Finn may have the strength of ten," he said, "but I notice that he's the one who's on the floor and not you. Allow me to congratulate you. It's the first time I've ever seen him lose a fight."

"Finn? What sort of name is that?"

"Irish," said Lucas.

"Ah. And you are Irish, as well?"

"No, I'm . . . a Gascon."

"I would not have known it! We are countrymen! I, too, am a Gascon! You have, perhaps, heard of my father? He was a well-known soldier."

"Indeed I have," said Lucas. "Which is why I advised my friend to refrain from crossing swords with you. We have gone through much together and I would have hated to lose a friend to a swordsman who was the son of the famous D'Artagnan. If you are half the man your father is, my friend would not have stood a chance. And it was only a misunderstanding, after all."

"Well, to tell the truth, I sought to provoke a duel," D'Artagnan said, rather sheepishly.

"Because your father advised you to."

"Indeed. He said that it is necessary to fight duels in order to gain respect and a reputation. You have my apologies, Monsieur. I would have hated to deprive a fellow Gascon of a friend."

"I understand," said Lucas. "One must respect a father's wishes, after all."

"What is your name, Monsieur, so I may know whom I have the honor of addressing?"

Lucas thought quickly. Priest was an English name and England was the enemy of France. "Dumas," he said. "Alexandre Dumas."

"I am pleased to make your acquaintance, Monsieur Dumas. And I hope that your friend will not be ill-disposed toward me when he regains his senses."

Finn groaned. He started to sit up slowly. The innkeeper brought him a bowl of water and a wet cloth. D'Artagnan went to help him to his feet.

"I trust you are not injured, sir, and that there remains no ill will between us. Monsieur Dumas has explained everything to me and I see that it was a misunderstanding, after all."

"Who?" said Finn.

"He is still a little dazed," said Lucas. "Surely you remember me, my friend—Alexandre Dumas? I hope that blow did not addle your senses. It seems that Monsieur D'Artagnan and I are countrymen. We are both from Gascony."

"You are, eh? What did you say your name was?"

"Dumas."

"That's what I thought you said. I just wasn't sure I heard right."

"I fear I have damaged him," D'Artagnan said, with genuine concern.

"Oh, no, he'll be all right," said Lucas. "The Irish are a hardheaded people."

As D'Artagnan was helping Delaney to his feet, the door to the inn opened and a party of men entered, laughing boisterously.

"Did you ever see such an animal in your whole life?" said one of them, a tall, dark-haired cavalier with a scar upon his cheek. "An orange horse! A fit steed for a pumpkin!"

D'Artagnan straightened suddenly, and Finn, deprived of his support, slipped to the floor again.

"Forgive me," said D'Artagnan, helping Delaney up again. "I think that man is laughing at my horse."

"Who laughs at a horse laughs at its master," Lucas said, remembering that it was at this very tavern that D'Artagnan first met the Count de Rochefort, and that the man who had just entered with the group of guards could be no other.

"Do you think so?" said D'Artagnan.

"Well, don't you?"

"Perhaps," D'Artagnan said. "But I would not wish to have yet another misunderstanding. No doubt the man means nothing by it."

"How, nothing?" Lucas said. "Clearly, he was making fun of you."

"Indeed? Well, you may be right. Still, it would not do to be too hasty. See, we sit here as friends and moments ago, I would have crossed swords with you."

"That was quite another matter," Lucas said. "This man is insolent and should be chastised."

"You may be right," D'Artagnan said. "Still, I would not wish to leap to the wrong conclusion. And my horse is, I am afraid, a somewhat amusing-looking steed."

"Well, I will not sit here and suffer a countryman of mine to be insulted," Lucas said. "You, sir! You with the scar!"

De Rochefort looked up.

"Yes, you! What are you laughing at?"

"I do not see that as being any concern of yours, Monsieur," said de Rochefort.

"I think it is," said Lucas, standing. "I heard what you said!"

"I was not speaking to you, Monsieur."

"Well, *I* am speaking to *you*! I do not like your laughter."

"I do not laugh often, sir," said de Rochefort, "but I retain the privilege of laughing when I please."

"And I, Monsieur, will allow no man to laugh when it displeases me," said Lucas. "Nor will I permit my friends to be the butt of jokes!"

"Please, Dumas," D'Artagnan said, "you do not need to stand up for me; this is my affair."

"Well, when you gentlemen settle it between yourselves, perhaps you will enlighten me as to what this affair may be," said de Rochefort.

"The horse tied up outside, which you were laughing at, is mine," D'Artagnan said. "And it does not suit me to be called a pumpkin!"

"I do not care about what suits you, Monsieur," said de Rochefort. "There are more important matters on my mind and you have already distracted me enough."

"I fear that I will prove to be much more than just a mere distraction, Monsieur," D'Artagnan said. He drew his rapier.

"You must be mad," said de Rochefort, turning away.

"Turn, sir! Turn or I will strike you down!"

"This is annoying," de Rochefort said to his men. "Do something about this insolent boy."

"Insolent, am I?" said D'Artagnan, striding forward. He pushed past one of the guards and reached for de Rochefort's shoulder. "I am not done with you, Monsieur! I—"

The guard he had brushed past picked up a chair and, with a swing that seemed almost nonchalant, he smashed it over D'Artagnan from behind. The Gascon crumpled to the floor. The innkeeper moaned over the loss of the second chair of the afternoon.

The guard turned back to face Lucas and Delaney. With a hand on the hilt of his sword, he approached them belligerently.

"You gentlemen don't have anything to add, do you?" he said; then, in the same breath, he whispered, "Mongoose."

Finn's eyebrows rose. "No, we don't have anything to add," he said. "In fact, we hardly even know that fellow."

"It appears to me that your friend has had too much to drink," the guard said, indicating Lucas. "I would strongly advise you to be on your way, before his drunkenness gets you into any more trouble."

"Certainly, Monsieur," said Finn. "The last thing that we want is trouble."

"Then be on your way," said the agent, adding in a quick whisper, "Moreau's Tavern on the Rue Férou. Say Legault sent you." He raised his voice. "Out with you! Now! And make it quick!"

4 _____

Something was wrong.

No one had seen Jacques Benoit for days. In anyone else's case, this would not have been particularly noteworthy, but Doctor Jacques was well known to be a creature of scrupulous habit. For the past week, Hunter had been making all the rounds, but ex-army surgeon Jack Bennett, known to his Parisian friends as Doctor Jacques Benoit, was nowhere to be found.

He wasn't at his home on the Rue St.-Honoré. His servants, Marie and Old Pierre, had found it necessary to turn away his patients, as they did not know where Doctor Jacques had gone or when he would return. This gave them cause for much concern, since their master never went anywhere without leaving them some word.

Moreau's Tavern, on the Rue Férou, where Doctor Jacques could be found every evening enjoying a bottle of wine and playing a game or two of chess, had not been graced by his presence for over a week. This upset Moreau somewhat, as Benoit was something of an attraction at the tavern. It was the way that he played chess. He would sit with his back to the board, at another table, carrying on idle conversation with onlookers. His opponent would announce his move, and then Benoit would announce his, "Knight to King's Bishop four" or whatever, all without looking at the board. He had yet to lose a game. These casual, friendly matches brought in customers and these customers frequently bet upon the outcome —at least, those who had not seen Benoit play before would bet.

Moreau knew Hunter as "Monsieur Laporte," an old friend of Jacques Benoit's from Reims. Insofar as Moreau knew, Monsieur Laporte was a gentleman, a man who liked to live quietly and who did not often come to Paris, but when he did, he always made a point of it to visit his old friend and to stop in to see Moreau.

"It is not like Doctor Jacques," Moreau was saying, as he poured both himself and Hunter some red wine. "He never goes anywhere without at least telling Marie and Old Pierre. He has always been considerate of his friends and especially his patients."

"He didn't say anything the last time you saw him?" Hunter said. "He did not say he was going to the country for some rest?"

Anytime Jack Bennett made a trip to Plus Time, he always said that he was "going to the country." Members of the underground who kept in frequent touch with one another had various code phrases such as that to pass on messages. "He didn't say anything at all?"

"No, Monsieur," Moreau said. "If he had said anything, I would most assuredly have remembered."

"I hope nothing has happened to him," Hunter said. "Paris can be dangerous at times, especially these days."

"Who would hurt Doctor Jacques?" Moreau said. He shook his head. "He hasn't an enemy in Paris. He has his peculiarities, true, but who can argue with his results? I, myself, have never understood why he looks down on bleeding, for example. He insists that it does more harm than good. Still, he has helped many people hereabouts, and he even extends himself to those who cannot afford to pay. He may ask some little service or, as in the case of Marcel's ailing father, take payment in a chicken or two, but . . . no, I cannot imagine anyone who would wish him harm. He is the soul of compassion. And well-liked and respected."

"Then what could have become of him?" said Hunter.

Moreau shrugged. "Perhaps he had some business with those friends of his, from Flanders."

Hunter frowned. "Friends from Flanders?"

"Yes, five of them," Moreau said. "They were with him the last time he was here. And the time before that, too."

"Can you tell me anything about them?" Hunter said. "It could be important."

"They were a rough lot," Moreau said. He shrugged again. "Still, Doctor Jacques has friends from all walks of life, no? Not my sort, though. Not my sort at all. They would all grow silent whenever I approached their table, as though afraid that I would overhear their conversation."

"What did they look like? Perhaps I know them."

"They were all large men," Moreau said. "All except one, who was very slight and thin. About like so," Moreau said, indicating his own chest level. "Three of them were dark, rough-looking, as I said. One was bald. Him I remember very well. He was a bull, that one, a giant of a man. They didn't speak much, at least, not to me, but they were not French, that much was certain."

"They did not know the language," Hunter said.

"Oh, no, they knew the language very well," Moreau said, "but they learned it elsewhere. They had some sort of accent, but I could not place it."

"What about the fifth man?" Hunter said. "The slight one?"

"Ah, yes, him. I thought he was a girl, at first." Moreau chuckled. "It was a bit embarrassing. I called him 'mademoiselle' and it seemed to amuse the others and it was only then that I saw he was a man. A very young man, no more than a boy, really. Some boys, in their youthfulness, well. . . ."

"Yes, I understand," said Hunter. "And some young girls look like young boys sometimes, especially if they are not wearing dresses."

"Quite so," Moreau said, visibly relieved. "Still, this one . . . he wore his hair quite long, much longer than is the fashion. And it was like spun gold, Monsieur. Most unsettling. *His* French, now, was flawless. A real gentleman, that one. I heard Doctor Jacques call him 'Adrian.'" Moreau lowered his voice. "An English name, no?"

"Could be," said Hunter. "I know no one by that name. This all sounds very mysterious, Moreau."

Moreau looked around, then leaned closer to Hunter. "Tell me, Monsieur," he said, "Doctor Jacques. . . . I have never known him to, that is, he has no . . . *political* leanings, has he?"

"I don't know," said Hunter. "What makes you say a thing like that?"

Moreau shrugged again. "One learns a thing or two in this business, Monsieur. After all, you must admit, it does look strange. Five strangers, four of whom are decidedly not French and the fifth with an English-sounding name, all speaking in low voices in the corner. . . ."

"I see what you mean," said Hunter. "But political intrigue? That does not sound like the Jacques Benoit I know."

"One never knows for sure, Monsieur," Moreau said. "Intrigue seems to be the watchword of the day. I would hate to learn that Doctor Jacques was in some sort of trouble."

"So would I, Moreau. So would I. Listen, if you should see him before I do, tell him that I'm staying at the Luxembourg. Ask him to come and see me on a matter of some importance."

"I will, Monsieur Laporte. And if you should see him first, you tell him that he has friends who will stand by him, eh? If there is trouble, you tell him to come to old Moreau."

Hunter looked at Moreau and smiled. The burly Frenchman had a face that looked like old leather and broad shoulders that suggested a previous trade more strenuous than being a tavernkeeper. If there would be trouble, Jack would do well to have someone like Moreau beside him.

"I'll tell him," Hunter said.

He left the tavern feeling very worried. Something was definitely wrong. Jack Bennett had disappeared without leaving behind any message whatsoever. With Jack, that sort of thing simply didn't happen, unless those men had something to do with it and he had not had time to leave a message. But then, according to Moreau, those men had been with Jack for at least a week and they would not have known the signals that Hunter and Jack had arranged between themselves. Jack should have been able to leave word if something out of the ordinary had occurred. But he hadn't.

Those "friends from Flanders" made Hunter nervous. Jack didn't have any friends in Flanders that he knew of. Then there was Moreau's description of them. *Large*. Spoke French excellently, but with an accent that Moreau, an ex-seaman, could not place. Perhaps it was because it was an accent unknown to this time.

"Where are you, Doc?" Hunter mumbled. "What have you gotten yourself into?"

He was so preoccupied, he didn't notice that he was being followed.

Andre realized that she owed Hunter a great deal, but there was a limit to any obligation. She had promised Hunter that she would learn to act like a lady, but she had never promised him to play that role continuously. Nor had she promised him to, as he had said it, "stay put" in their apartments.

He had brought her to another time, to another world, and he expected her to stay in their hotel unless told otherwise. Yes, she owed him a great deal, but she did not owe him blind, unquestioning obedience. He had developed a tendency to order her around and she didn't like it. She understood that he was only being protective, because he knew much and she knew little of this time, because he was in his element and she was in an alien environment. Still, that did not make her confinement easier to bear. She felt herself dependent upon Hunter and she didn't like having to depend on anyone. She never had. She liked feeling caged up even less.

In the 12th century, at least, she had known the rules. In England, she had been able to make her way alone. Hunter had spent many hours with her, teaching her to speak 17th-century French. The task was made easier by her knowledge of the Norman tongue, but it had proved bothersome when Hunter would not speak to her in any other language. He had explained that they would be in 17th-century Paris for an indefinite amount of time and that it was of paramount importance for her to know the language. Surprisingly, even though the constant repetition and the boring drills were tiresome, she had discovered that learning a new language came easily to her, far more easily than learning "the gentle art of acting like a lady,'' and only slightly less easily than learning how to use a rapier. Already, Hunter was no match for her. Her progress had astonished even him. Yet what was the point in knowing all these things if she was to be denied the opportunity to put them into practice? What was the use in learning how to act like a 17th-century Parisienne if she remained constantly within the walls of the Luxembourg Hotel, seeing no one, going nowhere?

"A lady never wanders through the streets of Paris unescorted," Hunter had said.

Well, perhaps a lady didn't. But then, she had never promised him that she would be a lady all the time.

She had inquired as to the whereabouts of the nearest tailor and the carriage took her to an exclusive little shop, patronized only by the wealthier citizens of Paris. The tailor had readily accepted her explanation that she was buying a surprise birthday present for her little brother, who was almost exactly the same size as herself. He had summoned a seamstress to measure her, telling Andre that when she presented the suit to her little brother, he would be more than happy to perform any necessary alterations free of charge. If the tailor or the seamstress were surprised at her unusual height and dimensions, they kept their comments to themselves. If the lady had arms and shoulders like a laborer's, that was no concern of theirs, especially since she didn't even remark upon the price.

The white silk shirt would feel good against her skin and the black brocade breeches would be infinitely more comfortable than skirts. The high leather boots would be a distinct improvement over her dainty little shoes. The doublet and cloak were also in rich black brocade, "the finest cloth available," the tailor had insisted. He had also insisted upon the "necessary lace adornments" about the collar, sleeves and boot tops, without which no proper gentleman could consider himself dressed. A dark red sash would complete the ensemble, along with an ornately plumed hat that would feel much more comfortable upon her head than that abominable wig. Attired in this manner, she would look like a dashing, well-to-do young cavalier. The tailor was ecstatic when she ordered two more suits, identical in nature. Still, he was not so ecstatic that his aesthetic sensibilities did not demand that he press upon her a change in color at the very least, if not in cloth. It made little difference to her, so she ordered one suit in burgundy and one in mauve. Delighted with himself, the tailor threw in several pairs of gauntlets in matching shades and two extra baldricks. "Oh, and a full complement of handkerchiefs, as well," he added, magnanimously. He thanked mademoiselle profusely for her business and promised that the clothes would be delivered to her hotel.

Andre spent the remainder of the morning driving around Paris. Hunter would be angry, but she didn't care. After all, it wasn't as though she was some pampered, helpless woman wandering about Paris alone and unprotected. She viewed the city from the safety of her carriage and she was perfectly capable of protecting herself if the need arose.

She didn't care for much of what she saw. Paris was dense and crowded and noisy beyond belief. How was it possible for people to live like this, like rabbits in a warren? If this was an example of what the future held in store for her, she wasn't at all certain that she wanted any part of it. Yet, on the other hand, there was a majesty to Paris, a beauty and elegance that far surpassed anything she had ever seen before. As the carriage passed the Louvre, she gasped. The Palais du Louvre was a far, far cry from the castle strongholds of her time. No builders of the 12th century would ever have been able to achieve such grandeur. Compared to Louis XIII, Prince John of Anjou was a peasant. The carriage took her along the Seine and she marveled at the Cathedral of Notre Dame, towering over all the other buildings on the Île de la Cité. How had its builders been able to construct such a massive edifice; how had they built the majestic flying buttresses? If this was what the architects of the 17th century could achieve, what wonders awaited her in the 27th? She drove through the Marais, where the Knights Templar had once held their fief—a large, vast fortress of a temple built in 1107. That reminded her of one Templar in particular and, for a moment, there was a sinking feeling in her stomach as she recalled Sir Brian de Bois-Guilbert, the man who had murdered her brother, Marcel. She had avenged her brother's death, but it had not made the pain of her loss easier to bear. At present there was no trace of the temple. The Marais was now a residential area, the square

filled with red brick and white stone buildings three stories
high with window surrounds. On past la Place Royale, the carriage drove by the Bastille. The Bassin de l'Arsenal brought
water from the Seine to the moat around the prison. Andre
looked upon the massive stone walls and thought of the people
rotting within them, never again to see the light of day. Hunter
had told her a great deal about Paris, but seeing it for herself
made her realize for the first time just how primitive she must
seem to him, a man to whom *this* wondrous city would seem
backward.

It was nearing noon and she decided it was time to turn
back. There was still much more of the city that she had yet to
see, but there was no point to trying to see it all in just one
day. It would have been impossible, at any rate. As they
passed the Carmes-Dechaux, Andre directed the coachman to
stop for a while. Here was a small pocket of silence in the bus-
tling city. She got out and walked slowly toward the convent, a
large and windowless building surrounded by barren fields.
Here, at least, there was something of the flavor of her time.
She walked along the side of the building, running her hand
along its wall. Curiously, although she had done nothing for
the past several hours more strenuous than sitting in the carriage, she felt exhausted. She would just rest here for a moment in the peaceful silence of the courtyard of the nunnery.
As she came to the corner of the building, almost to the inner
courtyard, she heard the sound of running footsteps and hesitated. Foolishly, she had left her rapier behind in the carriage,
along with her dagger. She was unarmed. She spun around
quickly, but the footsteps were not coming from behind her.
Cautiously, she peeked around the corner.

The running figure burst into the courtyard and paused a
moment, out of breath. It was a young man, blond and bedraggled, wearing old and dusty clothes and a rapier that
seemed far too long for him to handle. He glanced quickly
around the courtyard and his gaze fell upon an older man,
with a bandaged shoulder, dressed in the uniform of the king's
musketeers, sitting casually atop a hitching post and picking at
the mud upon his boots with his rapier.

"I trust I am not late, Monsieur?" said the blond youth.

The musketeer slowly raised his head, while he continued

prodding at his boot absently. "No, you are quite punctual," he said. "I, myself, have only just arrived moments ago. I shall, however, have to beg your indulgence for a short while, as I have asked two friends of mine to be my seconds and, as you can see, they have not yet arrived."

"Ah," said the young man. "Ah. Well. I must confess that, since I am new to Paris, I have no seconds, Monsieur."

"What, none at all? Do you not know anyone in Paris?"

"Well, Monsieur de Treville...."

"Yes, well, he would hardly do, would he? The captain of the musketeers is hardly in a position to disobey the edict against dueling. Well, I must say, this is most irregular. Dueling with a youth who has no seconds, not good for appearances at all, I am afraid. I'll have the air of a boy-slayer."

"Not so much so," said D'Artagnan, bowing slightly. "After all, you do me the honor of drawing a sword against me while you still suffer from a wounded shoulder. I am afraid it is I who shall suffer from appearances, Monsieur, if I should kill a man whose wound prevented him from properly defending himself."

"Well spoken. However, I shall take the left hand," said the musketeer. "I usually do so in such circumstances. I use both hands equally well and a left-handed swordsman can be quite troublesome to one who is not used to it. I fear that the disadvantage will be yours, Monsieur. I regret that I did not inform you of it earlier."

"That's quite considerate of you, Monsieur," D'Artagnan said. "I hope my inadvertent collision with you earlier this day has not overly aggravated your condition."

"Well, you hurt me devilishly, but I'll survive. Thank you for your concern."

"If I may, Monsieur," D'Artagnan said, "my mother has given me a wondrous balsam with miraculous healing properties. I am certain that, in three days time, it would effect a cure upon your wound and then, when you are less inconvenienced, I would still be honored to cross swords with you."

"Well, that is a generous offer, indeed," said the musketeer, "not that I would accept it for a moment, but it savors of a gentleman a league off. It seems that you are not at all the ill-mannered lout I took you for. I'm almost sorry that I'm going to have to kill you. *Merde*. Where *are* those two?''

Listening to this exchange of courtesies, Andre was pleased to note that chivalry still seemed alive in the 17th century. She decided to linger and watch the outcome of this meeting.

''If you are in haste, Monsieur, and anxious to dispatch me at once,'' D'Artagnan said, ''pray do not inconvenience yourself. I stand ready.''

''Well spoken once again,'' said the musketeer. ''I'm rather beginning to like you, young man. No, I think we'll wait for my seconds to arrive, if you don't mind. It would be the proper thing to do. Ah, here comes one of them right now.''

Andre saw a stout, swarthy-looking man dressed flamboyantly in a cerulean blue doublet, crimson velvet cloak and gold-worked baldrick strut into the courtyard. The young man seemed quite surprised at his appearance.

''What? Is your second Monsieur Porthos?'' he asked the musketeer.

''Yes,'' said the musketeer. ''Why, is that not acceptable to you?''

''Oh, no, not at all,'' D'Artagnan said. ''I'm perfectly agreeable.''

''And here comes—''

''Monsieur Aramis,'' D'Artagnan finished for him. A tall, handsome, slim man approached. He was dressed more simply, in dark hues, and he had a somewhat pale look about him. He wore a delicate, thin moustache and he moved with an air of graceful nonchalance.

''You know Aramis?'' said Athos.

''Only in a manner of speaking,'' said D'Artagnan, weakly.

''What, Athos!'' Porthos said. ''Don't tell me *this* is the man you're going to fight?''

''Yes,'' said Athos, ''he—''

''But he is the man *I* am to fight, as well!''

''But not until one o'clock,'' said D'Artagnan, somewhat sheepishly.

''But *I* am to fight him, also!'' said Aramis.

D'Artagnan cleared his throat uneasily. ''Ah, yes, at *two* o'clock, Monsieur.''

Andre, watching from concealment, suppressed a chuckle.

Athos raised his eyebrows. ''It seems you've had quite a

busy morning, my friend," he said to D'Artagnan. "And to think, you've only just arrived in Paris."

"Well, now that you three gentlemen are here together," said D'Artagnan, "permit me to offer you my excuses."

Athos frowned. "See here, young man," he said, "this is a most serious matter. If you—"

"Oh, no, you misunderstand me," said D'Artagnan. "I only meant to offer my excuses in the event that I am killed before I can give all of you your satisfaction, for Monsieur Athos has the right to kill me first, you see, and then Monsieur Porthos would come second and you, Monsieur Aramis, would be the third. I merely wish to apologize in advance in case I do not last out the afternoon."

"Very nicely said," said Porthos. "See here, Athos, what is your quarrel with this lad?"

"To tell the truth, I'm not sure I recall," said Athos. "He hurt my shoulder, I think; it arose somehow out of that."

"And what is your quarrel with him?" Aramis asked Porthos.

"Why, it's . . . it's . . . Damn me, I've forgotten! But it is of no matter, whatever it was, we'll settle it between ourselves. And what of you?"

"Ah, well, it was a matter of some delicacy—"

"Come, come, gentlemen," said Athos, "we're wasting time. For all we know, this youngster has other appointments to keep, at three, four and five o'clock, no doubt."

"On the contrary, Monsieur," D'Artagnan said, with some slight embarrassment. "I am at your disposal for the remainder of the afternoon." He drew his sword. "And now, if you're quite ready. . . ."

"Not now, not now," said Aramis. "The cardinal's guards, the cardinal's guards! Sheathe swords, gentlemen, quickly!"

Andre saw a company of red cloaked men-at-arms approaching quickly. At first, she was puzzled by the last remark she overheard, and then she recalled that the one named Athos had mentioned something about there being an edict against dueling. She felt disappointed. She had been looking forward to a display of swordsmanship, so that she might assess her own skills in relation to those of these men.

"Aha, what have we here?" said the leader of the guards.

"Musketeers dueling then, is it? And what's become of the edicts, eh?"

"Peace, Jussac," Athos said. "We were merely about to settle some small private matters. I promise you, were our roles reversed, we would not interfere with you in your own business."

"But you would not have to answer to the cardinal, Monsieur Athos," Jussac said. "No, I am afraid that I cannot allow it. I will have to ask you to sheathe your swords and follow me."

"I'm afraid that would be impossible," said Athos.

"You refuse, then?"

"I'm afraid we must."

"I warn you, sir, if you refuse to go along peaceably, we will have to charge you."

"Five against three," said Porthos, dryly. "Hardly the best of odds, I would say."

"Five against *four*," D'Artagnan said, stepping closer to them. "That is, if you'll allow me."

"We'll allow you, we'll allow you," Porthos said.

"Just one moment," Athos said. "He is not a musketeer. This is none of his affair, you know."

Aramis cleared his throat. "Uh, Athos, in case it has escaped your notice, there are *five* of them."

"But moments ago, we were to duel with him," said Athos.

"Just so," said Porthos. "We can kill him later, if you wish."

"Come, come, gentlemen," said Jussac. "What is it to be?"

"What is your name, young fellow?" Athos said.

"D'Artagnan."

"Well," he said, glancing at the oversized rapier, "I hope you know how to use that thing."

"But not *too* well," said Porthos, remembering their prior engagement.

The three musketeers drew their swords. "*All for one*," said Athos. The guards charged. "The hell with it," he said and sidestepped Jussac's rush.

Andre watched what followed with a great deal of interest

and not a little amusement. The combatants used the Florentine style, meaning that one hand held the rapier while the
other used a dagger, but to say that there was any style to their
combat was to stretch all definitions of the term. There was
none of the graceful intricacy which, according to Hunter,
characterized the art of fencing. As he might have said it himself, instead of swash and buckle, it was more like slash and
flail. Of all of them, only Jussac and Athos displayed some
semblance of the finer points of swordsmanship. Jussac's
manner of fighting was the closest to the classical form,
whereas Athos fought with a minimum of motion and wasted
effort, a sharp contrast to his comrades. Aramis moved like a
dancer, using his footwork to compensate for his lack of
strength. He played his opponent like a toreador working a
bull, deflecting the guard's blade and moving gracefully
sideways, causing the man's own forward momentum to carry
him past, whereupon Aramis's blade would describe a light-
ning-quick series of overly flamboyant arabesques over the
guard's exposed back and buttocks. Not one was a killing
stroke, but the cumulative effect of all those pretty slashes
would, if continued, result in his opponent bleeding to death.

Porthos was literally comical to watch. His movements were
exaggerated, jerky, and he appeared to fight as though he were
a man in abject panic. Yet, instead of fear, there was an expression of intense concentration on his face, forehead deeply
furrowed, eyebrows knitted, tongue protruding slightly from
his mouth. His footwork was that of a lumbering plough
horse, ponderous and clumsy, and he looked as though at any
moment he would trip over his own two feet. His thrusts and
slashes were the most pronounced of all the fighters.

Athos, by contrast, appeared totally relaxed and insouciant.
He was economy personified and he allowed his opponent to
come to him, preferring to work close. Andre soon saw the
reason why. At very close quarters, the bullish strength of the
elder musketeer was a decisive advantage. He used his dagger
sparingly, but when he did it was either to bludgeon his opponent with its blunt end or to attempt a stab into the upper
torso. Curiously, he seemed unconcerned about his defense
and, though he had avoided his opponent's rush at him and

disposed of the next guard quickly, Andre saw how a skilled swordsman, wary of being lured in close, could take advantage of his careless guard.

Of them all, the blond youth named D'Artagnan was the most interesting to watch. He, alone, disdained to use a dagger. In fact, he didn't seem to have one, though he did not seem to suffer from its absence. His style, if style it could be called, was the most peculiar, yet by the same token, it was the most effective. Quite obviously, the guards had never come across anyone who used his sword in quite the same manner as he did and they seemed at a loss to deal with him. He used his free hand to alternately take a two-handed grip upon his oversized rapier and to wrench his opponents about as though he were a wrestler. Andre had to chuckle as she saw him deal with two of the guards at once. He parried the thrust of the first with a vicious back-handed two-hand blow, using his rapier almost as though it were a quarterstaff. His parry almost spun the guard around completely and, as the second guard came at him, D'Artagnan stepped in close to the first, his hand darting out to grasp him by the throat. Unprepared for this unorthodox maneuver, the first guard was momentarily shocked, giving D'Artagnan just enough time to parry the thrust of the second guard, then slam a knee into the first guard's groin. The man sagged and D'Artagnan released him, to concentrate his attention upon the second guard. With a bizarre, two-handed circular parry, he brought the guard's rapier around and down to touch the ground. Then he stepped upon it and lunged in to smash the guard of his rapier into the man's face. A quick thrust and it was over; then he was rushing to help Porthos with his man.

Porthos gratefully relinquished his opponent to D'Artagnan, who attacked with exuberance and a boyish glee, grinning from ear to ear. In seconds, Jussac found himself sorely beset. Athos, having killed his man, joined Porthos, who was leaning against the hitching post and mopping his forehead with a handkerchief.

"Would that I could help him," Porthos said, breathing heavily, "but my breakfast still weighs heavily upon me and I fear that I am all worn out. Besides, he doesn't seem to require my assistance. God, did you see that? What a ghastly blow!

I've never seen the like of it! He handles his sword as though it were a garden hoe!''

"I would hate to be his garden, then," said Athos, dryly. "The lad fights amusingly, but devilishly well. The thought that I was to duel with him gives me acute discomfort.''

The guard matched up with Aramis, his uniform in tatters, was sidestepped by Aramis again and this time, taking advantage of his own forward momentum, he chose to continue in the same direction, taking flight and running directly toward Andre. She moved back into the shadows and pressed herself against the wall. He kept running until he was almost abreast of Andre, at which point he stopped, turned, and removed a pistol from his belt. As D'Artagnan ran Jussac through the shoulder, the guard stretched out his arm and took careful aim. Andre stepped out from the shadows and kicked high, knocking his pistol off the mark even as he fired. The ball went wide. The combination of being unaccustomed to her skirts and shoes and the slickness of the ground beneath her caused Andre to lose her balance and sit down hard into the muck, composed of mud from recent rain and the leavings of a horse which had earlier relieved itself upon that spot.

The look of rage upon the guard's face changed abruptly to one of immense frustration when he saw who had interfered with him. He sputtered incoherently for a moment, then caught his breath long enough to say, "*Really*, Mademoiselle!" He tucked his pistol back into his sash and took off at a run. Sitting on the ground, Andre sniffed and wrinkled her nose.

"Look at that!" said Aramis. "An angel in the mud!"

"She saved my life," said Athos.

"No, no, you are mistaken," Porthos said. "That shot was aimed at me."

"You are both wrong," said Aramis, "it was my life that she saved.''

"No, but clearly, it was mine," D'Artagnan said. "That guard was aiming straight at me.''

"Don't be ridiculous," said Aramis. "Your back was turned, how could you see?"

"Nevertheless, it was I who was the target," said D'Artagnan.

"My friend," said Porthos, "it is a miracle, indeed, that you are an accomplished swordsman, for clearly you are blind. I tell you, it was *me* she saved!"

"Gentlemen, gentlemen," said Aramis, "this matter can be settled easily. Let us go and pull the lady from the mud and ask her whom she meant to save."

Athos tapped him on the shoulder and pointed. There was no sign of Andre.

While they had been arguing, Andre had quickly made her way back to her carriage, directing the coachman to take her back to the Luxembourg Hotel. The coachman had raised his eyebrows when he saw her all covered with filth, but he made no comment. He was being well paid and if the lady chose to have an assignation in a puddle of manure, that was no concern of his. The recreational pursuits of the jaded well-to-do made little sense to him and he really didn't care. He counted himself fortunate to be employed.

Andre ignored the stares and wrinkled noses as she entered the lobby of the Luxembourg and made her way back to her rooms. She knew that Hunter would be furious. Doubtless, he had returned by now to find her gone with no word of explanation left. She had taken the carriage and some of their money and now she was returning, soiled and smelly, after having been gone all morning and much of the afternoon. She prepared herself to face his anger. Pausing at the door to their apartment, she took a deep breath and entered. There was no sign of Hunter. Relieved, she went into the bedroom to change her clothes.

Hunter was in bed, with the covers pulled up over his head. Quietly, so as not to wake him, she tiptoed to the closet. Then she noticed that the clean white sheets were stained with crimson. She jerked back the covers.

Hunter's throat was slashed from ear to ear.

5 _____

Moreau's Tavern was a noisy, friendly place, patronized mostly by the members of the working class and, on occasion, by gentlemen in search of some diversion. It was a rough-hewn sort of place, with cracked white walls, one of which was decorated with a mural placed there by a local artist with a decidedly erotic bent, cheap and sturdy furniture (the better to survive the occasional donnybrook) and heavy-timbered ceiling. Moreau's establishment was a tavern in search of a character and, in that, perhaps, lay its charm. Elderly men played chess at quiet tables in the corners, younger men played cards, gentlemen rubbed shoulders with common laborers as they drank their fill, and prostitutes solicited the patrons, albeit very politely and in a subdued, indirect manner. Moreau would not allow it any other way.

The aging seaman held court in his establishment with a charm and *joie de vivre* that made his tavern a popular spot, and he was tolerant of the excesses of his patrons, but only to a point. Although he was sixty-two years old, Moreau was still as strong as an ox and one did not argue with him unless one were deeply in his cups and, in such a case, the conclusion of such an argument could be sobering in the extreme.

Messrs. Dumas and D'Laine inquired as to the rooms their friend, Monsieur Legault, had arranged for them and Moreau had them sign the register for one of several rooms he let out on the tavern's second floor. Lucas raised his eyebrows when he saw Finn sign in as *Monsieur F. D'Laine*.

"Well, if you can be Alexander Dumas, *I* can be Francois D'Laine, so long as we're posing as Frenchmen."

"But D'Artagnan already knows you as Delaney," Lucas protested.

"So? If we run into him again, I've Frenchified my name for the sake of convenience."

"*Frenchified*?"

"Whatever."

Their room was spartan, nothing more than four walls, a couple of ramshackle beds, a small table, and a basin.

"If you'll be wanting anything more, it's extra," said Moreau.

Lucas assured him that if they needed anything, they would let him know.

"No food before eight o'clock," Moreau said, "and none after nine at night. And there'll be no eating in the rooms, if you please. If you're hungry, you come downstairs and get fed in the tavern. I'm trying to keep the rats down." He pointed at the foot of the bed in the corner. "Chamber pot is under there. When you're done, you fling it out the window in the hall, into the alley. Don't leave it sitting, stinking up the place. I run a clean establishment."

"So I see," said Lucas, eyeing a large roach as it scuttled across the floor. Moreau spat and hit the roach dead on, slowing its progress only for a moment. He shrugged.

"There's still a few around, but I'm getting rid of 'em."

"How?" said Finn.

"Snakes," Moreau replied. "Bought three of 'em from a sailor friend of mine. Don't you worry, though; they're not the poisonous sort. You find one in your bed, just toss it out upon the floor."

"The snakes will eat the rats, I think," said Lucas, "but I don't believe they'll eat the roaches."

"You sure?"

"I think so."

"Hmmph. That explains it, then. I was wondering why

there were still so many of them. What eats roaches, then?''

"Lizards."

"*Lizards*?"

"Lizards."

Moreau seemed to consider this a moment, then he shook his head. "No, then I'll be up to my ears in lizards."

"The snakes will eat the lizards," Finn suggested.

"And then I'll still have the roaches," Moreau said. "What's the point?"

"It does seem to pose a dilemma," Lucas said, "unless you get rid of the snakes. But then you'll have the rats."

Moreau considered this as well, then grunted. "I'll take the roaches."

"Wise choice," said Finn.

That night, he let out a yell and Lucas was out of his bed in an instant, rapier at the ready. Looking sheepish, Finn dropped a king snake down onto the floor. It slithered off somewhere into the shadows. "Springtime in Paris," Finn mumbled, sourly.

In the morning, someone knocked upon their door.

"Who is it?" Lucas said.

"Ratcatcher," said a voice from beyond the door.

"We've already got one," Finn said.

Lucas opened the door to reveal a gnarled and bent old man dressed in rags and smelling of garlic. He carried a cloth sack draped over his shoulder and a club-shaped stick in his left hand. He was filthy and his nose was running. He brushed past Lucas and entered the room.

"I'm afraid—" Lucas began, then stopped when the old man suddenly straightened, moving his shoulders to loosen the kinks.

"Mongoose," said the smelly old man.

"Mon—" Lucas halted in mid-word, then peered hard at the stranger. "I'll be damned."

"That's a pretty good disguise," said Finn, wrinkling his nose.

"I'm paid to be a lot more than 'pretty good,' Mr. Delaney," the agent said. He scratched himself. "Damn lice."

"Must be rough," said Lucas, sympathetically.

"It *is* rough, Captain, but it's the work I do best."

"God bless America," said Finn.

Mongoose looked at him for a moment, then an amused smile appeared on his face. "Working for a spook stings your professional pride, does it?" he said.

"Let's just say I'm less than happy with the arrangement," Finn said.

"I think I can understand that," Mongoose said. "Your dossiers were delivered to me yesterday. I memorized them, then destroyed them. In your particular case, there was quite a lot written between the lines. I think I know you, Delaney. We spooks are only supposed to do the groundwork, after all, right? Then you real pros come in to clean the situation up. Isn't that how it's supposed to work?" He grinned. "It might interest you to know that we have a lot in common. I was in the Corps myself and I also flunked out of RCS. My final thesis was just a bit too controversial, so I didn't make the grade, but I'm not bitter. I expected it. Just between you and me, I'm not that crazy about the agency myself. Too many diehards and nut cases."

"And where do you fit in?" said Delaney. "What's in it for you?"

Mongoose shrugged his shoulders. "A certain amount of thrill-seeking enters into it, I guess, but mostly, it's the life-style."

"The lifestyle?" Lucas said.

"I get bored rather easily," said Mongoose. "Playing the same game all the time gets tiresome. I like it when the rules keep changing."

Finn raised his eyebrows. "You're telling me you're in it for the sport?"

Mongoose smiled. "If you like. I suppose that's as good a way of saying it as any, although I'm not much on sportsmanship, if you know what I mean. I play to win. But it's not much of a challenge if the game's too easy."

"Jesus Christ," said Finn.

"You know, that's one scenario I haven't played yet," the agent said. "I've always wondered what it would be like to infiltrate the apostles. I doubt I'll ever get that chance, though.

There's a certain extreme sensitivity about some historical scenarios."

Finn glanced at Lucas. "Is he kidding?"

Lucas looked worried. "I don't know," he said. He glanced at Mongoose. "*Are* you?"

"I think so," said the agent. He grinned. "But I'm not really certain. The idea does have some intriguing possibilities, doesn't it?"

"I don't know who scares me more," Delaney said, "you or the Timekeepers."

The agent chuckled. "The Timekeepers have a cause. They're fanatics with a twisted idealism, but it's idealism just the same. That makes them amateurs. I'm a pro."

"Idealism doesn't matter, then?" said Finn. "History doesn't count for anything?"

"History lies," said Mongoose. "You should know that better than anyone. It always has and it always will. History is written by the winners to glorify their victories and if the losers ever have anything to say, they explain away defeat in whatever manner makes them look more dignified. If dignity is possible. If it isn't, then they make omissions. We've all seen things that never made the history books. Right and wrong depends on point of view. I'm not especially interested in the moral implications of what I do. Morality is totally subjective. To a thug who worships the goddess Kali, murder is a moral act. To a Communist, the end justifies the means. And in a democracy, majority rule means that the minority will be oppressed. Idealism? History? Neither is absolute. The nature of reality depends on the observer."

"God help us," Finn said, "a philosopher spy."

"In our profession, a philosophical attitude can be a definite asset," the agent said, his voice betraying his amusement. "What is an intelligence operative, after all, but one who seeks to be enlightened?"

"You're not a philosopher, Mongoose," Lucas said. "You're a cynic."

"Ah, yes," the agent said, leaning back against the wall and crossing his legs beneath him on the floor. "The condemnation of the righteous. In Oscar Wilde's words, 'A cynic is one

who knows the price of everything and the value of nothing.'
Well, when it comes to what I do, the price of failure is usually
death. And I happen to place a very high value on my life.
Now, diverting as it is discussing metaphysics with you, gentlemen, we do have certain matters to attend to. Our friends' demands have been rejected and the game is about to begin in
earnest. And to begin with, I think we can turn your blunder
into our advantage.''

"What blunder?" Finn said.

"Your encounter with our friend, D'Artagnan," Mongoose
said. "Or had you forgotten how you almost prevented his
run-in with the Count de Rochefort?"

"Oh, that," said Finn.

"Yes, that," said Mongoose. "Unfortunate, but not a
disaster, by any means. I had hoped that Rochefort's party
would arrive before he showed up and I would be able to contact you, but things didn't work out all that badly. I want you
to keep tabs on him. The fact that he knows you will make it
that much easier."

"I don't think he'll be very well disposed toward us after we
ran out on him like that," said Lucas.

"Who says you ran out on him?" said Mongoose. "Your
story is that you leaped valiantly to his defense the moment I
bashed him with that chair. You fought bravely, but you were
overwhelmed and taken into custody. Delaney was slightly
wounded in the process."

"But I wasn't wounded," said Delaney. "I mean, I'm not."

Mongoose produced a laser and aimed it at Finn.

"*Hey! Are you crazy?*"

A bright shaft of pencil-thin light lanced out at him, scar-
ring his cheek on the right side.

"To add verisimilitude," said Mongoose. "The girls in
Heidelberg would love you. It looks rather dashing, if I do say
so myself."

"You miserable son of a bitch, I'll. . . ." Finn stopped when
he saw the laser pointed at him still, the agent's thumb on the
beam-intensity control stud.

"A little cosmetic surgery and you'll be as good as new,"
said Mongoose. "Assuming you behave yourself and don't
give me any trouble. I told you before, I play to win."

"And we're the pawns, is that it?" Lucas said.

"To paraphrase Lord Tennyson, 'yours not to reason why, yours but to do.' We'll hope it doesn't come to die. Now if you'll sit down, Delaney, and keep your hands where I can see them, we'll continue."

Delaney sat down on the bed, holding his cheek gingerly, glowering at the agent.

"Thank you. Now, D'Artagnan was still unconscious when we left, so he'll never know what really transpired. Should he ask, and he undoubtedly will, you'll tell him that you managed to escape en route to Paris. You weren't pursued, doubtless because Rochefort didn't think that you were worth the trouble. When you see him, you'll be overjoyed to learn that that blow didn't kill him, as you thought it had. I want you to encourage his friendship, in the course of which you'll certainly meet the three musketeers. I want you to encourage their friendship, as well. If anyone should ask, you have found employment with Monsieur de Levasseur, a wealthy shipping merchant from Le Havre who occasionally stays in Paris and keeps apartments here for that purpose. He is currently absent from Paris and you are the custodians of his apartments and the possessions therein."

"What if he should return to Paris and run into us?" said Lucas.

"Then he will greet you warmly and acknowledge you," said Mongoose. "*I* am Monsieur de Levasseur."

"Since when?"

"Since this morning," said the agent. "I arrived in Paris at the crack of dawn, established myself at the Luxembourg Hotel, impressed them with my financial resources, then departed on pressing business with some people in the Marais. I informed the people at the hotel that they can expect you shortly, that you will be representing my business interests in Paris. When you arrive, you'll explain that my business took me back to Le Havre unexpectedly, but that you will be remaining in Paris, at the Luxembourg, as my principals. That will give you a somewhat more comfortable and more secure base of operations and provide you with a cover at the same time."

"Just one question," Lucas said. "If we follow this plan

you've outlined, our cover will be blown in a matter of days. You realize that, don't you? D'Artagnan had no friends when he arrived in Paris. Historically, we don't exist. If we establish a relationship with D'Artagnan and the musketeers, we might as well be announcing our presence here to the terrorists."

"If the Timekeepers' planned disruption involves the three musketeers, then your arrival on the scene will definitely make them nervous," said the agent. "However, history has never been totally complete. There are the inevitable undocumented details. They won't be sure about you. On the one hand, you might very well be exactly what you appear to be. On the other, you might be agents from the 27th century. They won't be certain and that will make them nervous. Nervous people make mistakes. That's what I'm counting on."

"That's what I thought," said Lucas. "I can see why you're so fond of these people, Finn," he said sarcastically. "He's setting us up. We're the bait to flush out the Timekeepers."

"Well you can fucking well forget that noise," said Finn, rising to his feet angrily. "That wasn't part of the deal. This is supposed to be *your* ballgame, Mongoose, or whatever the hell your name is. You seem to forget that we're not company men. We're soldiers. And damn expensive soldiers, at that, too damn expensive to be used as judas goats in your espionage games. This is supposed to be a TIA show. I didn't like it, but those were the orders. We're here just in case you people blow it. We're not even supposed to be involved in your investigation."

"That's where you're wrong, Delaney," Mongoose said. "You're *already* involved. You stepped into the game when you interfered in Meung and involved yourself with D'Artagnan. That was *your* mistake, not mine. It was your responsibility. You're going to have to live up to it."

"No way."

"You haven't got much choice, Delaney." The agent got to his feet. "You either do it my way or I'll blow your cover myself. The Timekeepers are here, there's no question of that, and knowing the way they work, I'll stake my reputation on the fact that they've manuevered themselves into positions that will enable them to strike at key figures in this scenario.

My job is to intercept them and I can't do that unless they reveal themselves. I'm not about to have a couple of commandos come in to clean up my mistakes. I don't make mistakes."

"Listen here," said Lucas, "what do you think this is, some interagency competition? Some sort of intramural game? We've got a potential timestream split here and you're worried about your record?"

The agent headed for the door. "Let's get one thing clear," he said. "This is *my* show and *I* call the shots. And I'm going to call them as I see them. I'd appreciate your cooperation, but remember one thing—I don't need it. You either work *with* me or you work *for* me, it's up to you."

"Or we work against you," Finn said.

The agent held up his laser casually. "I wouldn't advise that. These are perilous times. Keep in mind that adjustments are your specialty, gentlemen. Assassination's mine."

There was a soft knock at the door. For the second time that day, Andre panicked. She was not normally given to that emotion, but her emotions had been strained to the breaking point. Earlier that day, there had been another knock at the door to the apartments and her heart was in her mouth as she answered it. It was only a messenger from the tailor shop, delivering her clothes. She had been able to keep him out of the apartment, but she had been afraid that the boy would still sense that something was amiss. Hunter's body had been lying in the bedroom for two days. There had been no chance to get rid of it, no way of removing it without being discovered. It had been all that she could do to keep the maids out of the room. The lie was that "Monsieur Laporte" was very ill and could not be disturbed.

For two days, she had been in something like a state of shock. *Who* had killed him? *Why?* Nothing had been stolen. Had Hunter enemies in Paris, in this time? If so, why had he not warned her? Or perhaps he had, when he told her to remain in the hotel unless he accompanied her. What had happened? And worse than the shock of finding him dead, worse than not knowing why he had been killed or by whom, was the realization that she was now entirely alone, trapped in an unfamiliar city, in an unfamiliar *time*, with no way of escape. She literally had no place to go.

Cautiously, her nerves ragged, she went up to the door.

"Who is it?" Her voice seemed shrill to her. She swallowed hard, trying to calm herself.

"Doctor Jacques Benoit," came the soft reply, "to see Monsieur Laporte."

She leaned against the door with relief. It was a name she knew. Jacques Benoit—Jack Bennett—Hunter's friend. The man who was the reason for their journey to this time. Surely, he'd know what to do. She had no one else to turn to. Quickly, she opened the door and pulled him inside.

The old man looked confused. He had come to see an old friend and he now found himself facing an extremely agitated young woman dressed in nothing save her undergarments. His eyes took in the harried look that spoke of little, if any, sleep. He noticed the uncharacteristically short blonde hair, worn in a male fashion, the flushed cheeks, the nervous perspiration on her forehead. Then his professional senses took over and he saw deeper, or rather, he observed more closely. He noticed the woman's bearing, her unusual muscular development, her slightly bowlegged stance that spoke of years spent in the saddle. He saw her hands, which were not the hands of a pampered Parisienne, but the hands of one who worked at hard and possibly brutal labor. The calluses and scars told a tale of violence and survival.

She, in turn, saw a withered, kindly, avuncular old man with gray hair and crow's feet, wrinkled skin, and slightly stooped posture and her heart sank. How could this grandfatherly old man be of any help to her? Then her years of soldiering took over and she saw something else, which the casual observer might miss. His eyes. They were alert, sharp, distressingly blue, and deeply observant. He was taking her measure even as she took his.

"What is it?" said Jack Bennett. "Where is he?" He spoke in English.

She shut the door quickly, locked it, then jerked her head toward the bedroom. Before he reached the door, the old man knew. The knowledge stopped him in his tracks like a hammerblow.

"Oh, my God," he said, softly. "How long?"

"Two days."

"Sweet Jesus." He pulled back the sheet and his eyes became filled with pain at the sight. "It was because of me," he said, his voice hollow. "It was all my fault. He couldn't have known."

"He couldn't have known *what*?" said Andre.

"He was in the wrong place at the wrong time," said Bennett. "And they killed him for it. Because of me."

"*Who* killed him? *Why*? What had you to do with it? Speak, and be quick about it!"

Bennett turned and saw her standing in the door, a rapier in her hand. Under other circumstances, it might have been a comical or maybe even an erotic sight, a striking-looking woman in her underclothing, standing in the doorway to the bedroom with a sword in her right hand. But it was neither funny nor erotic. The soldier in Jack Bennett, though he had not fought in years, knew at once that this woman was extremely dangerous.

"Who are you?" he said, gently.

"Andre de la Croix."

"You speak English very well, but it's not your native language. And your French, from the little I heard, is less than perfect. Are you underground?"

She frowned for a moment, then remembered. "That was the purpose for our journey here. Hunter came to seek you out."

"You're a recent deserter, then. I thought as much."

"You thought wrong," she said. "I was never a part of the armies of the future. I am a Basque whose time is over four hundred years distant."

"Good Lord. You're a D.P.," said Bennett, astonished.

"What?"

"A displaced person. And Hunter brought you here to join the underground, to receive an implant?"

She nodded.

"You must be an extraordinary young woman," Bennett

said. "I can imagine what you must have been going through these past two days."

"I need your help," she said.

"You have it. It's the very least that I can do. God. Poor Hunter."

"Who did this?" Andre said. "Why was he killed? You say it was on your account?"

"I'm afraid so," Bennett said. "It must have been an accident. A horrible misunderstanding. There was no way he could have known. They must have thought that he was someone else. Yes, there could be no other explanation. They—"

"*Who?*" shouted Andre. "What kind of misunderstanding could have led to this? What could he not have known? Tell me, this instant!"

Bennett stared at her. "Yes, I'll tell you. I can't condone it any longer. They've gone too far. I've made a terrible mistake and now my friend of many years has paid for it. I'll tell you, but I don't know what in God's name we can do about it now."

"Precious little, I'm afraid," said another voice. Andre saw Bennett's eyes widen even before the man spoke and she was already spinning around to face the threat, but she was too late. She felt a sharp blow to her side and she fell into the bedroom, off balance and carried by the momentum of the kick to land at Bennett's feet. The rapier fell from her hand and clattered to the floor. She lunged for it, but Bennett stopped her.

"Don't!" he said, stepping on the sword with his foot.

"Are you *mad?*"

"I'd listen to the good doctor if I were you," the man said. She saw the little tube in his right hand. It was a weapon, one she didn't understand, but she knew what it could do. Hunter had shown her once. A deadly light that could cut through steel. The same light that had burned through the lock on her door could burn through her flesh as easily as a hot knife passing through fresh butter.

"A good thing Adrian decided to keep tabs on you, Doc," the terrorist said. "Seems like your commitment's slipping. We can't have that."

"Let the woman go, Silvera," Bennett said. "She doesn't know anything."

"But you were about to fix that, weren't you?" said Silvera. "No, you're expendable, Doc, but I'm afraid she's not. I got her partner, but Adrian's going to want this lady alive. We need to find out how many more of them there are, and where they are, and what they know."

"She's not an agent!" Bennett said.

"You'll have to do better than that, Doc."

"She's not, I tell you! And neither was he," he said, pointing at Hunter's body. "He was a friend of mine! He was in the underground!"

Silvera nodded. "That's what he kept saying. It makes for a good cover, doesn't it? He was good, I'll give him that. He didn't talk. But I think the lady will. Adrian's a little better at persuasion than I am."

"Silvera, *listen* to me! You're making a mistake, I swear it! Kill me, if you must, but let her go. She doesn't know a thing, she's a D.P., she's harmless to you!"

"Then why were you going to tell her everything?" Silvera said. "If she's not an agent, what good would it have done? Sorry, Doc, I'm afraid you're not very good at this game. It's too bad, really. You've been very helpful—"

For a moment, his eyes were not on Andre. That moment was all she needed. She reached behind her quickly, to the back of her neck, where hung a slim dagger in a sheath suspended from a thong. In one fast motion, she drew the dagger and hurled it. It buried itself in the terrorist's larynx. He fell, gurgling horribly, the laser beam cutting a crooked swath across the ceiling. She leaped to her feet and ran over to the fallen terrorist, kicking the deadly tube out of his hand. Then she kneeled by him, grasped the knife, and gave a vicious, sideways slash. Hunter was avenged.

Bennett stared at her, his jaw hanging slack. Andre went over to him and shook him, getting some blood on his shirt. "We cannot stay here," she said. "I understand none of this, but I understand the danger all too well. Collect your wits, Jack Bennett. We must flee."

Bennett came out of it. "Yes, you're quite right, we must. I have friends who will hide us. But we can't simply cut and run. We can't leave two bodies to be found in your apartment. We'll have troubles enough without being sought for murder.''

"What do you propose?"

"That we leave quietly, normally. That we pay your bill and move out, with all your things." He thought a moment. "Hunter has arranged other quarters for you. You'll be staying with friends, something of the sort. We'll have to clean up the mess as best we can."

"And what of the corpses?" Andre said.

Bennett bent down and picked up Silvera's laser. "It is both a weapon and a surgeon's tool," he said, "although I dread the use to which we must put it now." He pulled one of the clothing chests into the center of the room. "Use the sheets to line this chest," he said. "And we'll sprinkle lots of perfume on . . . the contents. It should help to hide the smell. I hope. Perhaps it would be best if you left the room. The sight will not be pleasant."

"You'll need help to pack the pieces," Andre said.

"Will you be able to stand it?"

"I've seen blood before," she said. "I will try not to think whose body we're dismembering. If it must be done, then let's set to it. The sooner we quit this place, the better."

"I was right," said Bennett. "You *are* an extraordinary woman."

Finn and Lucas moved to one side to let the porters carrying the heavy chests pass. Lucas wrinkled his nose as one chest went by. It reeked of perfume and the smell was powerful enough to make his head swim.

"God, what a stink!" he said.

"It covers up the body odor," Finn said, chuckling. "And there's one lady that must smell like something died inside her."

"Christ, Finn, that smell was bad enough."

"Shhh, I think here comes the perfumed doll herself," said Finn.

They moved to the left side of the stairs, allowing the old

man and the young woman to pass by on their right. His clothes were shabby compared to her ornate and obviously very expensive dress.

"There goes one father whose little girl will send him to the poorhouse," Finn said, turning to Lucas.

Lucas was standing on the stairs, looking after the old man and the young woman.

Finn chuckled. "Yes, she's very pretty, but can you stand her fragrance?"

"That's not it," said Lucas, thoughtfully. "That woman. . . . I've seen her somewhere, I'm certain of it."

"Probably reminds you of some old flame," said Finn.

"No, I've seen that face before," said Lucas. "But I just can't. . . ." He shook his head.

"Are you sure?" said Finn.

"I'm almost positive. But it just won't click. There's something. . . ." He frowned.

"Must be a coincidence," said Finn. "Hell, who do we know in 17th-century Paris?"

"Not in 17th-century Paris," Lucas said, "but somewhere else. I just don't remember where."

"You're not kidding, are you?"

"I'm telling you, Finn, *I know that face!*"

"That's good enough for me. Come on, we'll follow them and find out where they go. But just to play it safe, let's keep our distance. Worse comes to worst, we'll just waste an afternoon."

"What if worse doesn't come to worst?" said Lucas.

"You're asking me? You're the one who can't remember faces."

"I never forget a face. That's why this one bothers me. It hasn't been a long time, either." They watched the chests being loaded into a carriage, the old man and the young woman getting in. "Horses," Lucas said.

"What?"

"Horses. That face belongs with horses."

"Well, that should narrow it down," said Finn. "We haven't ridden horses in more than ninety percent of our missions."

"Something doesn't fit," said Lucas. "It's the right face, but somehow, it's all wrong."

"Well, I'm glad you cleared that up," said Finn. "Shall we see which way your right-wrong face is heading? I'd hate for this to keep you up all night."

"I have a feeling that it will. I'm not sure what memories go with her face, but I am sure that none of them is good."

6

"Vacated their rooms, you say?" said Adrian Taylor. "And no sign of Silvera?"

Jimmy Darcy stood uneasily before the terrorist leader. Only a short while ago, Adrian Taylor had been a small, whip-cord thin young man with violently blue eyes, a sharp, slightly crooked nose, and a thin, cruel mouth. He knew that Taylor was considerably older than he was, though by how much, he could not say. Taylor had appeared to be, judging by the standards used before the advent of antiagathic drugs, eighteen to twenty years of age. He was, Jimmy knew, at the very least three times that age. Now, however, Taylor was trans-formed.

The skills of Jack Bennett had reshaped his face, shortening and straightening out his nose and giving it a slight, delicate upward turn. His jawline had been restructured, more gently curved, the sharp planes of his face smoothed out, the cheeks rounded, the soft flesh around the eyes surgically altered to eliminate the beginning signs of age. His mouth was full and soft now, the lips were those of a voluptuary. The ears were small and shapely, without the pronounced lobes they had earlier possessed. A small beauty mark now graced Taylor's right cheek. His adam's apple had been removed and the skin of the throat smoothed out. Taylor's hairline had been depilated to give him a higher forehead. He had round, full breasts now and decidedly and unsettlingly feminine hips. The extensive operation had been a masterwork, complete right down to the very last detail. Taylor even had Milady's brand, the harlot's fleur-de-lis, burned into his shoulder.

Transsexual operations had been reversible for many years. The purpose of the procedure had simply been to enable Taylor to become a "woman" for the purpose of the mission. When it was over, Adrian Taylor would be able to have his male organs back, either exactly as they were or redesigned to his own specifications. But it had become much more than an elaborate disguise. Taylor took a perverse pleasure in being as he was now. With each succeeding day, he fell more and more in love with his new aspect.

Of all the Timekeepers, Taylor was the best known. The TIA had an extensive dossier on his activities. He was regarded as an expert in his field, ruthless, cold, and extremely dangerous. The one thing that no one outside the organization knew was what Taylor really looked like. Few people within the Timekeepers had ever glimpsed Taylor's real face. He changed his appearance almost as frequently as most people changed their style of clothing. Taylor was a true chameleon, but to Jimmy's knowledge, he had never gone so far before. It wasn't Taylor's sexual preferences that bothered Jimmy Darcy. There was nothing unusual in that. What frightened Jimmy Darcy was that Adrian Taylor appeared to have two personalities now. He was both Adrian Taylor *and* Milady. Sometimes he spoke as Adrian Taylor and acted like a man surgically disguised as a woman. Sometimes he spoke as Milady de Winter, living out the role. And sometimes, he spoke as Milady, referring to Adrian Taylor in the second person, as though Taylor existed elsewhere, as a separate and distinct being. He did so now.

"No sign of Silvera," he said once again, fingering his throat absently. "Adrian won't like that. I think we can safely assume that Silvera is no longer with us. Pity. He must have underestimated the opposition. You checked? You're certain? There was only Bennett and the woman?"

"They were seen getting into a carriage and driving away," said Jimmy.

"There can be no doubt that she's an agent," Taylor said. "Bennett has betrayed us."

"But he seemed totally committed to the cause," said Jimmy. "God, do you realize what this means? It's a complete disaster! They know who you are now! We're stopped before we've even started!"

"Not necessarily," said Taylor. He smiled. "That won't stop Adrian at all. Why should it?"

"I don't understand," said Jimmy. "How can we continue now?"

"You're not thinking, Jimmy." He was Adrian again, suddenly on his feet and pacing nervously. "Didn't I always tell you to have faith? All right, so they know that I've become Milady. So what? You forget that time is on our side."

"The chronoplate!" said Jimmy. "We can go back in time and outmaneuver them! Of course, we can go back and save Silvera and then—"

"Screw Silvera," Taylor said. "He made a mistake and he's paid for it. No, we don't need the plate, Jimmy, not yet. We can always use it as a last resort if need be, but we're still ahead. The scenario's progressing smoothly. They may know who I am, but for the moment, they don't know *where* I am. And, after all, we're the ones threatening to change history, remember? They're here to preserve the status quo. If they know that I've become de Winter, then they'll surely know that the real Milady's dead and that's just it. They *need* de Winter. Or, more precisely, they need *a* de Winter to insure that events in this period of history progress as they should. They can plant their own de Winter, but they wouldn't dare to do that as long as I'm around. No, they'd have to take me out first and that won't be so easy."

"But the very fact that they know," said Jimmy, "the fact that they're *here*—"

"Only serves to make the game more interesting," said Taylor.

"The game?" said Jimmy.

"Of course. It's a wonderful, fascinating game that just became more challenging. The TIA and I have been playing it for years and now it's reached its climax. They'll have their best people in on this, you can be sure of that. There's more than just the two we've spotted. The one Silvera killed was not one of the first-string or Silvera would not have taken him so easily. The woman, I'm not so sure about, but the man. . . . He was expendable. Maybe his only purpose was to flush us out. Yes, that would be the way he'd do it," Taylor said, nodding his head and smiling.

"Who?"

"My old friend Mongoose," Taylor said. He suddenly seemed very happy.

"Who's Mongoose?"

"We've been playing cat and mouse for years," said Taylor. "He's the TIA's best agent. He's my *doppelganger*. Neither of us knows what the other looks like. Oh, Jimmy, this is going to be fun! Sometimes I've beaten him, sometimes he's beaten me, but this time, *this* time, I'm going to get him! I'm going to take him, Jimmy. I'm going to take him and I'll keep him for a while, we'll talk about old times, and then I'll kill him. It's going to be wonderful."

There was no doubt in Jimmy Darcy's mind that Adrian Taylor was insane. About everything else, Jimmy had a great deal of doubt. He had joined the Temporal Preservation League because his older brother had died in the time wars. And for what? To protect his family? To defend his homeland? Had Danny's death *anything* to do with protecting his own, with patriotic loyalty, with anything at all that made any sort of sense? No, it had all been part of some grandiose game, wars fought on paper, move a decimal point and another hundred people die. Just an endless escalation to keep the machine oiled and running, to feed its momentum until, sooner or later, the inevitable would happen. Man had already split the atom and now he was threatening to split time. The only movement that made any sense at all was that of Albrecht Mensinger. There was no alternative. The time wars had to stop. They were mankind's greatest folly. In his attempts to master nature and his fate, Man had gone too far at last. He had poisoned himself and the environment he lived in, he had stripped the Earth of resources, he had shown contempt for all the works of God. Nor was it enough to imperil his future. Man was now threatening his past.

The leaders of the league were fond of quoting Thomas Jefferson, saying that government was far too important to be left up to the people. The people had demonstrated a staggering irresponsibility, electing leaders whose own criminal stupidity surpassed even that of those who put them into office. It was past time for the elite to lead. Someone had to show the way.

There were those within the league who went by the strictest principles set down by Albrecht Mensinger, but there were also those who thought that what the league was doing did not go far enough. It was to this more militant group that Jimmy Darcy had been attracted. It was from this group that he had been recruited into the Timekeepers.

Jimmy Darcy had a great deal of anger roiling away inside of him. It had fueled his terrorist activities. He saw no ethical contradiction in using violence to achieve peace. In thousands of years of human history, the passive way had never worked. The ideology of peace was alien to the warmongers. Violence was all they understood. There were those within the league who believed that the end did not justify the means. Jimmy had once believed that too. Since then, he had become a great deal more pragmatic, more realistic. He understood that it was not up to him to justify the means. His course had been forced upon him by people who remained steadfastly unaffected by any other course of action. Let *them* justify the means, Jimmy had shouted at the doves within the league. They have handed us our tools. Those who are morally right have no need of justifying anything. A resistance leader by the name of Arafat had once said, upon addressing the United Nations, "I come bearing an olive branch in one hand and a machine gun in the other. Do not let the olive branch fall from my hand."

The doves within the league held out the olive branch. It was repeatedly ignored. The Timekeepers fired the machine gun. To ignore it was to die.

At the core of his existence, Jimmy Darcy still believed in peace. It was what he fought for. He fought the war machine. When the war machine was beaten, he would be happy to let the machine gun fall from his hand into the dust, never to be fired again. He did not believe that Adrian would do the same. No, Adrian would find another battle, start his own war if need be. Even in the Timekeepers, Adrian was feared because

Adrian was always at war, with the world and with himself.
Yet they needed Adrian. He was effective. *They have handed
us our tools.*

"It isn't a game, Adrian," said Jimmy. "It's a struggle for
survival. Surely, you can see that, can't you?"

Adrian regarded him with amusement. "Of course I can see
that, Jimmy. Can't *you* see that the struggle for survival is the
most fascinating game of all? The stakes are high and it's win-
ner take all. Life is a game, Jimmy. The idea is to play to win.
And we're going to win, because for once, we control the
board. We're on the offensive. Milady wrote a letter to an
Englishman. Not just any Englishman, mind you. She wrote
to George Villiers, the Duke of Buckingham. It was a love letter. It wasn't from Milady, even though she wrote it. Buckingham will think it's from the Queen. He'll have received it
by now and, doubtless, it will have inflamed his passion for
the Queen anew. I do have a way with words, if I say so myself."

"I don't understand," said Jimmy.

"No, you wouldn't, but Richelieu will and that's what
really counts. He was quite pleased about it. In fact, he told
me that he wished he had thought of it himself. He'll take the
credit, of course, but that's all right. It all fits into the plan."

"I still don't—"

"Be patient, Jimmy, I'll explain it to you. There's a very
charming lady here in town by the name of Camille de Bois-
Tracy. She just loves intrigue, especially if it has to do with
love. She can't resist it. For quite some time now, she's been
an intermediary for Buckingham and Anne of Austria, a sort
of patron of the heart, a role she dearly loves. Richelieu's been
made aware of this, of course. It's brought Milady further
into his good graces. When he receives that letter, Buckingham will surely come to France. He might be on his way to
Paris even as we speak. He will come to Camille de Bois-Tracy
and a rendezvous will be arranged. Richelieu, of course, will
try to take him, Buckingham being an enemy of France."

"I remember now," said Jimmy. "Buckingham gets away,
according to history. Only we're going to change that, right?
Yes, it's a brilliant plan. If the musketeers are prevented from

helping Buckingham escape, then Richelieu has him. If not, then we can grab him and then we'll have a hostage. They'll have no choice but to listen to us! Either way, they'll have an adjustment on their hands, an adjustment made that much more complicated by our being here to interfere with it.''

"No, no, Jimmy, you see, you don't understand the game at all. I intend to make certain that Buckingham gets away.''

"But . . . why lure him to Paris in the first place, then?''

"To set up the next act in this scenario,'' Taylor said. "But you won't have to worry about any of that for now. You'll have another job to do. I want you and Tonio to find Jack Bennett and that agent. See if they'll lead you to any of the others. Find out what you can, then kill them.''

Jimmy left, feeling confused. Letting Buckingham get away made no sense whatsoever. Obviously, it would take an adjustment in order to attain their goal. The simple act of threatening to create a timestream split would never result in their demands being met by the warmongers. No, the threat would have to be brought home to them. They'd have to face an adjustment situation, one in which the interference of the Timekeepers would be a factor added to all the other difficulties inherent in such a task. They had a chronoplate now. That gave them the edge. They could create an adjustment situation, interfere with its resolution, and then clock out to another period and repeat the entire process. They could repeat their demands and continue to create one adjustment situation after another, forcing the warmongers to bring more and more attention to the problem, draining their financial reserves, putting a strain upon the Referee Corps and the TIA and the adjustment teams, nipping at the heels of the war machine until it was no longer cost-effective, until they realized that they could never win. It was the logical course of action.

But Adrian Taylor wasn't being logical. Or Jimmy couldn't see the logic. What was he planning? His cover was surely blown, yet he seemed completely unconcerned. He had created an excellent opportunity for an adjustment situation and he was walking away from it, using it to set up . . . what?

Jimmy was beginning to have a lot of doubts about the

operation. Terrorist tactics had to be hit-and-run in order for them to be successful. They had an opportunity to hit-and-run now, but Taylor wasn't taking it. He was building up to something else, to some more elaborate game. Somehow, the TIA had received intelligence about their operation and they had brought at least one team of agents in. That didn't bother Taylor. Taylor's cover had been blown. That didn't bother Taylor, either. One of the group had disappeared, killed most likely, possibly taken prisoner to be interrogated, to reveal all the members of their cell. That didn't bother Taylor. What *would* it take to bother Taylor? Why this pointless stalking of the traitor, Bennett, and the agents? Why take unnecessary risks when all it took was to create an adjustment situation quickly, cut and run, and repeat the process somewhere else, tying up the opposition's manpower until they realized that they only had one choice—capitulate or face a timestream split? A split was something no one wanted, not the warmongers, not the Timekeepers, and certainly not the league. The key to success was to walk that ragged edge between adjustment and disaster, to exhaust the Referee Corps with adjustments until they faced their folly and brought the time wars to a halt. But to Taylor, it was all a game, a senseless, crazy rivalry with the agent who had dogged his heels for years. It was putting the entire operation in jeopardy.

Jimmy was wondering if Taylor could be trusted with leading the operation. Based on recent evidence, the answer had to be a resounding *no*. But Taylor could not be relieved. It would not be a matter as simple as holding a meeting of the cell and voting him out of office. No, if it came to that, Taylor would have to be eliminated and that would not be easy. Taylor was dangerous. Taylor was suspicious to the point of being paranoid. Taylor had that musclebound German, Freytag, a homicidal brute who could snap him like a twig with just one hand. And Taylor had the chronoplate. Jimmy was alone. He could sound out Tonio, but he would have to be very careful, very subtle.

There was nothing to be done now except to follow Taylor's leadership. Bennett and the woman would be found, questioned, and killed. It would be risky, but there was nothing else to do. He would follow Taylor's orders, but the operation would come first. He would sound out Tonio, he would watch Taylor carefully, and he would bide his time. In the end, it always came down to time.

D'Artagnan was in love. More to the point, he was in lust, though he had not yet attained either the age or the experience that would enable him to tell the difference. He and the three musketeers, having become fast friends following their run-in with the cardinal's guards, had spent the better part of the evening discussing the mysterious woman who had intervened on their behalf. None of them had ever seen her before and each of them was fascinated by her. Each vowed to discover her identity, each maintained that it was he whom she had meant to save, and each had his own unspoken amorous designs upon the lady.

Over the next couple of days, their attention was occupied by this delightful mystery, but not to the exclusion of yet another illegal brawl with Richelieu's guards. Due to Treville's intervention with the king on their behalf and Louis's own secret delight at seeing Richelieu's men embarrassed, the musketeers were not only spared punishment, but they were given the sort of praise a master might lavish on his hounds upon discovering that they had torn apart a larger pack of dogs. The king had been especially delighted with Cadet D'Artagnan and, seeing that he was poor, he had gifted him with a purse containing the sum of forty pistoles.

The Gascon had celebrated by buying himself a fine new suit of clothes and procuring the services of a valet, a bedraggled, flea-bitten, scarecrow of a man whose name was Planchet. Porthos had found him sleeping in a garbage heap. He smelled terrible, but he was as grateful as a stray responding to the kindness of a stranger. All this was very pleasant to the Gascon, but it did nothing to assuage his mounting passion. D'Artagnan was a young man of extraordinary simplicity. His attention could be completely occupied by only one thing at a time. The new distraction appeared in the person of his landlord's wife, the pretty Constance Bonacieux. He already had the mystery woman of the mud puddle on his mind and he was preoccupied with his plans for courtship and seduction. However, the mystery woman was still a mystery, nowhere to be found, unknown, intangible. Constance, on the other hand, was very real; she was nearby and she was, it took no great perception to discern, available. D'Artagnan, being an eminently pragmatic youth, simply shifted gears and redirected his attention toward a more accessible objective.

The fact that Constance Bonacieux was also a woman of some mystery and the fact that she was married only served to add spice to the situation. In fact, her about-to-be-cuckolded husband had approached him just the other day, offering to forget about the rent if the dashing Monsieur D'Artagnan, who was already gaining something of a reputation as a swordsman, would help to rescue Constance from her abductors. This, in itself, had piqued the Gascon's curiosity.

It turned out that Constance's godfather was the cloakbearer to the queen and that he had secured for her a position in the palace as both maid and companion to Anne of Austria. It was in the palace that Constance had made her residence, coming home to see her much older husband twice a week. After she had missed a visit, Bonacieux had received a letter. He had shown it to D'Artagnan. It read: "Do not seek for your wife. She will be restored to you when there is no longer occasion for her. If you make a single step to find her, you are lost."

D'Artagnan had not been at all certain about how he would go about finding the lady, much less rescuing her from her abductors, but the story had intrigued him and he was in no position to turn down the offer of free room and board. He had barely given the matter any thought when two singularly interesting things happened. Bonacieux was arrested by the cardinal's guards and taken away for questioning and, in his absence, who but the kidnapped Constance should appear, having escaped from her captors by letting herself down from a window by the means of knotted sheets. She had made her way straight home to be sheltered by her husband, but in his place, she found D'Artagnan. The Gascon instantly perceived that it was a situation Madame Bonacieux found not at all unpleasant.

He saw that Constance was very young and pretty and quite obviously possessed of a strong sexual appetite. He knew that the opportunities for romantic diversion at the palace were not rare, but Constance, being a married woman, had her reputation to consider. At the palace, there would be no telling who was an informer. For many at court, it was a profitable occupation. Moreover, most of her time would be spent being a companion to the queen.

Constance did little to hide the fact that the possibility of a passionate and deliciously illicit romance so close at hand was having an effect on her. Her smoldering glances were not lost upon D'Artagnan. Her husband was much older than she was and the Gascon suspected that Madame Bonacieux's twice-weekly visits to her husband did little to satisfy her cravings. She had, after all, seen the handsome gentlemen at court and, compared with such cavaliers, Bonacieux paled into insignificance. D'Artagnan, on the other hand, was young, muscular, dashing, and good-looking and what he lacked in courtly manners he more than made up for in enthusiasm. What with the bowing, the hand-kissing, the putting of the arms around the shoulders to comfort an obviously distressed young woman, it took about twenty minutes for the comforting to travel from Bonacieux's front door to D'Artagnan's bedroom.

Between hugs and kisses and please-don'ts and no-I-really-shouldn'ts, Constance explained the circumstances of her abduction. She did not, however, go into too great detail. She did not tell D'Artagnan that word had reached Anne, through the usual secret channels, that the Duke of Buckingham had received her letter and had arrived in Paris in answer to her summons. Anne was understandably distressed, for she had written no such letter. Clearly, the whole thing was a trap to snare her lover, an enemy of France. Someone close to her was an informer, doubtless in the pay of Louis or, even worse, of Richelieu. Having no one else to trust, Anne had turned to Constance, pleading with her to go to the house of Camille de Bois-Tracy and warn the duke of treachery. She had been on her way to the house in the Rue de la Harpe when she had been taken by a group of men commanded by the Count de Rochefort.

The account she gave D'Artagnan was deliberately vague and it was accepted without prying questions because the Gascon's mind was less intent on conversation than on pressing his seduction of his landlord's pretty wife, which process

progressed with faint cries of protestation and only token
physical resistence. (*Please—no, don't, oh-monsieur-I'm-
only-a-weak-woman.*)

There had been a lengthy pause during which the extent of
her weakness was explored. All the while, Constance clung to
him and chattered on about the terrors of her captivity, as
though the shock of the ordeal had been so great that she did
not quite know what she was doing. Upon hearing her de-
nounce "that scar-faced lackey of the cardinal," D'Artagnan
recalled the man in Meung and he pressed her for details. In
due course, he learned that the man whose path had crossed
his in the tavern was none other than the Count de Rochefort,
Richelieu's right-hand man.

With the "explanation" out of the way, D'Artagnan was
able to think a bit more clearly. As he dressed, he came to the
conclusion that the house of Bonacieux would be the first
place the guards would look when they discovered that their
prisoner had escaped. Therefore, he elected to take Constance
to the home of his friend Athos for safekeeping. When they
arrived at Athos's apartment in the Rue Férou, the musketeer
was out. D'Artagnan had a key, however, and he let them in,
informing her whose house it was and that she would be safe
there. With Athos being out, something else occurred to D'Artagnan, but before she would agree to give him any further
"explanations," Constance prevailed upon him to undertake
an errand for her. He was to present himself at the wicket of
the Louvre, on the side of the Rue de l'Echelle, and ask for
one Germain.

"What then?" said D'Artagnan, feeling a great deal of im-
patience.

"He will ask you what you want," said Constance, "and
you will answer by these two words—Tours and Bruxelles. He
will immediately be at your command."

"And what shall I order him to do?" D'Artagnan said, not
so curious about the peculiar task as he was anxious to get it
out of the way.

"You shall ask him to go and fetch the queen's *valet de
chambre*," Constance said, "and then send him to me."

D'Artagnan left in a great hurry, mindful of the fact that

the sooner he returned, the sooner Constance could explain the whole affair to him. He did as he was told and he presented himself at the small gate at the Louvre. He gave the message to Germain and Germain replied, further perplexing him, by advising him to seek out a friend whose clock was too slow so that he would have an alibi, since the errand he was on could bring him trouble. It was all becoming quite mysterious.

D'Artagnan immediately set out to see Captain de Treville. Arriving there, he turned the clock back three-quarters of an hour and spent some time in idle talk with the old solider, during which discussion he made a point to remark upon the time. That being done and his alibi being secured in case someone should question him about his whereabouts that evening, D'Artagnan paused only long enough to turn the clock forward to the proper time before setting out to the house on the Rue Férou and a further explanation of these mysterious goings-on. En route, he thought of Constance and the good fortune that had brought him to his present state. He had left home penniless and now he was in Paris, a cadet soon to become a musketeer, with friends as illustrious as Athos, Aramis, and Porthos and a sponsor as distinguished as Captain de Treville. He had new clothes, a situation, comfortable quarters for which, having restored Constance to her husband, he would no longer have to pay and he now had a lover who, being married, would be in no position to make unreasonable demands upon him. All in all, he had done quite well for himself. It only remained for him to become a musketeer, to avenge himself upon that scoundrel, the Count de Rochefort, and to discover the identity and whereabouts of that mysterious woman he had seen at the Carmes-Dechaux. But for the moment, he had Constance.

To D'Artagnan, she was femininity incarnate. She had soft blue eyes and long dark hair, a pretty turned-up nose and a trim figure with a full bosom and long, slender legs. At twenty-five, she was a little older than he was, but that only served to make her more desirable. True, she was extremely talkative, but then there were advantages to that as well; he would be put to no great strain to supply entertaining conversation. And the fact that she seemed to be involved in some matter of questionable legality meant that she would require a protector—and who better suited to the job than he?

As he passed the Rue Cassette, he spied a figure hurrying furtively out of the Rue Servadoni. The wind blew back the hood of the figure's cloak and it was hurriedly pulled back in place, but not before D'Artagnan had seen that the person so stealthily abroad in the darkening streets of Paris was none other than Constance Bonacieux. Having told her that he would return as soon as the errand she had sent him on had been completed, he was puzzled to see her rushing through the streets, obviously intent on something. Keeping at a distance, he followed her through several streets and alleys until she came to the door of a house on the Rue de la Harpe. She knocked three times upon the door, glancing all about her, paused, then knocked three times more. The door was opened and she could be seen to have some words with someone inside the house. D'Artagnan watched, puzzled. A moment later, Constance stepped back and a tall man enveloped in a long cloak and wearing a large hat pulled low over his face appeared. He took her arm and together they hurried off into the night.

"So that's it!" thought D'Artagnan. "I am sent on some fool's errand to be got out of the way so that she can run off and see another lover!"

Outraged, D'Artagnan hurried after them. He caught up to them in an alley off the Rue Vaugirard. He passed them at a run, then turned and drew his rapier, blocking their path.

"So!" he said, "This is how I'm treated, is it?"

Constance gasped and backed off a step.

"Monsieur, I do not know you," said the stranger. "It seems that you have taken me for someone else. We have no quarrel. Kindly step aside."

"D'Artagnan, have you gone insane?" said Constance.

"You know this man?" the stranger said.

"Indeed, she knows me very well, Monsieur," D'Artagnan said. "And I would ask how it is that you come to know her."

"D'Artagnan, don't be a fool," said Constance. "This does not concern you."

"Does not concern me!"

"The lady's right," the stranger said, "this is none of your affair. You are interfering in something you know nothing about and it would be well for you to sheathe your sword and continue on your way."

"Sheathe my sword? No, Monsieur, better that you draw yours and give an accounting of yourself!"

"Very well, if you insist," said the stranger, throwing back his cloak and drawing his own rapier.

"Milord, please!" cried Constance.

D'Artagnan frowned. "*Milord?*"

"Yes, you fool," said Constance. "Milord, the Duke of Buckingham! And now you'll ruin us all!"

Suddenly, it all became quite clear. For the prime minister of England to be the lover of a lowly lady's maid in Paris was laughable. If he desired a lady's maid, there would be no scarcity of them in London. But if he desired that maid's mistress. . . .

"A thousand pardons, Milord," D'Artagnan said, lowering his sword. "I fear I've made a dreadful error. But I love her, you see, and I was jealous, and I. . . . Please pardon me, Your Grace, and say how I may serve you."

"You are a brave young man," said Buckingham. "You offer me your services and with the same frankness, I accept them. Follow us at a distance of twenty paces to the Louvre and if you see anyone watching us, be a good fellow and slay him."

Buckingham took Constance by the arm once again, having sheathed his sword, and they hurried off toward the Louvre. D'Artagnan kept his sword out, counted out twenty of their paces, and then followed, looking all about him to see if anyone was watching. He did not see anyone. But that was only because he was not very observant.

7

Finn and Lucas followed the carriage to a house on the Rue St. Honoré. It took some effort on their part, because although the carriage could not travel very fast through the crowded streets of Paris, it nevertheless proceeded at a fairly brisk pace. Twice, they almost lost it. As it pulled up in front of the elegant home on the Rue St. Honoré, Finn and Lucas watched from an alley across the street, trying to regain their wind.

"I just hope this doesn't turn out to be a wild goose chase," Lucas said, breathing heavily. "I'll feel like an awful sap if it turns out to have been nothing more than my memory playing tricks on me."

"I don't think there's anything wrong with your memory," said Finn. "Take a look at what that old man's carrying in his hand."

As the couple got out of the carriage, the old man glanced nervously up and down the street. It was getting late, but there was still enough light for them to see the slim metallic tube that the old man was holding in his hand.

"A laser," Lucas said. "And he's not even trying to hide it. He's holding it out in plain sight."

"Sure, why not?" said Finn. "Who'd know what it was?"

"That's just the point," said Lucas. "Anyone who would know what it was would be in the wrong place at the wrong time. The way he's waving it around, it's as if he *wants* someone to see it. Why would anyone be so obvious with a weapon unless he wanted whoever was watching to know that he was armed? You think maybe he knows we followed him?"

"It's possible," said Finn. "But why wave a laser around to scare off some would-be 17th-century muggers? I just had a rather nasty thought, old buddy."

"You think Mongoose blew our cover already?"

"I'm open to any other explanations."

They watched the chests being carried into the house. "All right," said Lucas, "let's try and think this through. The woman's the one who rang a bell with me, but the old man's got a laser. So that means that both of them aren't what they seem to be. They could be Timekeepers, but then I've never run across any of the Timekeepers before, at least not to my knowledge. I recall that face from a mission, I'm certain of it."

"A renegade soldier?" Finn said. "Right, Darrow said the terrorists made contact with someone in the underground."

"The only person in the underground we know is Hunter," Lucas said.

"That we *know*," said Finn. "We could've run across someone in the underground and not known it. Or the woman could be someone we've worked with before who's joined the underground since then. Or who's joined the Timekeepers. Come on, think, where did you see her face?"

"I just can't place it," Lucas said, exasperated. "It's driving me crazy, but there's something *wrong* about her and I can't figure out just what it is."

"Okay, leave it for now. It'll come to you. Let's get back to Mongoose. If he didn't blow our cover, then why's the old man waving a laser around?"

"Well, he wasn't waving it at us," said Lucas. "I don't think he knows we're watching him. But he thinks *someone's* watching him, someone from the future. Suppose Mongoose didn't blow our cover? What other explanation can there be?"

"That he blew *his* cover," Finn said. "Or that one of his people got careless and the Timekeepers know that someone's onto them."

"We're going to have to have a serious talk with him," said Lucas.

"Assuming that he's still alive," said Finn. "Damn spooks. They're going to make a mess of it, I just know it. They've got agents all over the place back here and the only one we know is Mongoose. And not only don't we know how to get in touch with him, we don't even know what he really looks like, with those damn disguises. All we can do is go back to the Luxembourg and wait to see if he or one of his people gets in touch with us."

"That does seem to be our only course of action," Lucas said.

"Maybe not," said Finn. "We could always push the panic button and see what happens."

The men exchanged glances. Pushing the panic button was always a last resort. It meant activating the implant that would send out a signal to be picked up by any members of the Observer Corps who might be in the area. It was standard operating procedure for the referees to send teams of observers out into any time period being used as a battle scenario. These observers, acting as undercover overseers, seldom got involved in direct action themselves. Their duties were primarily operational. They were equipped with chronoplates to enable them to quickly move about in time if need be and they generally functioned as supervisors over the Search and Retrieve teams and as the eyes of the Referee Corps in the field. The only thing was, this wasn't a typical scenario. Officially, it wasn't an adjustment, at least not yet. It was still a TIA mission.

"You're thinking that we'd be in a hell of a mess if we pushed the button and nobody answered," Finn said.

"Actually, that hadn't occurred to me, although now that you mention it, I see where that could be a problem. No, I was thinking that, officially, we still don't have any standing on this mission. If we pushed the panic button, we'd have to come up with some pretty convincing answers and we haven't got any. Not to mention the fact that activating the implant signals would enable the Timekeepers to trace us through their chronoplate."

Both men recalled only too well their last mission, when a similar situation, a stolen chronoplate in the hands of the opposition, had resulted in the enemy's being able to trace their movements through their implants. The technology was necessary to be able to trace the movements of Temporal Corps soldiers in battle scenarios. However, since their last mission, there had been a change in procedure. The implants of soldiers in commando adjustment squads had been modified so that they could not be traced through chronoplates. Commandos on an adjustment mission were completely on their own unless one of two things happened. If a commando was killed, then his implant would automatically be activated, sending out a termination signal that would enable the S&R teams to locate the body, unless it were destroyed and the implant along with it. Otherwise, a commando could "push the panic button," activating the implant to signal the Observers, in which case, as Lucas had pointed out, any chronoplate would be able to pick up the transmission.

"Looks like we're caught between a rock and a hard place," said Finn. "We've had the deck stacked on us again. These people have lasers and a chronoplate and God only knows what else, while we're equipped with nothing but swords and daggers and a couple of horses. Anything else we'd have to draw from Mongoose, only we don't know where he is or if he's still alive. If he is and we act on our own, he blows our cover. If he's bought the farm and we call for help, *we* blow our cover. You know, that still leaves us one other option."

"What's that?"

"Chucking it all and heading for the hills. I hear the Mediterranean is real nice this time of year. Now that we've got these fancy new implants that can't be traced unless we activate them, we could just disappear and take early retirement."

Lucas chuckled. "It's a tempting thought," he said. "There's only one thing wrong with it. Neither you nor I would last a month without going crazy. Besides, suppose the terrorists achieve a split and it turns up a future in which we were never born?"

"Can't happen," Finn said. "We've already been born. Our past is absolute. Mensinger proved—"

"Mensinger didn't prove anything when it came to temporal splits," said Lucas. "All he could do was theorize. No one's ever been affected by a split before. If it's all the same with you, I'd just as soon not be the first.''

"Yeah, well, I'm too young to retire anyway," said Finn. "It was just a thought."

"I think our best bet is to head back to the Luxembourg and wait to be contacted," Lucas said. "There's not much else we can do now, except find out who lives in that house across the street. You never know, we just might learn something."

They learned that the house on the Rue St. Honoré was occupied by Doctor Jacques Benoit and his two servants, Marie and "Old Pierre," an elderly married couple. No one seemed to know anything about "the mademoiselle." In fact, the question raised more than a few eyebrows in the neighborhood. Doctor Jacques, it seemed, was a paragon of virtue, the soul of kindness, a giant among physicians. No one had a bad word to say about Doctor Jacques, but their inquiries did yield one or two interesting points.

Unless Doctor Jacques had some secret source of income that no one knew about, he could not possibly be supporting himself as a physician. So far as anyone knew, he did not number anyone of the upper classes among his clientele, serving the common, working citizens of Paris exclusively. His methods of charging for his services were erratic, to say the least. From one man, he took whatever he felt he could afford to pay. From another family who were down on their luck, he took nothing whatsoever. The owner of a local business, whose mother he had treated, was allowed to pay "in trade" and another man's fee was the princely sum of three chickens. It was widely assumed that Doctor Jacques was independently wealthy as the result of a large inheritance.

From time to time, Doctor Jacques left Paris for parts unknown. Sometimes, he simply left word that he was "going to the country" for a few days. At other times, he left no word at all. During such times, Marie and Pierre filled in for him to the extent that they were able.

Doctor Jacques made house calls. So far as Finn and Lucas were able to ascertain, no one had ever been inside the house on the Rue St. Honoré except for the good doctor himself and his two servants. Except, occasionally, Doctor Jacques received visitors. These visitors seldom stayed for very long. No one had ever seen them before and only rarely were they ever seen again.

Doctor Jacques had been in residence in the house on the Rue St. Honoré for at least ten years, possibly more.

"That blows the terrorist angle," Finn said, as they walked back toward the hotel. "So our friend is underground."

"Either that, or he's a phony, having killed the real doctor and taken his place."

"I don't think so," Lucas said. "This Doctor Jacques obviously has medical knowledge."

"Easily acquired by implant education," Finn said. "The terrorists are not without the means to—"

"Yes, that's true," said Lucas. "You can teach the mind, but the hands are another thing entirely. Have you heard anyone say that he had ever failed to treat a patient? That, in itself, makes him stick out like a sore thumb. A doctor in this time period could be expected to have some patients die on him, if for no other reason than that he wouldn't possess the knowledge to treat diseases for which there would be no cure for years. If he's a terrorist, then he's very sloppy. No, Finn, he's underground. He just never expected anyone to be looking for him."

"Until now."

"Yes, until now. I think we've found our underground connection with the Timekeepers. That chronoplate might very well be in that house on the Rue St. Honoré."

"If it is, then we're making a mistake by not moving in," said Finn.

"And if it isn't?" Lucas said. "Either way, we're poorly equipped to handle the situation. Mongoose wants to call the shots, I say we let him. Or whoever takes over for him if he's been hit. Working at cross purposes with the TIA is going to buy us nothing but trouble."

"And if they blow the mission, it's going to buy us even more trouble."

"Yes, well, that's what we're here for, isn't it?"

"I was beginning to wonder."

There was the sound of running footsteps up ahead and shouting. Then the unmistakable clangor of steel upon steel filled the quiet night air. As they turned onto the Rue Dauphine, Finn and Lucas were greeted by the sight of a melee in progress. A young woman was pressed flat against a wall, her fists clenched at her mouth to stifle a scream. Two men were being hard pressed by seven of the cardinal's guard.

"Isn't that—"

"It's D'Artagnan," Lucas said, "and it looks like he's in trouble."

"Seven against two," said Finn. "Shall we make it seven against four?"

They drew their swords and waded in. No sooner had they joined the fight than the other man with D'Artagnan took advantage of their intervention by grabbing the woman and taking off at a dead run down the Rue Dauphine, disappearing into an alley.

"Who's your loyal friend?" Finn shouted, while doing his best to keep two of the cardinal's swordsmen at bay. Lucas engaged another two.

"Dumas!" D'Artagnan shouted. "And his Irish friend! I thought I'd seen the last of you!"

"You may yet," said Lucas, giving ground before his two opponents. "I see you're finally following your father's advice."

"I am not certain this is . . . quite what he . . . had in mind," D'Artagnan replied, engaging his opponent's blade and hooking it out of his hand. However, that left two more men to press in upon him and he was unable to follow it up with a killing thrust, so that the guard was able to retrieve his sword and rush to the attack once more. But just as he was about to come up on the Gascon from behind, a concentrated beam of light shot out from an alley and dropped him in his tracks. None of the combatants noticed it. Finn, using his superior strength, pulled one of his opponents away from him, then slashed his sword viciously across the face of the other. The man dropped his rapier and screamed, bringing both hands up to cover his face. Blood seeped between his fingers. Finn ran him through.

Lucas was backed against a wall, fighting a frantic defensive action against his two opponents. Confident in the odds of two against one, the guards grinned, spreading out to either side and moving in on him. Their maneuver gave Lucas the time to reverse the dagger in his hand and, holding it by the point, he hurled it at one of the guards, even as the other lunged. The dagger buried itself to the hilt in one guard's chest while Lucas parried the lunge of the other, then delivered a spinning back kick to his temple. The guard fell to the street, unconscious.

D'Artagnan, meanwhile, killed one of his men with a quick thrust while directing the lunge of the other past his side with his dagger. From the alley, Bruno Freytag kept a close watch on the combat. He was intrigued by the two strangers who had arrived to help the Gascon and he had not failed to notice that one of them had dropped an opponent with a move that marked him as an expert in Okinawan karate. His orders were to make certain that Buckingham got away and that nothing happened to D'Artagnan. His finger tensed on the firing stud of the laser, then relaxed as D'Artagnan delivered a brutal kick to the groin of his one remaining attacker, following it up with a sword thrust through the abdomen. As Finn easily disarmed the final remaining swordsman, the guard gave up and ran, leaving his rapier lying in the street behind him. Finn let him go. Seeing that D'Artagnan was safe, Freytag slipped away through the alley, heading toward the home of Camille de Bois-Tracy. He would keep a discreet watch over Buckingham until the prime minister was safely on his way across the channel.

"Well, I am fortunate, indeed, that you gentlemen happened by," D'Artagnan said, bending down to wipe the blade of his rapier upon one of the bodies. "And to think that I thought you had deserted me back in that tavern. I see now I was wrong." He indicated the wound on Delaney's cheek. "Was that received in Meung?"

"It was received on your account," said Finn, dryly.

"Well, then I am doubly indebted to you, Monsieur Finn."

"It's Francois now," Finn replied. "Francois D'Laine. Since we are in Paris, I—"

"Say no more," D'Artagnan said. "You are free to choose whatever *nom de guerre* you wish and I owe you a debt of gratitude, Monsieur, that I may never be able to repay. If not for you, that one there would have surely done for me."

He indicated one of the corpses with his sword.

"I didn't kill him," Finn said.

"Ah, then Monsieur Dumas—"

"I didn't kill him, either," Lucas said, frowning.

"Well, *one* of us must have killed him," said D'Artagnan. He turned the body over with his foot. "See? Run clean through the heart!"

Finn and Lucas exchanged glances. They knew that neither of them had killed the guard. What was more, they knew that D'Artagnan hadn't done it, either. The Gascon didn't have a laser.

Old Pierre took charge of the chest, dragging it away and showing a great deal more energy than his appearance would have indicated. Andre glanced at Jack with some concern.

"Don't worry," Bennett said. "He won't look inside. He won't even inquire as to why it stinks so much of perfume. Pierre's been with me for years and I trust him implicitly."

"What will he do with it?" Andre said.

"Incinerate it."

"Incinerate?"

"Burn it."

"But how? Surely it is too . . . damp to burn?"

"I have a fire that is more than sufficient for the task," said Bennett. "It's hardly a proper burial or even a proper cremation, but . . . Would you like to say some . . . words for Hunter or . . ." he trailed off, lamely.

"Prayer, you mean?" said Andre. She shook her head. "I do not think that Hunter was a man of God. And I do not think that any prayers from me would do much good. I have left behind too many bodies unattended and unprayed for."

Jack stared at her. "Yes, I believe you have," he said. "And so, for that matter, have I."

"What will happen now?"

"I don't really know," said Jack. "They'll be looking for me. They'll probably be looking for you, too. They've had me watched. They'll try to kill us now. We can't stay here for long; this will be the first place that they'll look. I am not without defenses here, but still, the sooner we leave, the better."

~"Why did we come here at all, if they know this place?"

"Because there are things here I can't leave unattended," Bennett said. "Things that don't belong to this time. I must see to it that they're all destroyed. That will take some time. Meanwhile, I have to get you out of here to where it's safe. There's a way out of here the Timekeepers don't know about. I've kept it a secret for just such an emergency. It will take you out under the street. You'll go with Marie; Pierre and I will join you as soon as I've taken care of what must be done here."

"What about your machine for traveling through time?" said Andre.

"They've taken that, I'm afraid." His eyes suddenly lit up. "Hunter's chronoplate! My God, I'd forgotten all about it! Where . . ." his voice trailed off when he saw the expression on her face.

"It was gone when I found him dead," she said. "But it will not do your friends much good. Only Hunter knew the proper way to make it work. If they attempt to—"

"Yes, I know, he'll have failsafed it to self-destruct if it should fall into the wrong hands. Mine works the same way. Unfortunately, I showed Taylor the proper sequence to. . . . God, I was a fool. Taylor will guess that Hunter will have failsafed his chronoplate and he won't tinker with it. It just gives him that much more of a reason to take you alive."

"But I do not know how to operate the machine," said Andre.

"Taylor won't know that. He thinks you're an agent from the future, someone sent to stop him."

"I still don't understand," said Andre. "Stop him from doing what? To what end is all this intrigue?"

"It would take far too long to explain it all now. I must get you to safety. Ah, Marie, this is Andre. We must—"

"Yes, I know, Doctor," said Marie. "Pierre told me that we must flee. What has happened? Who would want to—"

"There's no time for that, Marie. Take Andre and go through the secret passageway. Immediately. Can the two of you manage her chest?"

"We shall manage," said Marie, her wrinkled face grave with concern. "Where must we go?"

"Take her to your sister's. Take care that you're not followed. Have Marcel send word to Moreau asking him to meet us there. Say that there is trouble; Moreau will come. Tell him to take care that he's not followed."

Marie looked frightened.

"It's all right, Marie," said Jack, taking the plump little woman in his arms. "Everything will be all right. Now, go, please."

The two women picked up the chest containing Andre's belongings and went into Bennett's library. Andre was amazed to see so many books. Hunter had had books in his cottage in the forest, but Bennett had hundreds of them, arrayed upon shelves that covered all four walls. Marie had her put down the chest and then she went to one of the shelves and pulled out several volumes. She stuck her hand into the space where the books had been and fumbled around for a moment; then Andre heard a clicking sound and the entire shelf swung away to reveal a door, which Marie opened with a key.

"Come, Mademoiselle," the old woman said, "we must hurry."

"Wait," said Andre. "There is no need for us to be burdened with this chest. I do not need all these things."

"I have a bag," Marie said. "You will need at least a change of clothing. Wait here, I will go and fetch it."

As Marie ran off, moving like a pigeon trying to get out of the rain, Andre bent down and opened up the chest. She removed her rapier and her dagger, laid them down on Bennett's desk, then began to strip. When Marie returned, carrying a bulky cloth bag, she found a young cavalier waiting for her in the library. She took one look at the black-clad swordsman and gasped, bringing her hands up to her mouth.

"It's only me, Marie," said Andre.

"*Mademoiselle Andre?* But how—"

"They'll be looking for a woman," Andre said. "They won't look twice at a gentleman escorting an old woman home. Come, we'll pack just these few things. I will not need the rest."

Moments later, they were descending the stone steps down into the tunnel.

• • •

"Buckingham's away, then," Taylor said. "Good. We can now put our plan into motion. Did you have any trouble with the cardinal's guards?"

"No trouble," Freytag said, sipping from a glass of wine. "In fact, I hardly had to do anything at all. When the guards moved in, two men came to D'Artagnan's rescue."

"Ah, that would be our friends the musketeers," said Taylor.

"I don't think so," Freytag said. "Not unless one of them knows karate."

"Karate?"

Freytag nodded and took a big swallow of wine. He wiped his mouth with the back of his beefy hand. "One of them laid a spinning back kick on one of the guards," he said. "Dropped him with a heel right to the temple. Very pretty. I couldn't have done it better, myself. Their swordsmanship was very interesting. Textbook perfect. Unless I miss my guess, they've both had experience with swords other than rapiers. They showed some interesting variations. I'll lay odds that the big guy would be a mean man with a katana."

"What's that?"

"A large Japanese sword. Used by the samurai."

"Samurai!" Are you certain?"

"Weapons are my specialty, Adrian. You know that."

"Do you realize what that means? They've sent in commandos!"

"Well, you did say you liked a challenge."

"Not a word of this to Tonio or Jimmy, you understand? Jimmy already seems a little shaky to me. I think we'd best keep an eye on him."

"What does it matter?" Freytag said. "We don't need either him or Tonio. They were both expendable, right from the beginning, just like Silvera."

"They must never suspect that," Taylor said. "It's essential to the plan that they believe. . . ." His eyes seemed to glaze over for a moment. In a second, they became animated once again and a slow, sultry smile spread across the face of Milady de Winter. "You're quite right, Bruno. It doesn't really matter, does it? The more people they send in, the greater the risk of temporal contamination. That plays right into our hands.

Would you know these men if you saw them again?''

"It was dark. I'm afraid I didn't get a very good look at them. I couldn't say if I'd recognize them again."

"Well, no matter. I want you to take a letter to my good friend, the cardinal. After all, he has an interest in the Buckingham affair and it's time to prod him into the next stage of our operation."

8 ⸻

The carriage pulled up in front of the tavern on the outskirts of Paris. It was accompanied by a small troop of mounted guards. Rochefort dismounted and entered the tavern, followed by several of the guards. Two of them stationed themselves outside the front door. Another two grabbed the bewildered, suddenly frightened innkeeper and frogmarched him into the kitchen, where they stayed with him and the other help. Rochefort glanced around the tavern, seeing that he was quite alone. There was the sound of a door opening above him and he heard a soft footfall. His rapier sang free of its scabbard. He looked up and saw Milady de Winter standing at the railing above him, looking down.

"There is no one else here except my man," she said.

"Milady," Rochefort said. He crossed the room and went to the door, opening it and nodding at someone in the carriage. A man in a dark, long cloak and buff riding boots stepped out. He wore a large, slightly droopy hat pulled low over his face. He walked quickly to the front door of the tavern and entered. Rochefort stood aside to let him pass, bowing slightly as he did.

Once inside, the man removed his well-worn gloves and hat, revealing himself as a gray-haired, distinguished-looking gentleman of about thirty-six or thirty-seven years with piercing eyes, a prominent nose, and a sharply pointed imperial goatee surmounted by long, curled moustaches. He glanced up to see Milady de Winter descending the stairs toward him.

"This penchant of yours for mysterious, out-of-the-way assignations grows somewhat tiresome, Milady," he said, tossing his hat and gloves onto a table. "You did say it was important."

"I've come by some information that I believe you'll find to your advantage, Your Eminence," said Taylor, smiling at the cardinal.

"Why could this information not have been passed on to Rochefort?" Richelieu said, pulling out a chair for Milady to sit down.

"Because I don't like dealing with intermediaries," Taylor said, smiling as Rochefort stiffened. "I must be careful. I'm sure you appreciate that."

"I will tell you if I appreciate it after I have heard what you have to say," said Richelieu. "Our last contact brought less than satisfactory results."

"I cannot be blamed for Buckingham's escape," said Taylor. "I brought you all the necessary information. It was not my fault that your men were not up to the task."

"You did not tell me that he would be guarded by the musketeers," said Richelieu.

"I cannot know everything, Your Eminence. Obviously, your own informant was somewhat derelict in his duties."

"My own informant?"

"Did you not arrange to have Monsieur Bonacieux report to you concerning the activities of his wife?"

Richelieu raised his bushy eyebrows. "For one who claims that she cannot know everything, you are remarkably well informed, Milady. It occurs to me that you would make a very useful ally. Or a very dangerous antagonist."

"I will take that as a compliment, Your Eminence," said Taylor.

"It was not intended as one, Milady. What new information have you brought me? If it proves useful, you will not find me ungenerous."

"It concerns Milord, the Duke of Buckingham, Your Eminence."

"By now, he's back in London and well out of reach," said Richelieu. "He's had his assignation with the queen and made good his escape. I have lost my opportunity. Of what interest would he be to me now?''

"Well, he is still an enemy of France, Your Eminence, and I should think that any intelligence regarding an enemy would be welcome.''

"Let me be the judge of that.''

"And so you shall be. Buckingham has, indeed, returned to England. But he did not return empty-handed.''

"What do you mean?''

"I have reason to believe that the queen gave him something to take back with him. A token, a pledge of her affections.''

"This is not news to me,'' said Richelieu, "although I am surprised that you should know of it. The queen gave Buckingham a dozen diamond studs, which were a gift from Louis. Indiscreet, perhaps, but hardly incriminating. She could easily claim that they were lost or stolen or make up some other plausible excuse to explain their disappearance.''

"True,'' said Taylor. "But suppose, just for a moment, Your Eminence, that the king was to give a ball in honor of the queen. And suppose that he requested her, as an indulgence, to wear those very studs she gave to Buckingham.''

"She would be unable to produce them,'' Richelieu said. "Doubtless, she would make some sort of an excuse, as I have told you. Nothing could be proved.''

"Ah, but suppose again, Your Eminence, that when the queen claimed the diamond studs were stolen, you had two of them in your possession. Wouldn't it be interesting to see the queen's reaction when you explained how you happened to come by them?''

"I see,'' said Richelieu. "Yes, that would be quite interesting, indeed. What do you require of me?''

"Some money would be useful,'' Taylor said, "also some sort of authorization, in your own hand, that would enable me to act freely and without fear of compromise.''

Richelieu frowned. "Obviously, I can put nothing of this in writing,'' he said.

"It will not be necessary,'' Taylor said. "I do not require a detailed approval of my actions, only your *carte blanche*. I'm sure that you can word it appropriately.''

"That's asking a great deal,'' said Richelieu.

"The stakes are high, Your Eminence," said Taylor. "I need to protect myself."

"Very well," said Richelieu, after a moment's thought. "I will write you a *carte blanche*. The moment you have those studs in your possession, you will let me know."

"But, of course, Your Eminence."

The cardinal finished writing, then stood and put on his hat and began pulling on his gloves.

"I do not know why," he said, "but it makes me very nervous to deal with you, Milady. I am never entirely certain whom you serve."

"Why, only you, Your Eminence."

"If I believed that, then I would be a fool, indeed. Our interests seem to be allied for the moment, Milady. For the moment. Take care that we do not start working at cross purposes. I am France, Milady, and at this point in history, France cannot afford to be forgiving. See that you remember that."

"Who am I to go against the course of history, Your Eminence?"

Richelieu regarded Milady steadily. "Yes. Quite. Good day to you, Milady."

"Good day, Your Eminence."

Delaney awoke to find a knife held across his throat.

"If I was a terrorist, you'd be dead," said Mongoose. He was dressed as a cleaning woman in a shapeless dress, heavy shoes, and gray wig.

"You look ridiculous," Delaney said. "How did you get in? Oh, of course, these are your rooms, you have a key." He sat up slowly and groaned. "Oh, my head."

"You really think the Timekeepers would need a key?" said Mongoose. "Besides, you left the door open. Not even unlocked, for God's sakes, *open*. I would at least have thought that you'd be able to hold your liquor. You're a mess."

He went over to the bed where Lucas slept, dead to the world, and slapped him across the face several times.

"Come on, Priest, wake up, I haven't got all day."

Lucas shot up out of bed, making a grab, but the agent threw him on the floor.

"Commandos," he said, scornfully. "What a joke."

"Mongoose!" Lucas said, getting up unsteadily. "What the hell?"

Both men were still dressed, having fallen into bed fully clothed after a night of heavy drinking. D'Artagnan had insisted upon their meeting the other musketeers and celebrating.

"I take it that the musketeers drank you under the table last night," Mongoose said.

"Actually, D'Artagnan, Aramis, and Porthos were unconscious when we left," said Lucas, rinsing his face off with water from a bowl beside his bed. "Athos was still going strong. He seems to have had lots of experience."

"We saw Buckingham last night," said Finn. "In fact, we helped D'Artagnan save him from—"

"I know all about it, I was there," said Mongoose.

"So it was you!" said Lucas.

"If you're referring to the man killed by the laser, no, it wasn't me," the agent said. "It was a man named Freytag. A real nasty customer with a rather impressive record. I got a good look at him through my scope."

"A terrorist?" said Finn. "Why didn't you take him out?"

"A better question might be why didn't *he* take *you* out? He had a clear shot at both of you and it's a cinch he made you. French cavaliers don't usually know karate. You guys are about as subtle as a cavalry charge."

"I don't know what you're complaining about," said Lucas. "Wasn't that the general idea, using us to lure the terrorists out into the open?"

"I'm just puzzled as to why he didn't kill you," Mongoose said. "I find that very interesting. It was an ideal situation for a temporal disruption. All Freytag had to do was kill Buckingham and then take care of you. He could have killed D'Artagnan, too. That would have been one hell of a mess to straighten out."

"So why didn't he do it?" Finn said. "Not that I'm complaining."

"Good question. It would seem to suggest that they want Buckingham, D'Artagnan, and even the two of you alive."

"That doesn't make any sense," said Lucas.

"Perhaps it does, if the man who's giving the orders is who I think it is. This game is getting very interesting."

"Game?" said Finn.

"Oh, it would be a game to him," said Mongoose. "That would be his style."

"Sounds very melodramatic," Lucas said. "Do we get a name? A description, maybe?"

Mongoose smiled. His old woman's disguise was complete right down to the rotting teeth.

"His name is Adrian Taylor. I'm afraid we don't have a description on him. He's a cut above your average terrorist."

"What does that mean?" Finn said.

"It means that he's very good at what he does," the agent said. "Taylor's a mental case, a psychopath, completely unpredictable. But he's also a pro, which makes matters worse because he's capable of a deadly, systematic rationality. He can keep it on a rein and let it all loose when it suits him."

"Sounds like you know the fellow," Lucas said.

Mongoose nodded. "Our paths have crossed before. He's not like the others. I suppose it's possible that he believes all that fanatic bullshit the Timekeepers spout, but I doubt that that's what drives him. This one's in it for the money. And because he likes to hang it right out over the edge."

"Sorta reminds you of someone we know, doesn't he?" said Finn.

"He's worked with Freytag before," the agent continued, ignoring Delaney's jibe. "I tailed Freytag to the Rue Vaugirard and then I lost him. I don't think he knew that he was being followed, he was just being very careful."

"Which raises another question," Lucas said. "If they know we're onto them and they've got a chronoplate, why don't they simply abandon their plan to create a disruption here and clock out to another period? Our chances of latching onto them again would be practically nil."

"You don't know Taylor," Mongoose said. "He's not a quitter and he won't be intimidated. That's what I'm counting on. He knows that as long as we don't know where that plate is, he's got an edge and he'll hold off using it until the last possible moment."

"Then this should interest you," said Lucas. "Finn and I think we know where that chronoplate is. We followed an old man and a young woman from the Luxembourg to a house on the Rue St. Honoré. The old man had a laser. He—"

"That would be Jack Bennett," Mongoose said. "Alias Dr. Jacques Benoit. He's the underground link to the terrorists."

"You knew!"

"Of course I knew. What do you think I've been doing all this time, sitting on my hands?"

"But if you knew about Bennett, why didn't you let us in on it?" Lucas said.

Delaney snorted. "Silly question. There was no need for us to know. Right, Mata Hari?"

"For a guy who had a knife at his throat a couple of minutes ago, you're pretty cocky," Mongoose said.

"What's he talking about?" said Lucas.

"His bedside manner," Finn said. "Do you mind if I asked another silly question? If you knew about Bennett, why didn't you move in?"

"Because he doesn't have the chronoplate. The Timekeepers would never sit still for that. He might have given them access to it initially, but he's not part of their inner circle. Taylor will have taken it away from him."

"You had it all figured out, didn't you?" said Delaney. "You found out about Jack Bennett and you've probably had him under observation ever since, only it would seem that the terrorists got what they wanted from him and now he's out of the picture. So why leave him around? Easy, because he would make a perfect decoy. You figured that out, too, because you made sure that he knew he was under observation, hoping to scare him enough to lead you to the terrorists. If he did, you'd move in, and if he didn't, the terrorists would think their decoy plan was working. Meanwhile you anticipated the potential disruption scenarios and you've been Johnny-on-the-spot. You made sure to give us instructions that would involve us with the principals, so that the terrorists would make us, just like Freytag did last night. The idea was to dangle a little bait in front of them, a couple of decoys of your own. Freytag was supposed to spot us, if not last night, then at some other point, whenever we happened to intersect with the key figures in this scenario. You or one of your people would have been right there, because you've had us watched constantly. We were supposed to get killed. With us dead, the terrorists would feel more secure, since they'd seem to have gotten away with it. They'd get careless and you'd trail them to their hideout where they keep the chronoplate. All very neat. Only Freytag didn't kill us. That's why it bothers you. Not because they've passed up an opportunity, but because they're not improvising. They didn't take your bait. They're sticking to their original plan and you don't know what that is. What's more, you had a chance last night, when you made Freytag. You could have followed him to this Taylor character, but you blew it. Freytag didn't know that he was being followed? I don't buy it. He knew and he shook you and it only took him a couple of blocks to do it. He and Taylor probably had a good laugh about it.''

"Are you finished?"

"Not quite. How many people have you got on this mission? A dozen? *Two* dozen? *More?* You never even considered the possibility of an adjustment going down, did you? You brought enough people back here to spread a net, to cover all the possibilities. Only you needed someone the Timekeepers could spot, a target they could shoot at. As you said, someone to make them nervous. Agency personnel are too valuable to waste on something like that, right? A couple of soldiers would be just the thing. What did you do, go to the Referee Corps and requisition a couple of expendables? Sure, you can have Delaney. He's made a pain in the ass of himself before and he's up on charges now. He'll be just perfect. And Priest just happened to be there with me at the wrong time, so he got thrown into the deal. Is that how it went down?''

Mongoose regarded him with a steady gaze. "More or less," he said.

"*Damn,*" said Lucas. "I can't believe that Forrester would go along with that."

"He had no choice," said Finn, "assuming that he even knew about it."

"If it's worth anything," said Mongoose, "I don't think Major Forrester was fully briefed. There was no need for him to know."

"Well, that pretty much fits in with standard operating procedure, doesn't it?" said Finn. "The pawns are the least significant pieces in a game. There's no need for them to know the reasons for the moves they are required to make. That's all this mission is for you, isn't it? A game. It's a game for Taylor and it's a game for you. Except Taylor controls the board.

He's got a gameplan and you don't. He's castled and he's got all his most important pieces functioning freely. You've got your pieces spread out all over the board. Every agent you've got back here represents one more chance for something to go wrong. You're out of control, Mongoose. The only way you're going to win is if you get damn lucky.''

"You still only have part of the total picture, Delaney,'' said the agent. "To switch your chess metaphor to one of cards, I still have a few aces up my sleeve. Nor do I play a defensive game, as you imply. But that need not concern you. Granted, you've been used. But you can still be useful. Your survival depends upon the degree of your usefulness.''

"Suppose we don't choose to play?'' said Lucas.

"In that case, your usefulness will have ended,'' Mongoose said. "Freytag let you live, this one time. He obviously had a reason for doing so, although I confess that I'm at a loss to guess what that reason is. He could have killed you easily; Freytag is an accomplished assassin. He can and will do so whenever it suits Taylor's purpose. You're out in the open and extremely vulnerable.''

"Thanks to you,'' said Lucas.

"Yes, thanks to me,'' said Mongoose. "You do have several alternatives, though. One is to refuse to cooperate. You could push the panic button. I can tell you now that it would bring no results. We're the Observers on this mission. You could desert, but I don't think you'll do that. I don't think it's in you. You'd still be vulnerable. The Timekeepers could get you or, for that matter, my people could get you. It would be simple. You have no idea who they are, where they are, or how many of them there are. Frankly, there'd be no percentage in my having you sanctioned. I wouldn't waste my time. I don't think you'll desert, because you want to stop the Timekeepers as badly as I do. You could tell me to go to hell and try it on your own, but then you wouldn't have the benefit of whatever information I choose to pass on to you and I don't think I need to remind you that, without me, there's no way for you to get back home. Which brings us to your final alternative. You continue to work with me and let me call the shots.''

"Which means we've got no alternatives at all,'' said Lucas.

"I rather thought you'd come to that conclusion.''

"All right, you bastard," Finn said, "you win. We'll play it your way."

"I'm so glad," said Mongoose. "And just to prove to you that I'm not ungrateful, I'll pass on a useful bit of information. What you do with it is up to you. Before Jack Bennett deserted from the Temporal Corps some ten years ago, he was a medical officer. Specifically, he was a surgeon. A specialist in cosmetology, something you gentlemen should be familiar with. So when you go back out and start interacting with the principals in this scenario, you may want to exercise a little caution. One of them may not be what he seems."

Moreau came quickly. The old ex-seaman asked no questions, simply accepting that Doctor Jacques and "his gentleman friend" were in some kind of trouble and needed help. When Bennett told him that he would have to be extremely careful if any of the "gentlemen from Flanders" inquired as to his whereabouts, Moreau grunted, nodding his head as if to say that he had thought as much, and then told him to say no more, that he would take care of everything.

"There is one thing more that I must say," Bennett told him.

"There is no need of explaining anything to me, Doctor Jacques," Moreau said.

"Yes, I know that, old friend," Bennett said, "and I love you for it. But I must give you a warning. Be especially wary of Milady de Winter."

Moreau raised his eyebrows. There were few people in the know in Paris who had not heard of the infamous "Milady."

"*Merde*," said Moreau. "What have you gotten yourself into, Doctor? No, on second thought, don't tell me. I cannot tell what I don't know."

"I think that would be wise," Jack Bennett said.

"What would be wise would be to find a safe place for you right now and arrange for you and Monsieur Andre to leave Paris as soon as possible."

Andre, still being in her male guise, did not correct Moreau in his misconception and, following her cue, Marie, Pierre, and Bennett kept silent on the subject as well.

"I'm afraid that wouldn't do," said Jack. "We must find a safe place to hide for now, that's true, but we cannot possibly

leave Paris. There is more at stake than you would understand."

"It's your choice," Moreau said. "But they'll be looking
for you, won't they?"

"They'll be looking for Doctor Jacques," said Andre.
"They do not know about me as yet. That may give us some
freedom to act."

"I see," Moreau said. "Well, then, perhaps it would be best
if I were to arrange separate sanctuaries for you. If no one is
seeking you in connection with this matter, whatever it may
be, then you can come and stay at my establishment, Monsieur
Andre, as my guest."

"I would not wish to impose upon your generosity,"
Andre began, but Moreau interrupted her with a wave of his
hand.

"Think nothing of it. What I do, I do for Doctor Jacques,
and you are his friend. If helping you helps him, so much the
better. Now, where shall we put you, my friend?"

Moreau thought a moment.

"Ah, I have it. I have a friend who owes me for some
favors. He will be more than happy to get out of my debt so
cheaply. I will send you to stay with him. He has a house in the
Rue des Fossoyeurs, No. 14. What's more, he has a young
cadet who lodges with him, an expert swordsman, as I hear
tell. You should be safe there."

"Can your friend be trusted?" said Bennett.

"Bonacieux? He is an innocent and as simple as the day is
long, but he is also a bit of a chatterbox. He's a good man, but
I'm not certain that I would trust him with a secret. He might
blurt it out through no fault of his own. No, it would be best if
we were to concoct some sort of story to keep his curiosity ap-
peased."

"Have I met this Bonacieux?" said Bennett.

"It is entirely possible," said Moreau. "He frequents the
tavern now and then. A likeable, rather scatterbrained old
fellow, gray hair, spindly little legs, red nose, and chin just like
a spade."

Bennett shook his head. "Maybe, I don't know. His name
seems somehow familiar."

"Well, then doubtless you have met him. Either way, his
place will do. I'll tell him that you're my cousin, recently

returned from a life at sea. You know something of the sailing life, as I recall; that should make it easier in case he should become garrulous, which is very likely. He doesn't see his wife too often and laments for lack of company. We'll say that you've left the seaman's life behind because you've become somewhat infirm and need frequent rest. That should insure you some needed privacy.''

"I'll need to stay in touch with Andre," Bennett said.

"He can come and see you there, if he is not being sought," Moreau said. He shrugged. "Simple. We'll tell Bonacieux that he is your nephew on my sister's side, coming to look in on you from time to time. Bonacieux will doubtless find the whole thing very boring and you will doubtless find Bonacieux very boring, but at least you will be safe."

"Good, that will do then," Bennett said.

"Is there anything else that I can do for you, my friend?" Moreau said.

"One thing more, for now," Jack said. "I will leave some money with you. Those two downstairs—"

"Marie and Pierre?"

"Yes, I think it would be best if they did not know where I was, but you will look after them for me, won't you? They've been true and faithful friends."

"It will be my pleasure," said Moreau. "I think it would be best if the two of you were to stay here tonight. I will speak to Bonacieux after I leave and we can move you in tomorrow morning. Monsieur Andre, I should have your room ready for you by tomorrow afternoon. I will have to evict a deadbeat who insists on drinking up all his rent money. He's been drinking it all up in my tavern, so I haven't minded much, but I still come out behind. Make your way to the tavern after noon tomorrow."

"I shall," said Andre, "and thank you for your help."

"It's a small thing," said Moreau, shrugging. "I only hope that you two know what you're doing. If your path has crossed Milady's, well . . . she is said to have very powerful friends."

"I know that all too well, Moreau."

"Yes, well, goodnight then. I will return for you in the morning."

"Moreau?"

The burly old man turned.

"Please be careful."

Moreau chuckled. "I've weathered far worse storms."

When he left, Jack closed the door and turned to Andre. "I'm afraid that your disguise has resulted in there not being separate sleeping arrangements," he said. "I'm sorry for the inconvenience, but I'm very glad for your resourcefulness."

"Do not concern yourself," said Andre, sitting down upon a chair and resting her rapier across her knees.

"I must say, you gave me quite a turn when I first came in. I almost didn't recognize you. How is it that you—"

"I have lived most of my life passing for a man," she said. "It gave me more freedom. But that is not important. I've waited long enough. I know nothing of what has happened and it is past time for explanations."

"Of course," said Jack. "You have a right to know. It will take a while to explain."

"We have all night."

"Indeed. Well. I don't know how much Hunter told you, but you obviously know something about time travel and the future that we came from. I'll start from the beginning and tell you everything I can. Stop me if you require further explanation; I will do my best. The Temporal Corps was formed in. . . ."

Jack Bennett spoke for a long time, explaining everything he could to the best of his ability, answering questions, telling her about the time wars, the Referee and Observer Corps, the arbitration of temporal conflicts, and the work and theories of Albrecht Mensinger. When he finally stopped, at three o'clock in the morning, he was exhausted. He was also despondent, because of the role that he had played and because of the seeming futility of their situation.

"I was a fool to go along with them," he said, "an utter fool. But Taylor was persuasive, as was Darcy. You have to understand that I deserted all those years ago because I simply couldn't take it anymore. I could no longer give the system my sanction by being a part of it. It was lunacy. Mensinger told the world that it was lunacy and no one listened to him; why would anyone bother listening to me?

"No, if I couldn't change it, then I would no longer be a part of it. I had seen too much, I had realized all the dangers from firsthand experience and if the world was headed toward disaster, then at least I could have some small satisfaction in knowing that I had not been a part of it, that I had withheld my sanction. That I had washed my hands of it," he added, lamely, shaking his head.

"I deserted and I came here. I resolved to live out the remainder of my life here in France as a simple country doctor, removed from the city, away from all the foolishness of man. All told, it was a rather maudlin period during which I felt extremely self-satisfied, terminally righteous, and very much at peace. However, life doesn't necessarily work out the way you plan it.

"I don't know why I never destroyed my chronoplate. Now, I wish to God that I had, but at the time, I remember thinking that it was good to keep around as a sort of last resort. I was quite paranoid in those early days, convinced that even with my much modified, untraceable chronoplate they might still somehow find me. In that case, I would need to escape quickly. I think that, perhaps, I also knew that the plate would come in handy if I ever faced a situation that I would not be able to handle on the strength of my medical knowledge alone. That, in fact, is precisely what happened.

"An old farmer came to me with his wife and child—a man whom I had befriended and who had befriended me. They had always, from the very first, welcomed me into their home and made me feel a part of their lives. The child had cancer. The disease was fatal. It was in its advanced stages. It can occur that way, striking with very little warning. I knew at once what was the matter with the boy. They knew only that he was dying. I knew why he was dying, I knew what was killing him, and I knew how to cure it. But I could not cure it given the resources of this time. To do that, I had to travel back to my own time in order to obtain the necessary supplies. I was afraid, but I could not sit by and watch that child die, knowing that I had the knowledge to save him and was too afraid to utilize the means. That was when I made my first trip back to my own time. That was also when I first became aware of and made contact with the underground.

"I won't belabor you with the details of that story. What matters is that suddenly I was presented with an opportunity to *do* something about the time wars. I couldn't stop them, but I could help others to desert, to refuse to take part in the lunacy. I became part of the underground.

"That child was cured, but my life changed from that point on. I moved to Paris and established myself there as a physician. I would be a contact point in the underground and it's easier to conceal the comings and goings of people in a city teeming with people. That was how I first met Hunter.

"I kept returning to my own time, dangerous though it was, and contacting people in our organization who helped me to procure supplies. I had access to modern equipment, to stolen, modified implants, in short, I soon became a key figure in the organization. And on one of my trips back to my own time, I met the Timekeepers.

"There were people in my own time, members of the underground, who were involved with an organization known as the Temporal Preservation League. It was a group founded by Albrecht Mensinger and its aim was to stop the war machine. Most of the members of the league pursued this goal through peaceful means, but there were those who believed that they should stop at nothing to achieve their aims. These were the Timekeepers. Jimmy Darcy was a member of the Timekeepers, although when I first met him, I didn't know that. I simply thought he was a member of the league. In time, I came to learn the truth, and it was through him that I met Adrian Taylor.

"You must understand that I was and am against everything that the Timekeepers stand for. I could not and cannot condone terrorism. But they wove a very tempting web and drew me in. I'm not trying to excuse my actions, only to explain what motivated them.

"They had a plan to fight the war machine, an elegant plan that I believed could not fail to work. With my help, with access to my surgical skills and chronoplate, they could form a unit that would travel back in time and interfere with history. The plan was that they would announce their intent, then follow through on it if the ones in power refused to listen. They would refuse, of course; but in time, they would have no choice but to accede to our demands.

"We would go back to some period in the past and create a temporal disruption, set into motion a course of events that would interfere with history. We would then alert the Referee

Corps, giving them ample opportunity and time to effect an adjustment, thereby preserving the natural, historic course of events. Yet, even as they worked to bring their adjustment about, we would already be in yet another period, creating yet another disruption. We would repeat the process all over again and keep repeating it, putting a massive drain on the power, resources, and abilities of those who perpetuated the time wars. In time, they would be forced to realize that they could not stop us and they would have no choice but to listen to our demands. I was so naive, I actually believed that.

"I know now that that was never Taylor's plan. Taylor is insane. He's a killer. I'm convinced that he never meant to create a mere temporal disruption. No, his goal is far more ambitious. What Taylor wants to do is to create nothing less than a timestream split, to bring about the very disaster that the league and even his fellow terrorists wanted to avoid. And I helped him."

"Then it is up to you to stop him," Andre said.

"I wish I could," said Bennett. "I know I'm going to have to try, but I don't know what I can do. I'm just one man."

"One man who can move through time as easily as I can cross this room," said Andre. "A man who can make a beam of light cut better than the sharpest blade, who can transform a man into a woman. After what I have seen and learned, I no longer believe that there is anything that cannot be done. After all that, what must be done seems very simple. Taylor must be killed, along with those who serve him. You are not alone, Jack Bennett. I will help you."

"I'm afraid that killing Taylor is not a simple matter," Bennett said.

Andre smiled. "Nor is killing me."

9

Jimmy Darcy and Tonio Valenti had seen Bennett and the woman enter the house on the Rue St. Honoré. They had seen Bennett brandishing his laser.

"What do you think they did with Silvera?" Tonio said, scratching at his several-days'-old growth of thick black beard. Both he and Jimmy were dressed as common laborers.

"Could be they've taken him into custody and turned him over to other agents, maybe even clocked him out," said Jimmy. "Could be he's dead."

"That one chest seems pretty heavy," Tonio said. "What do you think they've got in there?"

Both men exchanged quick glances.

"This is really stupid," Jimmy said, beginning to test the waters. "There's absolutely no good reason to kill those two."

"Boss's orders," Tonio said. "Besides, they got Silvera. One way or another," he added, a bit more softly.

"So they got Silvera," Jimmy said. "Silvera screwed up. He never should've taken out that agent."

"He was the opposition," Tonio said.

"Christ, use your brain," said Jimmy. "They've probably got agents crawling over half of Paris; you really believe we can take them all on? What's the point? The only thing that matters is the plan and they have no idea what it is."

"Yeah, but maybe they can guess," said Tonio.

"Maybe, but I doubt it. Even if they do, so what? Stopping

it won't be so easy. Even if they do stop it, we've still got the plate. We cut and run and start all over in another period. And this time, there won't be any infiltrators to tell them where we are.''

"That bastard never had a chance to—"

"How *else* could they have found out about it? He must have lived long enough to leave a message."

"C'mon, Taylor left him with his guts all over the goddamn floor," said Tonio.

"Maybe that's just the point," said Jimmy. "Taylor didn't finish the job."

"Yeah, maybe."

"He thinks an agent known as Mongoose may be running the TIA operation," Jimmy said.

"Yeah? So?"

"The way I understand it, Taylor's got a pretty heavy grudge against him. It just makes me a little nervous, that's all. Taylor seems to want to get his hands on that guy pretty badly."

"You saying Taylor might be putting his vendetta or whatever ahead of the operation?"

"I don't know. Is that what I said?"

"No, not exactly. It's what you're not saying that interests me. Ever since that sex-change operation, he's been acting pretty strange."

"You noticed."

"Don't pussyfoot with me, son. Say what's on your mind."

"How long have you known Taylor?"

"Not as long as you."

"How do you feel about him?"

"What do you say we cut through all this crap?" said Tonio. "Either you level with me or you don't; make up your fucking mind."

"I think you know what I'm getting at."

"Yeah, but I want to hear you say it."

Jimmy nodded. "All right. Taylor is a pro. Unlike you and me, he's getting paid a bundle for this. I don't know how much, but I know it's pretty heavy. He makes all the right noises, but when it comes right down to it, he's an outsider."

"He's been with the organization for quite a while."

"He's worked *for* the organization," Jimmy said. "It's not

the same. He's still an outsider. A very well-paid outsider.''

''They have handed us our tools. . . .'' said Tonio.

''Yeah, sure. But it helps to know that you're using the right tool for the right job.''

''You don't trust him.''

Jimmy didn't reply for several seconds. ''You realize he's crazy, don't you?''

Tonio chuckled. ''Don't let Freytag hear you say that.''

''Well?''

Tonio stared at him. ''He's a paranoid schizophrenic most of the time, except when he's a psychopath. Does that answer your question?''

''Yes, that answers my question.''

''And you want to know what I'm going to do about that.''

''Yeah.''

''Absolutely nothing.''

''What?''

''You heard me.''

''I heard you, but I didn't understand you. You *agree* with me about Taylor and you're going to do *absolutely nothing?*''

''You bet. It's like you said, Taylor is a pro. I'm just an amateur. Going up against Taylor would be dangerous, but going up against Taylor and Freytag would be fucking suicide. Taylor I've got my doubts about, but I know for damn sure that Freytag doesn't give a good goddamn about Professor Mensinger, the Timekeepers or the time wars. Freytag's a mercenary and Taylor is his paymaster. Neither you nor I nor both of us together can afford to buy him off and, frankly, I'd rather go up against a dozen Jimmy Darcys than one Freytag. So I'm simply going to pretend this conversation never happened and if you're smart, you'll watch yourself. Besides, he might be madder than a mayfly, but with Taylor, there's a hell of a lot more chance of this whole thing coming off than without him. Okay?''

Jimmy nodded grimly. ''Okay.''

''Terrific. Now what do you say we go and get the job done? It's dark enough to slip in there without drawing attention to ourselves. We'll make it nice and quick and there's one less thing to worry about. All right?''

''Sure,'' said Jimmy. He took a deep breath and let it out slowly. ''Let's go and kill poor old Doc Bennett.''

"Just make sure you subdue the woman first," said Tonio. "She's an agent and she'll be the one to give us trouble."

Walking normally, they crossed the street and headed toward the house, going past it and then doubling back behind it. There was no back door, but they had been at Doc Bennett's house before and they knew the best way to break in. It didn't take them but a moment. They entered the house silently, weapons at the ready, listening for noise, the sound of conversation, footsteps, anything. There was no noise.

"Watch yourself," whispered Tonio.

It didn't take them very long to discover that their quarry had fled. The house was deserted and they saw that Bennett had taken care to destroy all of his equipment and supplies.

"We waited too long," said Tonio. "We should have moved in earlier."

"But how did they get out?"

"Obviously there's a way out of this house that we don't know about. Looks like Doc didn't tell us everything. Lucky for him."

"They must have just left," said Jimmy. "It took time to burn up all that stuff. Some of this slag is still hot."

Tonio had left the room and started searching the other rooms on the first floor. Moments later, he called Darcy into the library.

"Take a look at this," he said, indicating the chest on the floor in the center of the room. Most of Andre's clothes were still in it, several items hanging over the sides of the open chest, others on the floor around it. "Looks like she left in a hurry and repacked to travel light. But why repack in here?"

"The bookshelf," Jimmy said. He pointed to a space upon the shelf where several books were missing, having been placed upon the desk. Jimmy went over to the shelf and reached into the empty space, feeling around with his hand. "Jackpot," he said, as a click sounded and the shelf swung away to reveal the door behind it. He aimed his laser at the lock. "This should only take a second," he said and pressed the firing stud. The beam of light shot out for a moment and then he switched it off. He tapped the door with the palm of his hand and it swung open.

"Hold it right there!" someone said in English. Jimmy

bolted through the door. Tonio made the mistake of reacting. He started to spin around and fire, but nothing happened. There had been a brief flash of light and he heard a thump on the floor at his feet. Wondering why his laser hadn't fired, he looked down and saw his hand, still holding the weapon, lying on the floor.

He came to and found himself sitting in a chair, tied down securely. The room he was in was dark, the windows shuttered and covered with blankets so that no light seeped in. He could just barely make out several figures in the room, one of them seated backwards on a chair several feet in front of him.

"Good morning," said the one sitting before him.

"My hand," mumbled Tonio.

"We left it on the desk back in Jack Bennett's house," the man said. "If Doc ever gets back, he can use it as a paper-weight."

Tonio's mouth felt funny. He was having a hard time waking up and clearing his head.

"Oh, by the way," the man said, "we found your little cyanide capsules. Nice traditional touch. Your mouth feels funny because you're missing two molars. Our dental work isn't exactly top-notch quality, but that's the least of your worries."

"Mongoose?" Tonio felt lightheaded, wrapped in fog.

"Surprise, surprise," the agent said. "Right the first time. Adrian figured they'd send me, did he?"

"Bleeding . . ." mumbled Tonio.

"See to his mouth," said Mongoose.

Someone approached him and pried his mouth open with his fingers. Tonio tried to bite him, but received a stinging slap across the side of his head for his trouble. It seemed to him that he was moving in slow motion. Once again, the fingers pried open his mouth and he felt them reaching in, swabbing at where his teeth had been.

"We gave you a little shot, Tonio," said Mongoose. "We've already had a short chat, but you might not remember. You were still out of it. Blood stopped?"

Tonio tried to feel with his tongue. "Think so," he slurred.

"Good. You know there's no point in fighting it, of course.

You're going to tell us everything. If you try to fight it, it will just take a little longer, but not much longer. You know I'm right, don't you?''

Tonio nodded.

"Good. I know you're feeling a little woozy, but all you have to do is tell us what the plan is and we'll give you another little shot to make you sleep.''

"Going to kill me," Tonio said, thickly.

"No, Tonio, no one's going to kill you. I realize that there's no reason for you to take my word for it, but all you have to do is think about it for a minute and you'll see I'm telling you the truth. I could kill you, of course, but I'll get points for sending you back alive. It makes the agency look good. We'll just have us a nice little chat and we'll give you something to make you sleep and next thing you know, you'll be waking up in a nice warm prison cell back in the 27th century. Free room and board for the rest of your life, unless you decide to opt for re-education and enlistment in the Temporal Corps. No sweat, nice and easy.''

"Nice an' easy. . . .''

"Riiight.''

"Nie an' easy. . . .''

"What's the plan, Tonio?''

"B'ingham . . .''

"Buckingham, right, we guessed as much. Go on.''

"M'us'teers . . . Di'mon stus . . .''

"All right, now we're getting somewhere," Mongoose said. He turned to the agents standing behind him. "We'll have this wrapped up by tonight." He turned back to the terrorist. "All right, we know that the musketeers are going to be sent out to retrieve the diamond studs from Buckingham. What's Taylor going to—''

Tonio suddenly jerked back in his chair. Blood began pouring from his ears, mouth, nose and eyes.

"*Son of a bitch!*" Mongoose jumped up, toppling his chair. Furiously, he kicked the chair across the room. Tonio's head lolled grotesquely against the back of the chair he was tied to. Blood dripped down onto his clothing, made droplets on the floor.

"What the hell happened?" said one of the other agents, rushing up to inspect the body. "How could he—''

Mongoose turned away. "Explosive implant," he said, flatly. "Detonated by remote control. Poor bastard probably didn't even know about it. Those tooth capsules were there just to throw us off. Taylor hasn't missed a trick."

"Jesus."

"I took a long shot and it backfired," Mongoose said. "We should've taken Bennett right from the beginning, instead of using him as bait."

"Want us to bring him in now?"

Mongoose nodded. "Yeah. Bring him in. But don't be rough with him. He'll probably be very glad to see you. He's got no friends now and he'll be scared. I think he'll want to talk."

"Suppose he's got one of those explosive implants, too?"

"Not a chance. Taylor would've detonated it, instead of sending people after him. No, good ole Doc Bennett's probably the guy who did the operation. It's nice and simple. A little shot while you're asleep and five minutes later, presto, walking time bomb."

"Some doctor."

"You're wasting time. I want Bennett in my custody before nightfall. He gave us the slip with that clever secret passageway and it may cost him his life. Get out there and find him before Freytag does."

"You know what I've been thinking?" Finn asked Lucas.

Lucas belched and patted his stomach. "What?"

"I've been thinking that we got a raw deal. We soldier our damn buns off and all these characters ever do is drink and brawl and screw. Some life, huh? Join the king's musketeers and get paid for raising hell."

They had joined the musketeers for dinner at Moreau's Tavern and, after stuffing themselves until they couldn't possibly eat another mouthful, Finn and Lucas sat kicked back against the wall, sipping wine and watching as Porthos and D'Artagnan regaled the crowd with an impromptu demonstration of the finer points of swordsmanship. Several tables had been pushed aside for the two to occupy the center of the room, where Porthos was discoursing upon the advantages of the Parisian style of fencing over the Florentine style. The Parisian style, as defined by Porthos, consisted of holding a rapier in one hand and a wine goblet in the other. He kept up a steady stream of chatter as he parried D'Artagnan's playful thrusts with exaggerated flourishes of his sword and Moreau's customers were loving it, guffawing, shouting "Well struck!" and pounding on the tables.

Aramis, emphasizing that he was preparing for the clergy, occupied himself with trying to convert the prostitutes. One at a time, he took them upstairs to lecture them upon the virtues of clean living and piety.

"I keep thinking about what Mongoose said," said Lucas. "I just find it hard to believe that one of the musketeers could be an impostor. Surely, it can't be D'Artagnan. Porthos seems like the real thing, all right, and Aramis—"

"If one of them is an impostor," said Delaney, "I'd say that this is our most likely candidate, right here."

Athos came back to the table, having left to get more wine. He sat down heavily and set several bottles on the table, bottles that were refilled periodically from casks Moreau had in his cellar.

"This wine is swill," said Athos, "but my throat is parched and I'll settle for almost anything. Come, Francois, Alexandre, drink up. It's our duty to get rid of all this garbage so Moreau can go out and buy some decent wine."

They refilled their goblets. Athos kicked back his chair to lean against the wall beside them. He frowned as he saw Aramis heading upstairs with yet another potential convert.

"Women," he said, scornfully. "They'll be the death of him yet." He was slurring his words slightly. "It's a wonder he hasn't gotten himself poxed already."

"You don't much care for women, do you?" Lucas said.

"I have no use for them."

"No romance? Never been in love?"

Athos stared out into the center of the room, eyes unfocused, seeing something other than the swordplay and the crowd.

"Once," he said, softly.

"What, just once?"

"It was enough, my friend. I will say, rather, that it was much more than enough. I was young and foolish and *in love*," he said those words as though they were an epithet, "and I did not do well in my selection of a mistress." Jerking his head slightly, as if suddenly aware that he had said more than he meant to, he reached out and grabbed one of the bottles off the table, knocking over two others in the process.

"I have another mistress now," he said, loudly, brandishing the bottle. "She's loyal and true and never strays far from my reach. She never fails to satisfy me; she never lets me down. She fills me to the brim with her warmth of loving kindness and she does not deceive me. Veritas in vino!" he shouted, raising the bottle high in a violent gesture that toppled him from his chair. He fell to the floor and remained there, dead drunk.

Lucas glanced down at him. "You were saying?" he said to Finn.

"On the other hand, maybe it's one of the others," Finn said.

Lucas didn't say anything. Delaney glanced at him and saw that he was staring intently out toward the center of the room. A young, elegantly dressed cavalier had come down the stairs and he was circling around the mock combat in the center of the room, heading toward the door.

Misinterpreting his stare as an effort to keep his eyes in focus, Finn rocked his chair back down, away from the wall, and set his goblet down upon the table.

"Hell," he said, "I've had about enough. What do you say we call it a night?"

Lucas glanced at him sharply. "*What did you say?*"

"I said, what do you say we call it a night?"

Lucas rocked his chair forward so hard that the few remaining upright bottles on the table were knocked over, spilling their contents onto the floor and into Delaney's lap.

"Christ, what's with you?" said Delaney, jumping up.

Lucas stared at the door, through which the young cavalier had passed seconds earlier.

"*De la Croix*," he said, softly.

"What? Lucas, what's the matter with you? You look like you've just seen a ghost."

"I have," he said. "Come on."

"What? Where are we going?"

"Come *on*, I said! Hurry, before we lose him!"

"Lose *who?*"

"The red knight!"

"The . . . *what?*" Lucas was heading for the door, pushing his way through.

They followed the young cavalier carefully, keeping their distance and staying in the shadows.

"Lucas, are you *sure?*" said Finn. "It couldn't be a mistake?"

"I told you, I never forget a face," said Lucas, vehemently. "The last time I saw that face, it belonged to the woman who was with Jack Bennett. And the time before that, it was in 12th-century England."

Delaney shook his head. "That's crazy. You've had too much to drink. It's a physical resemblance, that's all. It *can't* be the same man!"

"Then what was he doing with Jack Bennett, an underground contact? I *told* you I saw that woman before. No wonder I couldn't recognize her! She was a man *dressed* as a woman! I'm telling you, Finn, that's Andre de la Croix!"

Finn thought back to their mission in the 12th century and to a mercenary knight who had sold his services to Prince John of Anjou. Lucas had met him in the lists at Ashby and had taken such a battering that he hadn't been able to see straight for hours.

"He must have been in the underground all the time!" said Finn. "What's he doing here?"

"That's what I intend to find out," said Lucas. They were in the Rue des Fossoyeurs. The cavalier went up to No. 14 and knocked on the door. "That's D'Artagnan's house!" said Lucas.

Finn glanced behind them, but he couldn't see anything in the dark streets. "If Mongoose has his people tailing us, I hope to hell they're not sleeping on the job," he said. "This could get nasty."

They crept up to the window and peered inside. The cavalier was seated at a table, talking with an old man whom they had last seen entering the house in the Rue St. Honoré.

"Jack Bennett," whispered Finn. "What the hell is going on here?"

"It looks like Mongoose was right," said Lucas. "Our

friend D'Artagnan is a Timekeeper."

"I can't believe it," said Delaney. "D'Artagnan *can't* be an impostor!"

"You have any other explanation?"

"No, but . . . it just doesn't fit. It would mean that they've had us made right from the very start, before we even arrived in Paris!"

"Well, there's only one way we're ever going to know for sure," said Lucas. He went over to the door and pounded on it.

Someone said, "Who knocks?"

In a perfect imitation of D'Artagnan's voice, Lucas said, "Damn you, Bonacieux, let me in! I've forgotten my key!"

A moment later, the door was unlatched and as the person on the other side started to open it, Lucas shouldered his way in with Finn following close behind.

Jack Bennett was knocked back into the wall. Andre de la Croix leapt up, rapier drawn.

"We meet again, Sir Knight," Lucas said, speaking in Norman.

De la Croix hesitated, obviously taken aback. Bennett clawed for something in his pocket, but the point of Finn's rapier was at his throat in an instant.

"Don't do it," Finn said, in English. "Let's have it. Slowly."

With a look of resignation, Bennett handed over his laser.

"Who *are* you?" said Andre.

"It is you, isn't it?" said Lucas. "Andre de la Croix. What do you call yourself in Paris?"

"How do you know me?"

"We've met before," said Lucas. "In the lists, on the field of Ashby."

"At *Ashby?* Impossible. I don't—"

"I'll refresh your memory," said Lucas, switching to English. "You wore red armor and had a fleury cross for your shield device. I wore white and my shield device was an uprooted oak. I remember being quite impressed with your abilities. I never dreamt that you were underground."

"She isn't," Bennett said. "At least, she wasn't then."

"She?"

"Take a good, close look," said Bennett. "Andre is a woman."

Finn had put away his sword and was now covering Bennett with the laser. "What is this?" he said. "What are you trying to pull?"

Moving slowly, keeping his hands in plain sight, Bennett walked over to a chair and sat down.

"You're commandos, aren't you?" he said. "An adjustment team?"

"That's right," said Finn, watching him closely.

Bennett seemed relieved. "Andre, we have to cooperate with these men. They are soldiers from the future."

Andre nodded. She put her rapier and her dagger down upon the table and slowly approached Lucas.

"That's far enough," said Lucas, when she was almost within arm's reach of him.

"I am unarmed," she said, "and your friend can kill me easily."

She held out her hands to Lucas.

"Your hand," she said.

Hesitantly, Lucas lowered his rapier and stretched out his free hand to her. She came closer and took his left hand in both of hers, pressing it against her chest, then slowly moving it down between her legs. There was nothing sexual in the contact at all. She kept her eyes on his, watching for a reaction. She was surprised at what she saw. It was not at all what she had expected.

Lucas raised his eyebrows only slightly and said, "All right, so you're a woman. What does that prove?"

She glanced at Bennett, uncertainly.

"She's a unique woman," Bennett said. "The term that's used is *displaced person*."

Now Lucas really looked surprised. "Are you telling me that—"

"That she is not now nor has she ever been a soldier of the Temporal Corps," said Bennett. "Briefly, she was born in the 12th century and orphaned as a child. She started passing for male at an early age and through a series of fascinating circumstances, she acquired the abilities that enabled her to become a mercenary knight errant. I don't know the full story, but she was brought to this time by a friend of mine whom she met in medieval England. Hunter had intended for her to—"

"*Reese Hunter?*" said Finn.

Now Bennett looked surprised. "You knew him?"

"Knew?" said Lucas. "Past tense?"

"Yes," said Bennett. "He's dead. Assassinated by a terrorist named Silvera, who believed him to be a TIA agent. Hunter came to Paris with Andre to seek me out for the purpose of obtaining a black market implant for Andre. I've been a major contact and supplier in the underground for many years. To my everlasting sorrow, Hunter arrived at a time when I was involved in a terrorist plot with the Timekeepers. I was with them when he came looking for me. In inquiring as to my whereabouts, Hunter must have attracted the attention of the Timekeepers, who took him to be an agent. They trailed him to his rooms at the Luxembourg Hotel—"

"The Luxembourg!" said Finn.

Bennett frowned. "Yes, that's right. I thought you looked familiar. You were the men we passed on the stairs."

"Continue," Lucas said.

Bennett sighed. "Hunter was followed to the Luxembourg and killed there. Fortunately, Andre was not there at the time. On the other hand, if she was there, she might have prevented it. She's altogether a remarkable young woman. Well. At any rate, they must have staked out the hotel. When I received word that Hunter was in Paris and staying at the Luxembourg, I immediately went to see him. That was when I met Andre. By that time, Hunter was already dead and she was alone in the hotel with his body, not knowing how to dispose of it, who had killed him, or why he had been killed. I was seen going into the hotel, to Hunter's room. Naturally, the Timekeepers assumed I had betrayed them to the TIA and Silvera broke into the room with the intention of killing me and taking Andre prisoner. However, Andre managed to kill Silvera first." Bennett was reciting the story in a flat and weary tone of voice. "We had to smuggle both bodies out of the hotel—"

"That perfumed chest," said Finn.

"Yes," said Bennett.

"You passed us on the stairs and I thought I recognized Andre," Lucas said, "only I couldn't place her face. Of course, the last time that I saw her, she wasn't dressed as a woman. When I saw her as she is now, leaving Moreau's

Tavern, I recognized her, but I thought she was a man passing as a woman. Instead, it was the other way around!''

"You followed us to the Rue St. Honoré?" Bennett said.

"That's right," said Finn. "When we saw you flashing that laser around—"

"You assumed I was a Timekeeper and that you had found the house where the chronoplate was being kept," Bennett finished for him. "You were almost right. However, I don't have my plate anymore. They took it from me. They have Hunter's plate, as well, but they don't know its fail-safe code. That's why they're after Andre. They don't realize that she's a displaced person and doesn't know how to operate it."

"And they want you dead because they think that you betrayed them to the agency," said Lucas.

"Kind of puts you in a tough spot, doesn't it?" said Finn. "As far as the agency team is concerned, you're with the Timekeepers. The Timekeepers think you've sold out to the agents. The question is, where *do* you stand?"

"Until a short while ago," said Bennett, "I stood with them. I'm against the time wars. That was why I joined the underground and it was why I became involved with the Temporal Preservation League."

"Then there *is* a connection between the league and the terrorists?" said Finn.

"Oh, yes. It's the most tenuous of connections, but it exists. I became convinced that the Timekeepers had a workable plan to bring pressure upon the Referee Corps to end the temporal conflicts."

"A timestream split is what you call a workable plan?" said Finn.

"That was only the announced intention," Bennett said. "The Timekeepers themselves never intended to bring about a split. The idea was to create adjustment situations throughout all of history, alerting the Referee Corps to each situation as it was created, so that they would be able to restore historical continuity, but at the price of extended manpower commitments, financial losses, and temporary historical instability."

"Interesting idea," Lucas said. "But surely you must have realized the chance that you were taking? Suppose one of those adjustment situations proved to be irreversible?"

"There was always that chance," said Bennett. "However, our aim was to conduct only the most controlled types of interference actions."

"What changed your mind?" said Finn.

"Adrian Taylor," Bennett said. "He's—"

"We know who Taylor is," said Lucas.

"Do you know that he's totally insane? That he is totally committed to creating a timestream split?"

"The agency is proceeding on that assumption," Lucas said.

"Then the TIA knows more than Taylor's own people do," said Bennett.

"Are you saying that the Timekeepers actually don't—"

"I *told* you what the plan was!" Bennett shouted. "But Taylor is uncontrollable! I became convinced of that when he killed the Countess de la Fère."

"But that's—"

"Milady de Winter," Bennett said. "Possibly the most important figure in this scenario. That was where my talents as a surgeon came in. I performed a transsexual operation upon Adrian Taylor. He is now Milady de Winter."

Finn put away his newly acquired laser. "Holy Christ," he said. "And Mongoose thought that one of the musketeers was an impostor."

"Ah, I see," said Bennett. "You followed Andre here and saw us in this house and you naturally assumed that D'Artagnan was a ringer. No, he's quite genuine, I assure you, as are the other musketeers. Moreau is an old friend of mine and he arranged this hiding place for me. Bonacieux owes him a favor. Bonacieux's name rang a bell with me, but what with everything that's been happening, I didn't put it all together until I arrived here and found out who his other tenant was. I was even toying with the idea of trying to get D'Artagnan to help me, until I realized how crazy it would be."

"Help you do what?" said Finn.

"I thought I had made that eminently clear," said Bennett. "Taylor must be killed."

"Where is he?"

"I can tell you where he was," said Bennett, "but it's a sure bet that he won't be there now. He's not a fool."

"I think you'd better have a talk with Mongoose," Lucas said.

"The agent in charge?" said Bennett. "I can't do that."

"You're not exactly in a position to say what you can or cannot do," said Lucas.

"You don't understand," said Bennett. "I'm an important figure in the underground. I know a great deal about the underground organization. Mongoose would have me arrested and clocked out, so that I could be interrogated. I won't jeopardize the lives of people whose only crime was in saying *no* to war."

"But you're willing to jeopardize the timestream," Lucas said.

"I told you, I want Taylor stopped as badly as you do. But I cannot allow myself to be taken into custody."

"Aren't you forgetting something?" Finn said. "You're already in our custody."

"Not exactly," Bennett said, producing another laser. Finn started and reached for the first weapon he had taken from Bennett, but Bennett fired his laser on low intensity, singeing Delaney's hand. "I don't want to do it," he said, "but if you force me to, I'll burn you where you stand. Don't forget that I'm a surgeon and I'm quite expert with this laser. Now take that weapon out very slowly and slide it to me across the floor."

Finn glanced at Lucas and did as he was told. As the laser slid across the floor toward Bennett, Lucas moved fast, grabbing Andre and jerking her around in front of him, holding her around the neck, his dagger at her side.

"Drop it or I'll cut her," he said.

The next thing Lucas knew, he was in mid-air and flying across the room. He hit the floor and rolled, coming up in a fighting stance, his dagger held ready. Andre was holding her own dagger by the point, ready to throw it.

"No!" shouted Bennett.

There was a fierce pounding on the door.

"Damn you, Bonacieux!" D'Artagnan shouted drunkenly from outside. "Let me in! I've forgotten my key!"

10

Nobody moved. The pounding continued, unabated.

"Bonacieux, God curse you! Wake up and open this door!"

From behind a door on the far side of the room, they could hear the old man getting up, mumbling in an irritated fashion.

"Quickly," Bennett said, "put away your weapons!"

Lucas and Andre both sheathed their daggers. She picked up Lucas's rapier and tossed it to him. Bennett, now in possession of both lasers, hid them from sight, but kept them both within easy reach. "Open this door," he told Finn.

Finn went to the door and opened it, admitting the besotted Gascon just as Bonacieux, dressed in a dirty nightshirt, came out of his bedroom, looking bleary-eyed.

"Ah, Francois!" D'Artagnan said, stumbling into the room. "What brings you here? And Dumas, as well! What a surprise! Is there some occasion that merits this celebration? It is not my birthday, is it?"

"Gentlemen, please!" said Bonacieux. "Cannot a poor man get some sleep? I really must insist on quiet after dark! I am not a young man, I need my rest! Monsieur D'Artagnan, I've spoken to you of this before! It is bad enough that you do not pay rent—"

"I do not pay rent, good Bonacieux, because it was our agreement," said D'Artagnan. "Did I not rescue your wife from her abductors? Did I not restore her to you?"

"For all that I see her, she might as well be held captive still," grumbled Bonacieux.

"Now, Bonacieux, I cannot be held responsible for your marital difficulties," said D'Artagnan, winking at Delaney. "If you did not exhaust yourself by staying up until odd hours and entertaining company all night, perhaps you'd be in better shape to satisfy her."

"I! I stay up until odd hours! Really, Monsieur, I—"

"Come on, now, off to bed with you, you old fossil," said D'Artagnan, putting his arm around Bonacieux and propelling him back into his bedroom. "This is a rooming house and not a tavern! Sensible people are in bed this time of night!"

Protesting weakly, Bonacieux allowed himself to be propelled back into his room. D'Artagnan placed his hand upon the old man's back and gave him a final shove, then slammed the door shut.

"Unreasonable man," he said. He peered at Andre. "I say, Monsieur, I don't believe I know you. Have you a sister?"

"Monsieur Andre de la Croix," said Lucas, performing the introductions, "and Doc—"

"Monsieur D'Artagnan and I have already met," said Bennett, hastily. "Andre is my nephew."

"A pleasure to make your acquaintance, Monsieur," D'Artagnan said. "Now, about your sister . . ."

"My sister?" Andre said, uncertainly.

"Yes, you have a sister, do you not? Surely, you must be her brother, the family resemblance is remarkable. I refer to the woman who saved my life at the Carmes-Dechaux recently. I have been searching for her ever since, so that I might properly express my gratitude. I never expected that fate should bring her brother to my door, but—"

Someone knocked upon the door.

"What, more visitors?" D'Artagnan said. "Francois, be a good fellow and tell whoever it is to go away."

"Go away," said Delaney.

"But I *must* speak to Monsieur D'Artagnan!" came the distinctly feminine reply. "Oh! Goodness, who is in there?"

"Constance!" said D'Artagnan.

With an elaborate gesture, Finn opened the door. "Why not?" he said. "Everybody else is here."

Constance rushed in, all aflutter. "D'Artagnan!"

"Constance!"

"Constance?" Bonacieux croaked from his bedroom. "What, is my wife there?"

"Oh, I *cannot* see him now!" said Constance. "I mustn't! He is a spy for Richelieu!" She glanced around at all the others. "Goodness, who *are* these men?"

"We are *not* spies for Richelieu," said Finn.

"These are my friends," D'Artagnan said, expansively.

"Is my wife there?" said Bonacieux, from behind his bedroom door.

"No," shouted D'Artagnan. "Go back to sleep!"

"But I thought I heard her voice," said Bonacieux, opening his bedroom door.

"You were dreaming," said D'Artagnan, pushing him back into the bedroom with a hand upon his face, then booting the door closed. "Quickly, up to my room," said D'Artagnan.

"But these gentlemen . . ." said Constance.

"Will wait their turn," D'Artagnan said.

"What?"

"He means to speak with him, madame," said Lucas.

"Oh!" Constance said, looking very much relieved.

"My wife . . ." said Bonacieux, opening his door again.

D'Artagnan shoved it closed and a heavy thump could be heard from the other side. "Upstairs, now, quickly," he said.

Constance ran upstairs to the Gascon's room. They heard his door open and close as she went inside and then Bonacieux peered out again, rubbing his head.

"What happened?" he said.

"You were walking in your sleep," D'Artagnan said.

"I *was*?"

"Yes, and you struck your head. You'd best be careful, you could injure yourself that way."

"I thought I heard my wife. . . ."

"You were dreaming," said D'Artagnan. "Dreaming and walking and talking in your sleep; really, Bonacieux, this is too much. If this sort of thing continues, I fear I shall have to seek other quarters!"

"Oh, no, Monsieur D'Artagnan, it will not happen again, I assure you!"

"Good, see that it does not. I grow weary of these constant disturbances. Go to bed, Bonacieux."

"Yes, yes, I will."

"Good night, then."

"Good night to you, Monsieur."

Bonacieux went back to bed.

"You will excuse me, gentlemen?" D'Artagnan said. He grabbed a bottle off the table and staggered up the stairs.

Finn immediately reached for his rapier, but Bennett had both lasers out at once, covering both him and Lucas.

"Andre, take one of these and watch them for a moment, will you?" Bennett said.

"This is ridiculous, Bennett," Lucas said. "You need our help. If you really want to—"

"Sssh," said Bennett, removing a small box, about the size of a package of cigarettes, from his pocket. He flipped a tiny switch on it.

"*—terrible thing!*" Constance's voice came from the box. "*You've simply got to help—*"

"You bugged his room!" said Lucas.

Bennett glanced up at him impatiently. "You mind?"

"*—anything I can, dear darling Constance, just let me—*"

"*Now now!*"

"*Oh, but Constance, I burn with the flame of desire, I am consumed with—*"

There were the sounds of a brief struggle, followed by the sound of water being thrown and D'Artagnan sputtering.

"I think she just extinguished his flame with the water from his washbasin," Bennett said.

"*Pooh, you stink!*"

"Correction, not his washbasin," Bennett said.

"*Now will you listen to me?*"

"*Lord, Constance, that was my best doublet!*"

"*The devil with your doublet! The queen is in dire danger and all you can think about is sex!*"

"*What, the queen in danger? Well then, why didn't you say so? Here, just let me remove this foul-smelling doublet. . . .*"

"*The king has ordered a ball to be held in honor of the queen,*" said Constance. "*And he has asked her to wear the diamond studs he gave her . . .*"

"Yes, go on, I'll just remove these soiled breeches. . . ."

"But the queen gave her diamond studs to Milord Buckingham," said Constance. *"Richelieu must have found out about it, his spies are everywhere."*

"Indeed. Here, come over to the bed and help me pull these boots off. . . ."

"If the queen does not get back her diamond studs in time, she will be ruined! She has given me a letter to Milord Buckingham. You must go to London and bring back the studs or—"

"Yes, of course, I'll depart first thing in the morning."

"Oh! D'Artagnan!"

"Sssh, you'll wake your husband."

"Oh! Stop it!" There was a ripping sound. *"My dress!"*

"I'll buy you another. I'll buy you a whole closetful of dresses—"

Bennett switched off the speaker. "Well, that's it," he said. "Taylor's made his move. It's started."

"What's the plan?" said Lucas.

"I don't know for certain," Bennett said. "Somehow, he's going to interfere with the musketeers and prevent them from delivering the studs. The queen's affair with the prime minister of England will be made public and her reputation will be ruined. She may even be accused of treason."

"Then we're going to have to make sure that she gets her studs back," Lucas said. "We're not going to be able to do that unless you cooperate with us."

"I can't allow myself to be arrested," Bennett said.

"Look, if Mongoose wanted to arrest you, he could have done so at any time," said Finn. "He knows all about you, who you are and what you do. He's had you watched."

"You were being used by both sides, Bennett," Lucas said. "Look, Mongoose isn't interested in your connection with the underground. He doesn't care. All he wants is to get Taylor."

"So I tell him what I've told you and he lets me go, is that it? You really expect me to believe that? I've told you men everything I know. There isn't anything further that I can—"

The door was kicked in and five men dressed in the uniform of Richelieu's guard burst into the room, knocking Delaney to the floor. Bennett reacted immediately, firing his laser. One of the men fell dead, another fired a laser of his own at Bennett, killing him instantly. There was a crash of glass as Andre dove through a window. From outside, someone shouted and there was the sound of several pairs of running footsteps. Mongoose entered the room, dressed in the uniform of a captain in the cardinal's guard. He glanced briefly at Bennett's body.

"The fool could have saved himself a lot of trouble," he said.

Bonacieux came hobbling out, looking like a startled chicken.

"What is it? What's the matter? What is the reason for this ruckus? Can't a poor man get some—" He saw the agents in the uniform of the cardinal's guard and instantly fell silent, eyes wide with terror.

"Back in your room!" said Mongoose.

Bonacieux gave a little yelp, then ducked back into his bedroom like a frightened rabbit darting back into its hole. The door slammed and they heard the key turn in the lock.

"All right, get him out of here," said Mongoose, indicating Bennett's body. Two of the agents lifted Bennett's body from the chair, each draping an arm around their shoulders. They started toward the door when there was the sound of a door slamming upstairs and then D'Artagnan appeared, standing at the head of the stairs, shirtless and shoeless, holding a rapier in one hand while he attempted to fasten his trousers with the other. His drunken gaze fell on the agents and he gave a shout.

"Hark! An invasion! To arms, my friends! One for all and one for—"

He lost his balance and fell headlong down the stairs to collapse in an unconscious heap upon the floor, his pants around his knees.

Mongoose bent over him for a moment, then straightened. "Well, he's alive," he said. "It's a miracle he didn't bust his head open." He glanced up the stairs toward D'Artagnan's room, then back down at the senseless Gascon. "Looks like Madame Bonacieux is going to have some explaining to do," he said.

"You had the house bugged," Lucas said.

Mongoose sighed. "Priest, you seem to be a master of stating the obvious."

"How did you know to bug D'Artagnan?"

"I had D'Artagnan's house bugged, I had Athos, Aramis, and Porthos bugged, I had Treville bugged, and I had Richelieu's private chambers bugged," said Mongoose. "The king and queen haven't been able to fart without my knowing about it and I've had Buckingham under surveillance in London. I'm not here to fool around, Priest, I'm here to stop a terrorist plot. Now if you gentlemen don't mind, we've got work to do. Let's go."

They were taken to an unassuming house on the Rue Servadoni, one of several places the agency had established as safehouses. There were no other tenants and the landlord had been given a long vacation in the country. One of the agents made them coffee and brought them cigarettes, which they gratefully accepted.

"Looks like you blew it, Mata Hari," Finn said. "You had everyone under surveillance except the one person who really mattered. Milady was a natural, right? A perfect pawn for the terrorists to use. It was so obvious, I'll bet you figured they wouldn't come within a mile of her."

"You're becoming very tiresome, Delaney," Mongoose said.

"I love you too, sweetheart."

"Your constant efforts to provoke me are not going to succeed," he said. "I have a job to do and, for that matter, so do you. When it's over, I'll be more than happy to accommodate your barroom instincts, but until then, put a lid on it."

Finn nodded. "You've a date, friend."

"And you've just bought yourself a long stay in the hospital, assuming you survive the next few days," said Mongoose. "As a matter of fact, you're wrong about Milady, or Taylor, as the case may be. I *had* her house bugged. You know what I got? A lot of stupid chatter with gentleman callers about the weather, fashion, court intrigue and other senseless babble. I had my men move in tonight. Know what they found?"

"A lot of prerecorded conversations," Lucas said. "Taylor anticipated you."

"Exactly. In that sense, I'm willing to concede your point, Delaney. I did blow it. Taylor put in an appearance every now and then and did some entertaining to keep up the illusion, but no real business was ever conducted in that house. I must admit, I never even considered the fact that he might have killed the real Milady de Winter and taken her place. It was a master stroke.''

"What about Bennett?" Lucas said.

"What about him? He ceased being an important factor once we heard what we needed to know."

"I'm just interested to know what you would have done with him if he hadn't fired on your men. Or was that the whole purpose of busting in like that, to provoke him?"

"Now what would have been the point in that?" said Mongoose. "If he hadn't been a suicidal fool, I'd have placed him under arrest and clocked him out and he'd still be alive."

"You mean he'd be alive to be interrogated for the purpose of tracking down as many members of the underground as he kept in touch with," Lucas said.

"You surprise me, Priest. I wouldn't have thought that you had any sympathy for deserters. Besides, that would be none of my concern. It would've had nothing to do with the job at hand. Thanks to Bennett, it's almost over now. There's only one thing left for you to do."

"Let me guess," said Finn. "You want us to go along to London with the musketeers, just to make sure everything runs smoothly."

"That shouldn't be too hard," said Mongoose. "I'll have things covered from both ends. I've got my people in position both here and in London and you'll be covered from the air en route."

"From the *air*?" said Finn.

"That's right. I'll have two agents equipped with Airborne issue floater paks doing recon for you."

"That should work just fine so long as nobody looks up," said Finn.

"The risk is negligible. Suppose one of the musketeers does spot them? So what? You think anyone is going to take them seriously if they come back with stories about flying people? They're not exactly known for their sobriety. Our primary concern is to prevent the split. Everything else is of secondary importance. You'll be equipped with miniature comsets that will enable you to keep in contact with the recon party. Our man in London is prepared for your arrival there, so if Taylor doesn't make his move before then, he'll be picking you up and giving you your instructions. You will also be issued lasers. It should be a piece of cake.''

"Except for just one little thing," said Finn. "Taylor still has that chronoplate.''

Mongoose grinned. "Well, you didn't want it *too* easy, did you?''

"I was just wondering what you intended to do in case Taylor and company decided that they'd reached the point of diminishing returns and skipped out to another time period," said Lucas. "You've never quite answered that to my satisfaction.''

"There's always that risk, of course," said Mongoose. "But from what I know of Taylor, I'm willing to bet that he'll take it right down to the wire. He'll exhaust every possibility before he gives up on his operation. He'll use that chronoplate to try and outmaneuver us in this time period before he attempts to escape to another one.''

"Suppose he does?" said Lucas.

"If he does, he'll find it very difficult to mount another operation," Mongoose said. "He'll need more financing and more manpower." Mongoose smiled. "A short while ago tonight, one of my men clocked out with a recorded testimony, in Jack Bennett's own words, proving conclusively that there has been and continues to be a link between the underground, the Timekeepers and the Temporal Preservation League. That, added to the other evidence we've gathered, will constitute all the proof the Referee Corps needs to order the arrest and interrogation of every known member of the Temporal Preservation League. The interrogation sessions will result in all the others being rounded up, as well. It will break the back of the anti-war effort.''

"And result in the arrest, interrogation . . . what is that term you people use? Oh, yes. Interrogation with extreme prejudice," said Finn. "It will mean the arrest, re-education and forcible induction of a lot of innocent people whose only crime was in disagreeing with temporal policy. That will make things very convenient for the Referee Corps, won't it? They'll be able to draft all their political enemies.''

"That shouldn't bother you, Delaney," Mongoose said. "After all, you're already in the service, aren't you?"

The door opened and an agent entered, very out of breath.

"She got away," he said.

"What? What happened?"

"She got Zebra with that damn laser," said the agent. "I hit the dirt when she fired and when I got up, she was gone."

"You idiot," said Mongoose. "Get out there and find her! I want her wasted, you understand?"

"Seems like you've thought of everything, Mongoose," said Delaney. "Now all you've got to worry about is a displaced person on the loose in Paris with a laser."

"She won't be on the loose for long," the agent said, grimly.

"I wouldn't know about that," Lucas said. "We ran into her on our last mission in 12th-century England and she struck me as being extremely capable. Jack Bennett was the only friend she had in this time period. How do you think she feels about the people who killed him?"

"Are you seriously suggesting that she'd try to take us on?" said Mongoose. He laughed. "In that case, she's as good as dead. We haven't got anything to worry about."

"Just the same," said Lucas, "I'd watch my back if I were you."

"I'm telling you, we have to get out *now*," said Jimmy Darcy. "They got Tonio. They must know everything by now! It's over, Adrian!"

"Don't be silly, Jimmy," said Milady, smiling faintly. "Nothing is over. Adrian knows what he's doing."

"*Stop it! Stop it!* Christ, Adrian, you're losing it! You're not Milady, for God's sake!"

"Jimmy, settle down. This is a most unfortunate display. There's nothing to be served by your losing control and panicking."

Darcy glanced at Freytag in exasperation. "Bruno, for

God's sake, don't just sit there!''

Freytag smoked a cigarette, regarding him silently. Darcy went up to him and took him by the shoulders.

"Bruno, listen to me. There's no way we can succeed, not here, not now. They've got us hopelessly outnumbered. We've lost. They know the plan!"

"They know nothing of the sort," Milady said.

"What are you talking about?" said Darcy, spinning to face Taylor. "They *know* we're going to try to prevent the musketeers from bringing back the diamond studs! They'll have all their manpower focused on—''

"Who said that was the plan?" said Milady, softly.

Jimmy stared at Taylor. He looked back at Freytag, then at Taylor once again.

"What are you talking about? Of course that was the plan! We worked it all out! You said—''

"I never said any such thing," said Milady. "Adrian might have mentioned something of the sort, but that was only for your benefit."

Darcy looked bewildered. "What? I don't understand."

Milady got up and crossed the room, moving gracefully to the window. She looked out at the sun rising over Paris.

"The opposition has greater resources than we have," she said, without turning around. "Adrian always knew and understood that. He knew that the only way we could succeed was by using misdirection." She turned around to look at Darcy and smiled. "For security reasons, only Adrian and Bruno, and of course, myself, knew what the real plan was. And now you'll be able to appreciate why that was necessary.

"In a short while, D'Artagnan and the musketeers will be departing for London in order to see Lord Buckingham and get back the diamond studs in time for the queen to wear them to the ball. Unbeknownst to the musketeers, they will be supported in their efforts by the entire might of the Temporal Intelligence Agency team. I've made certain that Cardinal Richelieu knows all about the mission of the musketeers and he will have his men attempt to intercept them at several points along their route. All of this works in our favor. Mongoose will have no way of knowing if the men who will be attacking the musketeers are Richelieu's people or Timekeepers. In fact, we won't be involved at all. They will all be off on a fool's errand, a wild goose chase.

"When they reach London, should they get that far—and with the help of the TIA, I have no doubt that they will—they will collect the studs from Buckingham and start back, only to face further attempts to stop them on their return trip. Mongoose will be handicapped by history. He will be forced to use a certain amount of restraint in protecting the musketeers, since the historical progression of events must be preserved. The tension will build. They won't know when they can expect us to strike. They won't know exactly what to expect."

"What *can* they expect?" said Darcy, hesitantly.

"They can expect a crushing defeat when they return," said Milady. "Oh, I have no doubt that they will return safely with the diamond studs. I'm certain that, after that, it won't take them long to guess my plan. By that time, Richelieu, Queen Anne, and King Louis will have been assassinated."

"*Assassinated!*" Darcy's voice was little more than a whisper. "My God, Adrian, you can't do that! Don't you realize what that would *mean?* It would cause a timestream split!"

"A rather massive one, I should think. With all three of them dead, France will be forced to abandon the siege of La Rochelle in the face of much greater problems. It will, without a doubt, affect France's participation in The Thirty Years' War and, of course, it would prevent the birth of Louis XIV. I should think it would be an absolute disaster, well beyond the hope of any effort at historical adjustment. And with Mongoose and his agents running about like chickens with their heads cut off, it shouldn't be too difficult to isolate him and settle an old and outstanding score. Brilliant, don't you think?"

Darcy's mouth worked soundlessly for a moment and his hands began to shake. "*You're mad*," he said at last. "Bruno, surely you can see he's mad! Our purpose, our whole reason for existence is to stop the war machine before something happens that will irreversibly affect the course of history and that's precisely what he intends to do! He wants to cause the greatest disaster ever to befall mankind! It's megalomaniacal lunacy!"

Taylor stiffened and his eyes glazed over for a moment.

"Bruno, for God's sake, we've *got* to stop him!"

"Why?" said Freytag, softly.

Darcy turned pale. "You're both insane," he said. He pulled out his laser. "I'm not going to let you do it, Adrian. I won't let you throw away everything we've worked for all these years. It ends right here."

"You're right, Jimmy," Taylor said, his hand in a fold of his dress. "It ends right here . . . for you." He pressed a button.

Darcy gave a violent jerk, like a hooked trout breaking the surface of the water. His head snapped back and blood erupted from his nose and mouth. It trickled down his cheeks, seeping from his eyes, and it flowed from his ears and down his neck. He was dead before his body hit the floor.

"Now we can say that Doctor Bennett has fully served his purpose," Taylor said. "Bruno, will you join me in a glass of wine?"

11

D'Artagnan was awakened rudely, revived by a bucket of water dashed in his face. He sputtered and shook his head, then opened his eyes to see a frightened Constance peering down at him anxiously.

"That's the second time tonight you've doused me," he said. He ran his hand through his wet hair and sniffed it. "At least this time it was water."

"I was terrified," said Constance, clutching her torn dress about herself. "I thought you were killed!"

"I almost wish I was," D'Artagnan said, getting up slowly and rubbing his head. Almost as an afterthought, he pulled his pants up. "What happened?"

"The cardinal's men arrested your two friends," she said.

"This is the second time they've run afoul of Richelieu's men on my account," D'Artagnan said. "I must get my clothes—"

"I've brought them down for you," she said. Somewhat sheepishly, she added, "If you were dead, then I thought it best to dress you, so that you would not be found so. . . ."

"Yes, I quite understand," D'Artagnan said, putting on his clothes. "Thank you."

"What are you going to do?"

"What time is it?"

"Almost midnight."

"Then there is no time to lose. I must first go to Athos, Porthos, and Aramis, then together we must go to Captain de Treville. Perhaps he will be able to intercede for Francois and Alexandre. In any case, we will have to obtain leave from him to go to London. I will tell him that we go in the queen's name, he will understand. We must leave tonight."

"What do you want me to do?"

"Go to the queen," D'Artagnan said. "Tell her that we will bring back the diamond studs. And stay with her. She will be able to protect you from Richelieu's men. But you cannot go looking like that."

"I have other clothing in the palace," Constance said. "It will do until you buy me that closetful of dresses."

D'Artagnan looked pained.

"I can wrap myself in my cloak," said Constance. "Do not worry about me. Just save the queen."

"We must move quickly, then," D'Artagnan said. "If we do not reach Milord Buckingham with all possible speed, then Richelieu will surely win the day. I will escort you as far as the Louvre, then I must fly like the wind. Come, quickly. There is much to be done before the night is out."

He took her hand and together they left the house, rushing off into the night. No sooner had the door closed behind them, than Bonacieux peeked out from his room, where he had been listening.

"So, the musketeers are off to London, eh?" he mumbled to himself, furious at having been deceived. "That little piece of information should be worth something to my friend, the Count de Rochefort."

He threw on his cloak and hurried out into the street, heading toward the Rue des Bons Enfans.

Andre had nowhere to go. Jack Bennett had been her only friend in Paris and now he was dead, killed by men with laser weapons. He had told her that they must cooperate with the soldiers from the future, the men he had called commandos. The men who had killed him had been from the future also. All Andre knew was that they had attacked both Bennett and the commandos; therefore, they had to be the enemy, the men Bennett called the Timekeepers.

She was confused. She did not understand this timestream split they had spoken of, this changing of history. All she knew was that Bennett had said that they must help the soldiers, that even though the soldiers had seemed to be at odds with Bennett, they had not harmed him, even though they had ample opportunity. Hunter had explained that to her. Both Hunter and Bennett had been underground, men who had deserted from the army of the future. It was understandable that the soldiers should want to apprehend them, but they had recognized that there was a more important task at hand.

She kept thinking about the soldier who had spoken to her in Norman, the one who had said that they had met before, upon the field of battle, in the lists at Ashby.

She remembered that day very well. The white knight with the uprooted oak upon his shield had challenged all the knights upon the Norman side. He had killed Front-de-Boeuf and unhorsed both De Bracy and Bois-Guilbert. When her turn had come, they rode at each other several times and the white knight had won, in spite of the wondrous armor that she had been given by her benefactor, the man who had learned her secret and had forced her into his service as payment for not revealing it.

She knew now that the man who had given her the strange, magical-seeming armor had been from the future also. Hunter had told her later that the armor had been crafted from a material known as nysteel, far lighter than the armor of her time, much more flexible and virtually impregnable. She had been caught in a battle between two opposing forces from the future and it was that which led to her meeting Hunter.

It still seemed like sorcery to her. They called it science, but it was all far beyond her understanding. Hunter had attempted to explain "technology" to her and she had understood some of what he said, but it still seemed like magic. In a short time, her entire world had been turned upside down. She had become involved with people who could do things that defied belief; and yet, it was impossible to disbelieve, for she had seen these things. She was here, in Paris, centuries removed from her own time, their "science" had made it possible. She had longed to understand it all. Hunter had promised her that, with an implant, all would be made clear to her. She was not even certain what an "implant" was, but now the man who could have given it to her was dead, killed by the Timekeepers. The man who had brought her to this time was dead, killed by the Timekeepers. And the soldiers from the future, one of whom she had met with in the lists and who had treated her much more than fairly when he won, had been taken prisoner —again, by the Timekeepers.

Her course seemed clear. Her fate was tied to the soldiers from the future, the commandos, as Jack Bennett had called them. Her allegiance seemed clear, too. The leader of the Timekeepers, the man called Taylor who was now the woman called Milady, must die. From what she had understood, this Taylor was not merely disguising himself as a woman in the same manner as she disguised herself as a man. Somehow, with Jack Bennett's help, he had *become* a woman. Nothing surprised her anymore. After what she had seen, she was convinced that these people could do anything. She had to help the two commandos somehow. If she helped them to defeat their enemy, perhaps they would give her the implant Hunter had promised her. Perhaps they would take her to their own time, where a woman could live as the equal of a man. The only other alternative was for her to live out the remainder of her life in Paris, in this time. Her choice was clear.

After she had escaped from her pursuers, she carefully doubled back to the house in the Rue des Fossoyeurs. She arrived in time to see, from the shelter of an alley across the street, the soldiers from the future being led away by the men who had killed Jack Bennett. They were not bound in any way, but then, she reflected, given the sort of weapons these men possessed, there was no need for it. Stealthily, she trailed them to a house in the Rue Servadoni.

She was uncertain as to what she should do next. She felt the laser in her pocket. She wasn't comfortable with so terrible a weapon. She had only used it once, on one of her pursuers, and its effectiveness was frightening. Still, she did not think that she could attack that house all by herself. There were more men in there than she could handle, each with a weapon just as devastating. She would have to bide her time and wait for an opportunity. At least she was relatively certain that the two soldiers were still alive. If the Timekeepers had wanted them dead, they would have killed them instead of taking them prisoner. Perhaps they were being tortured even as she waited. She bit her lower lip. For the moment, she could think of nothing she could do.

As she waited and watched, one of the men left the house and started walking briskly down the street. Perhaps, she thought, this would provide an opportunity. She followed him, being careful to keep her distance and not be seen. The night aided her in her efforts. The streets were poorly lit and full of shadows.

The man she followed was being cautious, constantly checking the street behind him, but in her black clothing, she was easily able to blend in with the shadows. After several blocks, he seemed more confident and did not check behind him, but walked purposefully through an alley and into the Rue Férou. He walked for a short distance down the street, then slowed to a casual stroll. Andre decided that it was time to make her move. Slowly, she closed the distance between them. Then the man stopped.

Andre pressed herself flat against a building wall. She was so close to him that she could hear the low, almost inaudible whistle that he gave, three short notes, the third one rising, like a bird call. He waited a moment, then repeated it.

She heard an answering whistle, reversing the progression. The man ducked into an alley.

Andre kept to the side of the building, running up to the mouth of the alley. She could hear his footsteps going down the alley, then stop. The night was perfectly still. Somewhere, a baby cried.

Slowly, edging around the side of the building's corner so that she would not be silhouetted at the mouth of the alley, Andre crept into the alley.

"Freytag?" said the man that she had followed.

"Right here," said another voice, and she saw a giant shadow detach itself from the side of the building opposite. She stifled a gasp. The man was huge, monstrous.

"Everything's all set," said the first man. "I think it'll be tonight. The musketeers will probably be leaving around dawn or shortly before then. D'Artagnan was out like a light when we left, but Sparrow will make sure he comes around." He chuckled. "Our phony Madame Bonacieux has that Gascon cretin wrapped around her little finger."

"What about the two commandos?" Freytag said.

"They'll be exactly where I want them. By the time it all goes down, they'll be miles away, galloping across the French countryside with Richelieu's men harassing them every step of the way."

"What about your people?"

"Spread out. Most of them are already in position along the route that the musketeers will be taking. They'll be standing by just to make sure that everything goes smoothly and according to the scenario. As soon as D'Artagnan gets the musketeers together, I'll send our two soldier boys out to join the party. Their story will be that the cardinal's guards were none too gentle in their questioning, but since they didn't know anything, they were released. And of course, they immediately rushed back to see if their friend D'Artagnan was all right. It will give them the perfect excuse to join the musketeers on their trip to London."

"You'd better be right," said Freytag. "Personally, I'm not too crazy about having commandos underfoot."

"Don't worry about them. I told you, I'll take care of it. The refs stuck me with those soldiers, but I've got them so hamstrung, they can't tell the players without a scorecard. They won't be any trouble. I'll make sure they never even get near you and Taylor. How's he holding up, by the way?"

"He's fragmenting. Half the time, I'm not even sure *he* knows who he is. Part of the reason that he's been so good is that he's always been able to immerse himself in his characterizations, but this time, he's added a new wrinkle. He speaks of himself in the third person these days. He keeps vacillating between being himself, being Milady de Winter, and being some weird combination of the two. I tell you, it's a little scary."

"Can you keep him under control long enough to get the job done? I don't want him going off the deep end on me before I'm ready."

"Frankly, I don't know," said Freytag. "He's very volatile and you never know what he's liable to do next. He killed Darcy, you know. That guy gives me the creeps. Darcy's a bloody mess upon the floor and he pours out some wine and asks me to join him in a drink. I'm the only one he's got left now, so you'd think my position would be pretty well secure, but Taylor's crazy. He doesn't really think that he needs anybody. I could be next."

"You losing your nerve, Bruno?"

"I'm not ashamed to admit that I'm a little scared. It's a close game that we're playing. It's pretty goddamn risky."

"I know it's risky, but I've gone to a lot of trouble to set this operation up and we're going to see it through to the end. I'm going to pull this off and I don't need you getting paranoid on me. You pull yourself together and do what you're told."

"Once Mongoose gets his teeth into something, he just doesn't let go, is that it? You know, it's funny how much you and Taylor have in common. I just hope to hell you know what you're doing."

"Count on it."

"Looks like I'm going to have to. I'd best be getting back."

"Good night."

"Yeah. Good luck."

Andre dropped to the ground, lying close against the wall, face down behind a foul-smelling pile of refuse. The man whom she had followed passed so close beside her that she could have reached out and touched him. The other man, the one called Freytag, went out the other way.

She remained there for several minutes, thinking furiously, trying hard to understand what she had overheard. What did it all mean? She had become involved in some complicated plot in which it appeared that no one was who or what they seemed. Constance was not Constance, but somebody named Sparrow. Taylor, the leader of the Timekeepers, had become Milady. The man called Freytag was with Taylor, yet he answered to the man called Mongoose. She had heard the soldiers use the name of Mongoose when they spoke of someone who was "in charge." They had wanted Jack Bennett to speak with Mongoose. Mongoose, then, was in a position of authority over the soldiers, yet now it seemed that he planned somehow to betray them, with the help of the man named Freytag. She could make no sense of it. What was going on? Who was on whose side and where were the battle lines drawn?

Perhaps the two soldiers would understand it, if she could figure out a way to reach them and tell them what she had overheard. She felt the laser in her pocket and took comfort in the sword and dagger at her side. It felt as though she were wading into a battle in which there were no allies, only enemies. She had trusted Bennett and the old man had helped her. Bennett said to help the soldiers. She could think of nothing else to do. She hoped that taking the side of the soldiers was the right thing to do. In any case, her fate was linked with theirs.

She hurried back to the house on the Rue Servadoni.

Finn and Lucas did not get much sleep. They had rested for a little over an hour when Mongoose came into their room and said, "All right, let's go."

He issued them their lasers and their comsets, the latter being tiny units consisting of a miniature receiver that was worn inside the ear and a miniature transmitter that was taped in place over the larynx and covered with a sheer, flesh-colored strip of adhesive that rendered it invisible.

"Okay, listen up," said Mongoose, "we're running short of time and I only want to go over this once. At this moment, D'Artagnan is with Captain de Treville, securing leave for himself and the musketeers to go to London. He has already contacted Athos, Porthos, and Aramis. They will all be meeting at D'Artagnan's house. You'll meet them there. You're going to be extremely angry at having been arrested and detained by the cardinal's men and at having been accused of plotting against France. You didn't know anything, however, and you were able to prove to their satisfaction that you are employed by the wealthy Monsieur Levasseur, who has influential friends at court. This is only in case you should be asked; don't volunteer anything. The gist of it all is that you were concerned about your friend, furious with the cardinal's guards, and anxious to even up the score. D'Artagnan will undoubtedly welcome your offer to go with them to London, knowing they'll need all the help that they can get. You'll have back-up all the way and the two floaters will be giving you recon reports periodically. Remember, I want Taylor alive if possible. You'll need horses. Yours are waiting in the stalls in the Rue Cassette. You can pick them up on the way. Any questions?''

"Where are you going to be?" said Lucas.

"I'll be in position at the palace, just in case anything goes wrong and Taylor tries a last-minute play of some kind. Remember, he's still got that chronoplate; but if we can take him out, we won't have to worry about it. If we take him alive, we'll find the plate. If not, then we can just forget about it. It'll be protected by its fail-safe code and the first person who tries to mess with it will also be the last. Now the floaters will start monitoring you as soon as they get in the air, which should be around an hour from now. They'll be picking you up sometime after you get past the barrier of St. Denis. I doubt you'll have any trouble until you're well away from Paris, but to play it safe, the floaters will be tracking you with nightscopes until daylight, just in case. Any questions? No? All right, get moving.''

They put on their cloaks and took their weapons and went out into the street, walking quickly toward the house in the Rue des Fossoyeurs.

"What do you think?" said Finn.

"I think I'm not going to like this very much," said Lucas. "Mongoose has the whole thing laid out like a major operation, but we're still working blind. We'll be going through a lot of wooded areas en route to the channel and the floater scouts won't be much use to us if they can't penetrate the cover of the trees. We know Taylor has lasers, we know he's got a chronoplate, God knows what other ordnance he might have available. Any way you look at it, we're still cannon fodder. When Taylor makes his move, the floater scouts may spot him, but we might be dead by then.''

"That's about what I was thinking," said Delaney.

"You know what else I think?" said Lucas. "I think we're being followed.''

Delaney didn't turn around. "Where?"

"About half a block back and closing," Lucas said. "One man, I think.''

"Think Mongoose has someone trailing us to provide security?''

"If he does, he didn't mention it. Duck into the next alley."

They walked about another three hundred feet and turned right into a dark and smelly narrow alley between two rows of buildings. Finn stepped on something and almost lost his balance. The rat squealed angrily, tried to bite him through his boot, and then scuttled away into the piles of garbage. Finn spat in disgust. Lucas motioned him to stand against the far wall while he took up a post at the corner, right next to the entrance to the alley. They waited several seconds and then heard running footsteps approaching. Lucas held his breath as the footsteps slowed to a walk, then stopped altogether just around the corner. He reached for his laser. For a moment, nothing happened. Lucas could barely make out Finn, standing across the way, almost invisible in the darkness.

"I am not an enemy," came a soft voice from just around the corner from where Lucas was standing. "I must speak with you. It is a matter of utmost urgency!"

Lucas licked his lips nervously. He seemed to recognize the voice, but it could be a trap.

"Clasp your hands over your head and step into the alley, slowly," he said.

Hands clasped over her head, Andre stepped into the alley.

"Here," said Lucas.

Andre turned toward him and Finn immediately came up behind her with his laser.

"Don't move a muscle," he said.

"De la Croix!" said Lucas.

"May I bring my hands down?" she said.

"You just leave them where they are for the time being," said Finn. "What do you want?"

"You are going to be betrayed," she said.

Lucas glanced at Finn quickly, then looked at Andre and put his finger to his lips, shaking his head. She looked puzzled, but nodded that she understood. Lucas glanced at Finn and pointed to his throat. Moments later, they had both removed the miniature transmitters from their throats. Lucas held his hand out and Finn gave him his transmitter; then Lucas took off his gauntlet, placed both units inside the thumb of the gauntlet, rolled it up, and tucked it into his boot.

"All right," he said, "talk quickly and quietly. What do

you mean we're going to be betrayed? How do you know? What's your interest in this?''

"I have no one else to turn to," she said, softly. "Although I did not know Jack Bennett long, he was my friend. He said we had to help you. Without you, I am trapped here in this time. I have no desire to remain here."

"What do you want?"

"I want you to take me with you to your future time," she said. "I want this implant Hunter promised me."

Finn and Lucas exchanged looks.

"We'll see," said Lucas. "If you convince us, we'll both do what we can. But we have to be convinced."

She nodded. "I thought that the men who broke into D'Artagnan's house and killed Jack Bennett were your enemies," she said. "The ones you call the Timekeepers. They gave chase when I fled, but I killed one of them and escaped the other. Then I returned to the house, only to see you being led away. I thought you had been taken prisoner. I followed you to the house on the Rue Servadoni, thinking that I had to help you, but I could not think how at once. While I watched and waited for an opportunity, I saw a man leave that house. I learned it was the one called 'Mongoose.' I followed him."

"Why?" said Finn.

"I thought perhaps that I could take him prisoner and then ransom you with him."

"Go on."

"I trailed him to the Rue Férou and was about to take him when he stopped and gave a little whistle, like a bird. He waited, then whistled again, and this time someone answered and he stepped into an alley. I followed, keeping to the shadows. He met a man, a very large man, a giant. He called him Freytag."

"*Freytag!*" said Delaney.

"You know the man?"

"Go on, go on!"

"I did not completely understand what was said between them . . ."

"Can you repeat it? As much as you can remember?" Lucas said.

"I will try. The one called Mongoose said that it would be

tonight, that the musketeers will be leaving at dawn or shortly before. He did not say where, but he said something about Constance Bonacieux. He called her 'Sparrow' and said that she had D'Artagnan wrapped around her little finger.''

Finn gave a low whistle.

"Continue, quickly," Lucas said.

"The one called Freytag asked about you, and Mongoose said that you would be right where he wanted you, riding across the countryside, harassed by Richelieu's men. Then he said that his people would be spread out, in position along the route that the musketeers would take. He said that he would send you out to join them.''

"He did," said Lucas. "You're doing fine, keep going."

"Freytag seemed concerned about you, but Mongoose reassured him, telling him that he would make certain that the two of you would be nowhere near him and Taylor. Then they spoke about Taylor. This was a part that I did not fully understand. Freytag said that there was something wrong with Taylor, that he was not sure who he was, I think. Mongoose asked Freytag if he could control Taylor long enough to get the job done and Freytag said that he did not know, that Taylor was crazy. He said that he killed Darcy. He said that he was the only one Taylor had left now, but that Taylor did not believe he needed anyone and that he—Freytag—could be next. Then Mongoose asked Freytag if he was losing his nerve. Freytag said that he was not ashamed to admit that he was frightened, that there was a great deal of risk involved. Mongoose replied that he had gone to a great deal of trouble to arrange things and he told Freytag to do as he was told. Freytag was reluctant, but he seemed to have no choice but to obey. There was no mention made of what it is they plan to do. No details were discussed. Freytag said that he had to return. He wished the man called Mongoose luck and they went their separate ways. I remained in hiding until they had gone. I do not know where Freytag went, but the man called Mongoose returned to the house in the Rue Servadoni and a short while later, you came out and I followed you.''

"You can put your hands down, Andre," Lucas said. "You've convinced us. You couldn't have made that up."

"I do not understand this peculiar plot," she said, "but I

can offer you my services, if I can be of any help.''

"Maybe you can," said Lucas. "It looks like we're going to need all the help that we can get.''

"Mongoose and Freytag," said Delaney. "Can you believe it? Obviously, we can't join the musketeers. The whole idea was to decoy us away. But why?''

"At this point," said Lucas, "your guess is as good as mine. I don't know what the hell is going on, but one thing is for sure. We've really been had.''

"Damn," said Finn. "This whole thing is crazy. It's been wrong right from the start. We've been used and lied to from the very beginning. Mongoose has had our hands tied ever since we got here.''

"The thing is, what can we do about it?" Lucas said. "We're totally dependent upon Mongoose. We can't push the panic button because it would only alert Mongoose. This isn't a military operation, it's a TIA show and we're essentially auxiliary personnel. Andre, I don't doubt your word for one moment, but the sad thing is that we don't have any proof. It'll be the word of a member of the underground against a high-ranking TIA agent. And without Mongoose, there's no way we can get home.''

"Worse than that," said Finn, "with Mongoose in charge of the operation, there's no way the TIA can stop the terrorists. It's ironic, isn't it? The agency got wind of this plot because they managed to infiltrate the Timekeepers, so they put one of their best men in charge of the operation and he turns out to be on the other side, playing the double game. I've got to hand it to the Timekeepers—subverting a TIA agent. I wonder how long Mongoose has been one of them?''

"Does it matter?" Lucas said. "The point is that they got to him. Or maybe he got to them. I think I can even understand why he must have done it. Mongoose is a thrill junkie, he's in it for the risk, to play the game. What game can be more risky than burning the candle at both ends? If the Timekeepers succeed in creating a timestream split, it will probably mean chaos, and people like Mongoose thrive on chaos. Just think of the opportunities.''

"It's crazy," Finn said.

"The time wars are crazy," Lucas said with a sigh, "but

nobody twisted our arms to get involved. We both had a chance to get out, only you stayed in and I wound up re-enlisting. Maybe we're not so different from Mongoose, after all."

"If it's all the same with you," said Finn, "we can get into the philosophical implications of this thing some other time. Right now, we've got to figure out a way to stop the split from going down."

"The musketeers are going to be leaving Paris soon," said Lucas. "If we go with them, we're being decoyed away and we're playing right into their hands. If we don't go with them, Mongoose will know about it as soon as the musketeers get out of Paris and the floater scouts pick up the party. They'll notice that two people are missing, not to mention the fact that we won't be able to communicate with them." He reached into his boot and pulled out the gauntlet with the comsets wrapped inside. "What's the range of these things, anyhow?"

"I don't know," said Finn, "but I know what you're thinking and you just said why it wouldn't work. They'll be scouting from the air and they'll know that two people are missing. Besides, if these things are short range, we're out of luck. If they're not, it still makes no difference. It looks like whatever they're planning is going to go down in Paris. If we can stop them here, they've still got the chronoplates. Unless we stop them dead, they can outflank us and attack the musketeers. We can't be in two places at once."

"Not necessarily," said Lucas. He looked at Andre. "There's three of us now. One of us can take Andre and go along with the musketeers to cover them. That may fool the floaters and it will leave one of us to stay behind in Paris and go after Mongoose."

Finn took a deep breath and let it out slowly. "Just one of us? That's what I call a long shot."

"Unless you can think of something else real quick, it's the only shot we've got. Mongoose said that he'd be in position at the palace. I think that's exactly where he's going to be. They'll think that we're out of the way and they'll feel safe to make their move. Now what could they do that would create a major disruption in history? I think they might go after

Richelieu. Maybe the king or queen, maybe even all three of them.''

"God, it's Mensinger's worst nightmare," said Finn. "If they assassinate their target in front of witnesses, it will be next to impossible to adjust. And even if plants can be arranged in time, which I doubt, we're talking about major historical figures here. Even with genetic engineering, what are the odds of coming up with an adequate substitute Louis XIV? Each time an adjustment necessitates a substitution, you're risking a temporal disruption that could lead to a split. This one would guarantee it.''

"There's always the chance that Mensinger was wrong," said Lucas, not very hopefully.

"Right. And we're only going to find out the hard way," Finn said. "Damn. Whichever one of us is going to stay behind is going to be completely on his own, with Mongoose manipulating the TIA people under his command. What do you think his chances are going to be?''

Lucas shrugged. "Whichever one of us takes Andre and joins the musketeers stands a good chance of not making it back. The one who stays in Paris is going to have to stay alive long enough to kill Mongoose, Taylor, and Freytag. Frankly, I'd rather not think about what our chances are.''

"I knew I was going to hate this mission," Finn said. "All right, who stays and who goes?''

Lucas removed a coin from his pocket. He held it in his hand, staring at it for a moment, then he tossed it in the air.

"Call it.''

12 ─────────────

Shortly before dawn, ten people on horseback left Paris by the barrier of St. Denis. The group consisted of Aramis and his servent, Bazin, a somber man of forty who dressed in black and affected a priestly air; Porthos and Musqueton, his lackey, an amiable peasant of about thirty-five who was dressed considerably better than his fellows in his master's cast-off clothes; Athos and his man, Grimaud, whose taciturn demeanor matched his name; and D'Artagnan and Planchet, the comical scarecrow of a man whose aimless, spirited babble more than compensated for Grimaud's and Bazin's glum reserve. They were just about to leave when their party was increased by two new arrivals.

Andre was readily accepted, both because Lucas vouched for "him" and because D'Artagnan, in a moment of careless exuberance, had let it slip that Andrew was the "brother" of that fascinating woman who had taken their side against the cardinal's guards at the abbey. That woman had been an object of intrigue and speculation among the musketeers ever since and now, with the appearance of her "brother" on the scene, each musketeer secretly hoped to obtain a private introduction. D'Artagnan was furious with himself for not having kept his mouth shut and thereby losing an advantage. In spite of their precarious situation, Lucas was quite amused by the musketeers' exaggerated overtures of friendship toward

Andre and the sudden, boisterous camaraderie.

Of necessity, no one but D'Artagnan was to know the true nature of their mission, since the honor of the queen was at stake. Andre and Lucas knew, of course, but they feigned ignorance. As for the other musketeers, all they were told was that it was to be a mission of great importance and that they had to go to London and very possibly get killed along the way. D'Artagnan told them that he had been entrusted with a letter and that, should he fall, one of the others would have to deliver it. Save for a few brief instructions regarding that delivery, the three musketeers knew nothing. Initially, Porthos had raised some doubts, but following a brief discussion of the risks involved and the reasons for their going, Athos settled the matter once and for all.

"Gentlemen," he had said, "is the king accustomed to giving you reasons for doing everything that you must do? No. He says to you, very simply, 'Gentlemen, there is fighting going on in Gascony or Flanders; go and fight,' and you go there. No, here are our three leaves of absence, which came from Captain de Treville, and here are three hundred pistoles, which came from I know not where. So let us go and get killed where we are told to go. Is life worth the trouble of so many questions?"

The issue settled, they departed for Calais, which was the quickest route to London. Finn had given Andre his cloak in place of her much more ornate one in an effort to fool the floaters. It was still dark and Lucas and Andre rode at the tail end of the group. Shortly after they left Paris, Lucas received his first contact from the floaters.

"Hawk One to Ground Squirrel, Hawk One to Ground Squirrel. Do you read? Over."

The throat transmitter enabled Lucas to speak softly, so that the others would not overhear him, but they would not have heard in any case, since they were all ahead of him and the group was in full gallop. Andre did not have a comset, so she was oblivious of the contact, but Lucas burst into laughter.

"Hawk One to Ground Squirrel, I'm getting a lot of noise. Are you reading me loud and clear? Over."

"You're getting a lot of noise because I'm laughing my ass off," Lucas said.

"Did you say 'over'?"

"Yeah, yeah, over, roger-willco," Lucas said. "What's with this Ground Squirrel shit? Who the hell is Ground Squirrel?"

There was a slight pause.

"What do you mean, who's Ground Squirrel? You're Ground Squirrel."

"No kidding?"

"Didn't Mongoose give you your call-sign? How the hell are you supposed to respond if you don't know your call-sign?"

"I *am* responding, you nitwit."

This time, the pause was appreciably longer. Lucas couldn't stop laughing.

"I don't see what's so funny, Priest."

"Well, Christ, if you know my name, why don't you use it?"

"Well, it would be a bit irregular, but I suppose there's no reason why—"

"Look, have you got something to report or are you just providing comic relief?" said Lucas.

There was a slightly longer pause. Finally, "Hawk One" came on and said, rather tersely, *"All clear up ahead."*

"Assholes," mumbled Lucas. There was no further contact until they reached Chantilly.

The group arrived at a roadhouse a little after eight o'clock. They left the horses saddled, in case they should have to depart in a hurry, and entered the inn to have a quick breakfast. The only other patron besides themselves was a drunk who greeted them with exaggerated bonhomie. They exchanged token pleasantries and nothing more was said between them until it came time for them to leave, at which point the drunk lurched to his feet, holding a wine goblet aloft and swaying unsteadily.

"Gentlemen, a toast!" he shouted, nearly overbalancing. He clutched at Porthos's baldrick for support, then lurched back several feet, accomplishing the act, miraculously, without spilling a single drop of wine. "A toast to the health of His Eminence, Cardinal Richelieu! Gentlemen, will you join me?"

"I have no objection," Porthos said, "if you, in turn, will join with us to drink the health of good King Louis."

The drunk spat upon the floor. "Pah! I recognize no king other than His Eminence!"

"You're drunk," said Porthos. "Otherwise, I might not so easily forgive your insolence."

"Drunk, am I?" said the man, reaching for his rapier and missing it. He grasped at air in the vicinity of his waist until his hand found his sword and he pulled it from its scabbard. "Well, we'll see who's drunk!"

"That was foolish," Athos said to Porthos. "Still, there's nothing to be done about it now. Kill the fellow and rejoin us as quickly as you can."

Porthos shrugged and drew his own rapier. The drunk came on guard with a sudden, remarkable sobriety. As they left the roadhouse with the sound of clanging steel behind them, Lucas suggested that it might be simpler, since there were ten of them in all, to gang up on the man and quickly get it over with. Athos looked at him with shock.

"My dear fellow," he said, in tones of strict rebuke, "that sort of thing simply isn't done!"

"Why?"

Athos gave him a pained expression for his answer, mounted up and galloped off.

"It *would* be a bit dishonorable," Andre ventured, cautiously.

Lucas shook his head. "Boy, have you got a lot to learn," he said. They mounted up and galloped off after the musketeers.

"Ground Squirrel to Goony Bird," said Lucas.

"*That's 'Hawk One,'*" came the annoyed reply.

"Says you. Where's the other birdbrain?"

There was a short silence.

"*Hawk Two is scouting up ahead. I'm at ten thousand feet, keeping you on scope.*"

"How come you didn't report that character in the tavern?" Lucas said.

"*What character?*"

"Jesus, you're a lot of help."

"*You expect me to see indoors from way up here? Give me a break, I'm doing the best I can.*"

"Then we're in a lot of trouble."

"*Not yet, but you're going to be. Hawk Two just reported an armed party about a mile outside Beauvais.*"

"I didn't hear anything."

"*He's on another frequency.*"

Lucas rolled his eyes. "Well, aren't your people supposed to be providing back-up on this ride? We're still well away from there. Move your agents in and clear the way."

"*They're moving into position, but we can only take defensive action in case the terrorists are among them. If they're not, you're on your own.*"

"You've got to be kidding."

"*Sorry. Orders.*"

"Okay, look, is there another road that we can take to get around them?"

"*No go,*" said the floater. "*This is part of the original scenario. You've got to go on through.*"

"Terrific," Lucas said.

They stopped at Beauvais for two hours, both to rest and walk their horses around to cool them off and to wait for Porthos. Lucas motioned Andre over to him. "Look," he said, "there may be some trouble up ahead. How good are you on horseback, out of armor, I mean?"

"I have been riding since I was a child," she said. "Why?"

"Well, there's a little trick I learned from the Sioux Indians at the Little Big Horn. Now listen carefully. . . ."

The two hours passed and Porthos did not arrive. "I fear we must assume the worst," D'Artagnan said. "We can wait no longer, gentlemen. To horse!"

They mounted up and proceeded on their way at a rapid clip. After they had ridden for about one mile, they reached a section of the road that was banked steeply on both sides.

"*Watch yourself,*" said Hawk One.

Lucas gave Andre a prearranged signal and, as she rode up even with him, men popped up on either side of the road, firing upon the party with muskets. Musqueton was hit immediately and he tumbled from his horse. Aramis took a ball in the shoulder and he reeled in the saddle, but he hung on and spurred for dear life. Andre and Lucas, riding side by side, both dropped out of their saddles to hang on the sides of their horses, using the animals' bodies as shields. Since they were riding behind the others, their maneuver went unnoticed. As soon as they had ridden beyond the ambush, they both swung up into their saddles.

"An excellent tactic!" Andre said. "I must remember it."

Lucas looked at her, grinning, then the grin disappeared as he saw that she had lost her hat. Almost immediately, Hawk One came on.

"*Nice trick,*" he said, "*but I've got just one question. Since when is Private Delaney a blonde?*"

Finn was getting tired of alleys. He had been sitting in the dark alleyway across the street from the TIA house in the Rue Servadoni for hours and his legs were beginning to feel stiff. The smell was offending his nostrils and once someone with a second-floor window facing out onto the alley dumped a chamber pot out and the contents landed right next to Finn, missing him by inches. He had lasered several rats that had become too curious, but there was one big one, almost the size of a house cat, that proved to be too quick for him. Clearly regarding the alley as its turf, it was annoyed at his presence and twice it attacked him. The first time, it sank its teeth into his boot and he kicked it away. The second time, he fired at it with his laser, but missed. Thereafter, it remained in the shelter of a large pile of rotting garbage and he could see its lambent little eyes glaring at him malevolently. Finn occupied himself by spitting at it.

Mongoose hadn't moved. Finn knew he was inside, but he could do nothing but wait and watch the house. He wondered how Lucas was doing. Finn had called "Heads" and won the coin toss. He elected to remain behind. He had tried to read Lucas's expression then, but whatever he had been feeling, Priest had hidden it well. Finn wondered what he had felt. They both knew that he had chosen the more dangerous course. Finn knew that Lucas, had he won, would have done the same. He wondered if he would ever be seeing him again.

He hated times like this, times when he was alone and inactive, with time to think. Liquor helped at such times and he had none now. Wine only gave him headaches if he drank too much of it. It never numbed his nerves.

There was a scratching, scuttling sound that came quickly toward him and he glanced up in time to see the huge rat scrabbling closer. It froze when it saw him looking at it and its feral gaze met his. Finn spat at it and hit it squarely in the snout. It squealed angrily and darted back into its pile of rotting garbage.

"If you had any class at all, you'd spit right back," said Finn, meeting the rat's ferocious gaze. He tried to stare it down, then realized what a ridiculous thing he was doing and looked back at the house across the street.

Mongoose had just walked out the door. He almost missed him.

They made another two hours of hard riding before Aramis said that he could go no further. He had lost some blood and he was pale. It was all he could do to remain in the saddle until they reached Crèvecoeur, where they left him at a cabaret with Bazin to look after him.

Lucas had refused to discuss the matter of Delaney's suddenly becoming a blonde with Hawk One and, after pressing him several times without success, the floater became strangely silent. It made Lucas very apprehensive. There was no further communication with Hawk One until they reached the inn of the Lis d'Or.

They arrived at about midnight and the innkeeper, dressed in nightgown and nightcap and carrying a candle, received them solicitously, but apologized for having only two rooms, at opposite ends of the hotel. Athos found this suspicious, but it was decided that he and D'Artagnan would share one room while Monsieur Dumas and Andre shared the other. As a further safeguard, Grimaud was ordered to sleep in the stables with the horses and Planchet firmly announced his intention to protect his master by sleeping on a pile of straw before his door. Shortly after they had separated to go to their rooms, Lucas heard the floater's voice inside his ear.

"All right, Priest, you're going to have a visitor in a little while. It'll be one of us, so don't get twitchy. You've got some explaining to do."

Lucas warned Andre and they settled down to wait. He had no idea what to expect. Just in case, they both kept their weapons ready. Twenty minutes passed and Lucas began to feel very nervous; then there was a soft knock at their door.

"It's open," Lucas said.

The door opened and a man dressed in a red doublet and black cloak entered. He paused when he saw Lucas holding his laser pointed at him and he looked long and hard at Andre. Then he slowly turned around and closed the door behind him.

"The name's Cobra," he said, "and spare me the wise-cracks. I'm the number-two agent on this operation." He took another long look at Andre. "You want to tell me about it?"

"Sure," said Lucas. "What do you want to know?"

"Don't get cute. What's *she* doing here? Where's De-laney?"

"Back in Paris."

"Why?"

"He's got saddle sores."

The agent stared at him silently for a moment. "You're not in any position to play games, Captain. Mongoose has disappeared and now I find out that Delaney stayed behind in Paris. The last time anyone saw *her*," he said, glancing at Andre, "one of our agents got burned. Now I'm giving you the chance to explain. I'm trying to be reasonable. I don't much like what I'm thinking, so you'd better set my mind at ease and do it fast."

Lucas sat silently for a moment, debating. He took a deep breath.

"Suppose you don't believe my explanation?"

"Make me believe it. I'm willing to listen."

"All right," said Lucas, "but you're not going to like it."

"Try me."

"There's good reason to believe that this ride is nothing but a smokescreen. The terrorists never intended to interfere with the musketeers. We're all being decoyed away from where the real disruption is going to occur."

"Who's decoying us away?"

"Mongoose," Lucas said. "He's either been a double agent all along or he's gone over to the Timekeepers."

"You're right," said Cobra, "I don't like it. You can't seriously expect me to believe that?"

"I didn't think you would," said Lucas. "That's why Finn stayed behind in Paris, to keep an eye on him. Mongoose was followed to a secret meeting with Bruno Freytag and—"

"Followed by *whom?*"

Lucas sighed. "Andre followed him."

The agent snorted. "That's your proof? You've just made one whale of an accusation, Mister. You're going to have to come up with better evidence than that."

"I can't," said Lucas. "At least, not now. I told you, I didn't expect you to believe me. But suppose, just for one moment, that Mongoose went over. Where would that leave you? What would be my motive for lying to you?"

"Well, let's suppose that *you* went over," Cobra said. "We know that Delaney, at least, has some sympathy for the league. And you were out of the service for a period of time. Who knows what you were doing? Not to mention the fact that you're here with someone who burned one of our agents."

"She did that in self-defense and you know it," Lucas said, angrily. "Besides, you know our records. They speak for themselves."

"So does Mongoose's."

"All right, then, pull us off the mission," Lucas said. "But ask yourself why, if I'm not on the level, I haven't taken advantage of all the opportunities I've had to sabotage this mission. Finn and I could easily have taken Mongoose out. We could easily have killed any one of the musketeers or even all of them. Besides, you picked me for this mission. Can you afford to take the chance that I'm not telling you the truth? Can you afford not to check it out?"

"You're putting me in a very bad position, Priest." The agent thought a moment. Lucas found that his palms were sweating. Finally, Cobra nodded. "You're right," he said. "I can't afford to take the chance. All right. I'll take some men and return to Paris. It means pulling some people off this operation and I don't like that. You'd damn well better be right.''

"Fine," said Lucas. "Let's go."

"You're not going anywhere," said Cobra. "You two are going to finish out this ride. You'll be covered every inch of the way. You make one wrong move and you've both had it, understand? And I'll take those lasers."

He held his hand out, palm up.

"No way," said Lucas.

"I'm not asking you, I'm telling you," the agent said. "You want me to stick my neck way out for you. You're asking me to consider your position; well, I'm asking you to consider mine. You'll still have your daggers and your rapiers, but after this, I'd have to be insane to let you keep your lasers. Now let's have them."

Lucas licked his lips nervously and glanced at Andre.

"He is only asking for a gesture of good faith," she said.

"He's asking a lot more than that," said Lucas, "but I'm afraid I see his point."

He reversed his laser and handed it over. Andre did the same.

"Okay," said Cobra. "I'll take some men and leave right away. Where can I find Delaney?"

"I don't know," said Lucas. "He's probably trailing Mongoose, wherever he is."

"He still wearing his comset?"

"I doubt it," Lucas said. "With Mongoose in charge, he would be wide open if he was transmitting. Which reminds me, just how far do these things go?" he said, pointing at his throat.

"Not to Paris, if that's what you're thinking. They're short-range. Assuming what you're saying is true, and Mongoose is a renegade, Delaney will have every reason to expect hostility from us. Can you think of anything that I can do to convince him that I'm giving you a chance to prove your allegations?"

Lucas thought a moment. "Yeah. Tell him that I wish he had called 'Tails.' He'll know what it means."

Finn followed Mongoose to the same alley in the Rue Férou where Andre had seen him confer with Freytag. Mongoose was being sloppy. He didn't expect anyone to be on his trail, so he didn't even bother to check to see if he was being followed. Just the same, Finn gave him plenty of room. It was late and the darkness made it easier. As the agent stepped into the alley, Finn quickly ran across the street. He would be in good position to fire at them in the alley, but then he'd have no idea where Taylor was. He debated the question of whether or not to go for the sure thing and kill the two of them now, hoping to catch Taylor on his own, or follow them to Taylor and try taking them out all at once.

It was tempting. All he had to do was step into the mouth of the alley and sweep it quickly with the laser and it would be all over for Mongoose and Freytag. But then it would mean cutting it very close with Taylor. Finn's cover did not gain him admission to the palace, whereas Taylor's did. He'd either have to sneak into the palace somehow and catch "Milady" inside, which would be next to impossible considering the odds, or get Taylor before he went into the palace, and there was no way of knowing for certain which entrance he would use. Finn could not cover all of them at once.

Staying low and keeping to the shadows, Finn glanced into the alley. He could just barely make out two shapes in there. The big one had to be Freytag. On the floor directly above him, a man and a woman were screaming at each other and there was the occasional crash of crockery. The noise made it impossible for him to overhear anything that went on inside the alley. He cursed the quarreling couple, but didn't want to risk getting any closer. He felt the laser in his right hand and wished that he could get it over with right now, but he fought down the impulse to fire. Two of them would not be good enough. He'd have to get all three. He steeled himself and waited. They would lead him to Taylor. They *had* to.

"All right, let's do it," Mongoose said.

Freytag smiled. "Sure. Anything you say. Adrian would just love to see you."

Mongoose looked down at the slim laser in Freytag's hand. It was aimed directly at his midsection.

"What the hell is this?"

"Just don't move a muscle, friend, or I'll fry your guts right here," said Freytag, reaching out with his other hand and patting him down. He relieved Mongoose of his weapon.

"I thought we had a deal," said Mongoose.

"Immunity from prosecution and a blanket pardon in return for handing Taylor over to you personally?" Freytag chuckled. "That's not what I call a very attractive deal. It won't put any money in my pocket."

"How much do you want?"

"You must really take me for a fool," said Freytag. "Once you had Taylor, you'd hang me, as well. You should've tried your pitch on Darcy. He might've been stupid enough to go for it; but then, he's dead."

"Don't be a fool, Bruno. You'll never get away with this."

"Who's to stop me?" Freytag said. "You wanted Taylor to yourself so badly that you sent all your people off on a wild goose chase. Your own colossal ego did you in, Mongoose. If not for that, you might've stopped us, but you blew it. You did just what Taylor said you would. You know, I didn't believe him. I told him that nobody could be that stupid. But here you are."

Casually, Mongoose reached up as if to scratch himself. Freytag slapped his hand down.

"You go for that panic button one more time and you've had it," he said.

"Taylor wouldn't like that," Mongoose said. "I'm sure he'd be real disappointed if you didn't bring me in alive."

"I'm sure he would be, but nothing says I gotta bring you in with both your hands still attached to your wrists."

"I'm afraid you've got a point," said Mongoose.

"All right. Now we're going to take a little walk. You walk in front of me, nice and easy. I'll tell you where to go. And don't get any ideas. You try anything and I'll burn your legs off at the knees and carry you the rest of the way. Now let's go."

Finn could hardly see inside the alley. Occasionally, he would catch some motion in there, but it was hard to make out what was happening. There was a fresh burst of screaming from the couple fighting upstairs and a crash as a thrown footstool hurtled through the window and out into the alley. Finn ducked down, quickly. When he looked up, both men had moved out into the center of the alley and were silhouetted as they walked out the other end. He followed, keeping at a distance.

They went several blocks, walking casually down the street until they came to a familiar neighborhood. With a shock, Finn realized that they were heading straight toward Moreau's Tavern. They passed the entrance to the tavern and went into the house right beside it.

"Jesus Christ," said Finn. "They were that close all the time!"

There was a light burning on the second floor, on the right side of the building. Finn looked up at the second floor of Moreau's Tavern, where the rooms were rented out. It was possible that he might get a shot—

"Don't move, Delaney."

A hand of ice clutched at his intestines and he froze, damning himself for not being more careful. *If I turn around fast and fire,* he thought. . . .

"Priest said that you should've called 'Tails.' "

Slowly, Finn turned around, holding his laser pointed at the ground.

"I saw the muscles in your neck and shoulders tense," the man said. "It's a bad habit. You should learn to control it. You telegraph that way. The name's Cobra, TIA."

There were two men standing with him, all three were wearing black cloaks. *Cloak-and-dagger,* thought Finn, stifling a chuckle.

"I should have been more careful," he said. "How long have you been tailing me?"

"We picked you up about two blocks back," said Cobra. "It's a lucky thing you kept your comset. We don't like to lose our equipment, so we set it up with tracing signals."

Finn reached into his pocket and pulled out the comset, wrapped in a handkerchief.

"I should've thrown the damn thing away," he said. "Seems like I have lots of bad habits. I don't like to lose equipment, either."

"Fortunately for you," said Cobra, "that's one habit that worked for you. We caught onto your little switch and I had a chat with Captain Priest. He told me Mongoose was working both sides of the street. I wouldn't have believed it if I hadn't seen it for myself." He nodded toward the building they were in.

"What made you believe it enough to check it out?" said Finn.

"Well, it was pointed out to me by Captain Priest that I could not afford to take the chance that he was not telling me the truth," said Cobra. "Also, I've been at this for a while. After a few years, it gets so that you don't trust anybody. You don't take things for granted; that way you live longer."

"I never thought I'd see the day when I'd be thankful for spook paranoia," Finn said.

"I'll take that as a compliment, though I'm sure you didn't mean it as one," said Cobra, with a mirthless, tight-lipped smile. "And now I really think we ought to do something about those three in there."

"At least the odds are on our side," said Finn. "Four against three."

"Six against three, actually," said Cobra. "I've already got two men in that tavern there. They should be in position in that room opposite the window on the second floor there. If there's anybody in that room, they'll be temporarily inconvenienced, I'm afraid."

Even as he spoke, an agent came running out of the tavern, approaching them.

"All set," he said. "It was one of the whores' rooms. Jaguar's got a prosty in there, but she's unconscious. Used a nerve pinch. When she wakes up, she won't even know what happened."

"Good work. How's it look up there?"

"We're in luck. There's a window directly across the way. It's shuttered, but that shouldn't present much of a problem. We'll be able to swing right across and break through."

"Sounds almost too easy," Finn said.

"Nothing ever is," said Cobra. "Fortunately, they won't be expecting anything. They'll be thinking that we're all miles away."

"It will still have to be pretty tight, though," Finn said. "Remember, they've still got at least one chronoplate. Which reminds me, where's yours?''

"Back at the safehouse," Cobra said. "I've got a man stationed there. We lucked out there, too. Mongoose didn't take his plate with him. He must've figured on returning. This must be some last-minute conference. I get the shakes when I think about the fact that we'd all be clocking in back there one at a time when we'd finished covering the musketeers. He would've been able to take us all out with no sweat." Cobra took a deep breath. "It was a close call for me. Soon as the floater said one of the commandos was an imposter, I clocked right back to check with Mongoose. He must've just left. If he'd still been there when I arrived and if I had told him. . . ." He let it hang.

"We've all had close calls," said Finn. "I'm thinking that breaking in on them might not be a good idea. Why not just get them as they come out?"

Cobra shook his head. "That might work, but I don't want to take the chance that any of them might be using that plate to get into position for whatever it is that they've got planned. You think it's a hit?"

"I think it's a hit."

"Give me that comset," Cobra said. He took it from him and handed it to the agent who had just come from Moreau's. "Take this and give it to Jaguar. I've got one on me." He pulled a tiny box out of his pocket. "Tell him to put it on, but to keep his mouth shut, just in case. You never know. Don't even breathe hard. Have him get ready to swing over. We're going in the front way. We'll burn through the lock and get as close to them as we can. When I say *now*, we hit 'em from both sides. You stay in that room and cover Jaguar as he goes across. Delaney, you stay right here, in case any of them get by us. Cover the street."

"I'd much rather be going in with you," said Finn.

"I know," said Cobra. "But odds are someone's going to get burned breaking in there. It was our man that went bad. I figure we owe you one."

"What are you going to do with Mongoose?"

"If I can, I'll try to take him alive," said Cobra. "But I'm not going to try too hard."

13

Neither Lucas nor Andre even bothered trying to get any sleep. The situation was extremely volatile. At four o'clock in the morning, someone knocked softly at their door.

There had been no warning over the comset telling them to expect visitors. Both of them drew their rapiers and slowly approached the door, ready for anything. In French, Lucas asked who was there, affecting a sleepy sounding voice. The reply was scarcely above a whisper, but they recognized that it was Athos. Lucas opened the door.

"Good, I see you are both still dressed," said the musketeer, quietly. "I could not get to sleep in this pestilential hole, either. Planchet has seen strangers about. We'd best quit this place and be on our way. Ah, here comes D'Artagnan and Planchet. Softly, now, let us be off. Planchet, did you tell Grimaud to saddle the horses?"

"Yes, Monsieur Athos. I told him to move with stealth, just as you said."

"Excellent," said Athos. "I do not much care for running away like a thief in the night, but it would be the prudent thing to do. I did not like the look of our innkeeper. He was a shade too friendly for having been wakened in the middle of the night."

Moving on tiptoe, they crept down the stairs and out the door, heading for the stables. Their horses were all saddled and awaiting them, but there was no sign of Grimaud. Athos glanced about him, searching for his servant.

"Grimaud!" he called, softly.

There was no reply.

"Grimaud, damn you for a laggard, where the devil are you?"

An answering moan came from within a pile of straw, from which a boot could be seen sticking out. Athos rushed over to the straw pile and, pulling by the foot, dragged out Grimaud, who appeared to have been bashed over the head. He was semiconscious and bleeding profusely from the scalp. At that very moment, they were attacked.

A group of men dressed as peasants, yet betrayed by the fine rapiers which they brandished, leapt out at them from all corners of the stable. One appeared over the stall behind D'Artagnan, stabbing down viciously with a dagger. The quick-witted Gascon ducked aside and caught the man's arm, dragging him over the stall and flipping him down onto the ground. He twisted the dagger out of the would-be assassin's hand and stabbed him with his own weapon, plunging the blade into the man's chest. He sidestepped a lunge from another and dropped him with a right across the jaw, then swung into the saddle and yanked free his rapier.

Lucas and Andre both drew their swords and daggers and met the men who charged them. Lucas turned a sword away from his attacker and booted its wielder in the groin. He quickly slashed his dagger across the man's face, then turned to meet his next opponent. D'Artagnan came riding up at that moment, rearing his horse and interposing it between Lucas and two swordsmen, giving him time to swing up into the saddle. The stables became filled with the sounds of ringing steel.

Andre parried one sword-thrust with her dagger and engaged another with her blade. She executed a quick beat and disengage, then quickly thrust the point of her rapier into her opponent's eye. The second swordsman lunged again and she twisted her body, feeling the blade ripping through her cloak and passing perilously close to her ribs. She moved into the thrust, trapping the man's blade and stabbing her dagger deep into his abdomen. The man fell, clutching at her and dragging her off balance, taking her down with him. She fought free and started to get up, turning in time to see another man bearing down on her. D'Artagnan ran him down with his horse and she took four running steps and leaped over the hindquarters of her horse and into the saddle.

Athos had pulled out his pistols and fired at the first onrush, dropping two of his attackers. He barely had the time to drop his pistols and draw his sword before he found himself beset by three opponents. He dodged a thrown dagger and it embedded itself in a post behind him. However, his ducking the dagger had given his opponents time to hem him in and he stood braced with his back against the post, fending off the three rapiers that darted in at him. He parried one thrust, kicked the man in the groin as he parried yet another, and felt the third blade scrape along his arm. He lunged quickly and killed one man, but that one was immediately replaced by another. Andre had already bulled her way through on horseback to the outside and Lucas and D'Artagnan were both mounted up and by the door, keeping attackers at bay.

"I am taken!" Athos shouted. "Go on, D'Artagnan! Spur! *Spur!*"

D'Artagnan only paused long enough to hurl his dagger at one of Athos's attackers, seeing it thud home into his back.

"*One for all—*" D'Artagnan shouted.

"*Get the devil out of here!*" screamed Athos.

They set spurs to their horses and galloped off after Andre, their number now reduced to four. Planchet, alone, had managed to leap into the saddle and gallop out the stable door before their attackers had closed in on them. He was waiting for them further down the road, looking terrified.

"Coward!" D'Artagnan shouted at him, leaning over in the saddle and flailing at him with his hat. "You should have stayed and fought!"

"With what, Master?" Planchet cringed, attempting to ward off the blows. "I don't have a sword!"

They rode at breakneck speed for St. Omer, beyond which lay Calais.

"Hawk One, where the hell were you?" Lucas said, furiously.

There was no reply.

"Hawk One!"

Silence.

"*Damn you, Hawk One. . . .*" It suddenly occurred to Lucas why Hawk One was not responding. He simply wasn't there. Cobra had said that he would pull several men off the operation to check his allegations against Mongoose. He had been coldly efficient in making his selection. If what Lucas had said was true, then the Timekeepers would be striking back in Paris and manpower would be needed there. If Lucas had lied, then he had been disarmed of his most effective weapon and, as a traitor, would not require reconnaissance reports. The second floater could very well be overhead and he most likely was. Cobra had said that they would be covered every inch of the way. But Hawk Two was on a different frequency and, in any case, until the truth was known, he would not be reporting in to Lucas. Effectively, they were on their own.

Thus far, everything had happened according to the original scenario. History reported that D'Artagnan and all three musketeers survived the mission, but Andre and Lucas were both extraneous factors. That gave fate a lot of leeway.

A short distance outside Calais, D'Artagnan's horse collapsed. Planchet's animal was all done in as well, so Lucas and Andre each took a passenger and they barely reached Calais, their horses totally exhausted. Dismounting, they made it to the port on foot and sought out the captain of a small skiff, who was already engaged in a discussion with another gentleman. D'Artagnan ran up to them and interrupted, asking if they could set sail at once to England.

"I say, sir," said the well-dressed gentleman, somewhat taken aback at the Gascon's rudeness, but the captain raised a hand, silencing them both.

"As I was about to tell this gentleman," the captain told D'Artagnan, "I am able to set sail at once. However, this morning an order arrived stating that no one should be allowed to cross without permission from the cardinal."

"I *have* that permission," said the well-dressed gentleman, taking out a paper and holding it out.

"It must be examined by the governor of the port," the captain said.

"And where shall I find him?"

"At his country house. You can see it from here, at the foot of that little hill. The slated roof."

With an arch glance at D'Artagnan, the man departed with his servant, heading toward the house of the governor of the port. D'Artagnan returned, crestfallen, to confer with Andre and Lucas.

"We are undone," he said. "The cardinal has ordered that no one—"

"Yes, we heard," said Lucas. "No one can cross without his express permission. So? What is the problem?"

"But we have no such permission!"

"True," said Lucas, turning to look after the departing gentleman, "but that man does."

D'Artagnan followed his gaze and he frowned, then understanding dawned. "Ah, yes! Of course, how stupid of me. We'll simply take it from him." He reached for his sword, but Lucas stayed his hand.

"Not *here*," he said. "Follow him. Discreetly, eh? Andre and I will remain here and make sure that no one else tries to book passage."

D'Artagnan and Planchet followed the gentleman and Andre and Lucas took a little time to get some much-needed rest.

"What happens now?" said Andre.

"We wait," said Lucas. "Our orders are to finish out the ride, so that means we'll have to go to England and to Buckingham. You heard what Cobra said. If we make one wrong move, we'll be killed."

"But no one is about," she said. "They could not have known that we departed for Calais in such a hurry, before dawn."

"They know," said Lucas. "And I'll bet you they're watching us right now. We'll just have to play it by ear, that's all. If Finn still has his comset, Cobra said that he could trace him when he clocked in to Paris. If Finn gives him a chance to explain, then maybe they'll be able to stop Mongoose, if it isn't already too late. That's an awful lot of *ifs*."

"What if Mongoose cannot be stopped?" said Andre.

"I'd rather not even think about it," Lucas said.

After a short while, D'Artagnan returned with permission

to sail, made out in the name of the Count de Wardes. D'Artagnan reported that the count had been unreasonably un-
cooperative, so he had left him bleeding on the ground with
his hapless servant tied to a nearby tree. De Wardes was still
alive when they had left, so just to be on the safe side, the
Gascon had given the governor of the port a precise description of "D'Artagnan," whom the governor had been ordered
to arrest if he arrived in Calais. The description D'Artagnan
had given the governor was that of the Count de Wardes.
Lucas congratulated him on his initiative and, with their
clearance secured, they set sail for England. It was just as well
that they had not eaten, for alone of the four, Lucas was the
only one who was not seasick. But then, a little trip across the
channel was nothing to a man who had sailed under Lord
Nelson and served under John Paul Jones.

They arrived in England at ten o'clock and obtained post-
horses for their trip to London. It was at this point that D'Artagnan realized that there were two aspects of the mission's
planning that he had entirely overlooked. This knowledge
came to him with something of a shock the moment he set foot
in England. For one thing, he had no idea how to get to London, and for another, he didn't speak a word of English. Fortunately for the Gascon, Lucas both spoke English and knew
the way to London, so they immediately headed for the residence of Lord Buckingham.

Upon arriving there, they were told that the duke was at
Windsor, hunting with the king. Patrick, the duke's valet, offered to conduct them personally when told that they had
come upon a mission of life and death, and he quickly had
a horse saddled for himself and they were off to Windsor
Castle. Once there, they were directed to the marshes, where
Buckingham was hawking with the king. When they came
within sight of the hunting party, Patrick bade them to wait at
a distance while he rode up to the duke and informed him of
their arrival.

"How shall I announce you to His Lordship?" the valet had
asked.

"Tell him it is the young man who sought a quarrel with
him one night in the Rue Vaugirard," D'Artagnan said.

Patrick raised his eyebrows. "A most unusual introduction," he said.

"I think you will find that it will be sufficient," said D'Artagnan.

Patrick rode off and, moments later, returned with George Villiers, the Duke of Buckingham, at his side. He had, of course, instantly remembered D'Artagnan and he was most concerned that some misfortune had befallen the queen. As Buckingham was fluent in French, there was no need for Lucas to act as an interpreter, so he and Andre drew away when they noticed Patrick beckoning to them.

"Glad you made it, Priest," said Patrick. "Wolverine, TIA."

Lucas shook his head in amazement. "Boy, when you people infiltrate, you don't kid around, do you?"

"I've been expecting you," said the agent. "I've heard all about it, of course. I received a message from the safehouse a little while ago. Terrible business."

"Then Cobra's contacted Delaney?" Lucas said, anxiously. "He's got his proof?"

"I'm afraid I have some bad news for you," the agent said. "Very bad news."

Using a laser, Cobra burned through the lock upon the door and quietly took his men inside. Finn waited, tensely, in the street.

From where he stood, Delaney could see the front door, the lighted window where the conspirators were, and the room on the second floor of Moreau's Tavern, where the two TIA agents had taken up their posts. He knew that Cobra thought that he was doing him a favor by placing him in the least dangerous position, but just the same, he would have felt a great deal better if he had gone along with them inside. Still, the raid looked almost foolproof. If Cobra hit them hard and fast, with the element of surprise upon his side, the chances of any of the Timekeepers being able to escape via chronoplate were virtually nil.

As Finn watched, the window on the second floor of Moreau's Tavern was opened quietly. He saw agent Jaguar peer out, cautiously, then he saw him raise his hand toward the wall of the other building, just across a narrow alley. The agent had some sort of object in his hand, which he seemed to be aiming at the wall. A moment later, Finn heard a faint popping sound and a metallic sounding clink and he realized what the TIA man had done. Aiming at a spot on the wall considerably higher than the shuttered window, he had fired a metal dart attached to a length of nysteel line into the opposite wall. It would enable him to swing across. He saw the agent taking position, crouching in the window frame, his feet on the very edge, his hands holding the nysteel line taut. Any second now, thought Finn. As soon as Cobra gives the word. He held his laser ready.

Jaguar glanced down at him for a brief moment and nodded, then swayed for an agonizing second and, as Finn watched, horrified, he lost his balance, shouted "*Shit!*" and swung out into the air.

"*Jesus . . .*" Finn whispered.

The agent swung across the narrow alley, but instead of jackknifing and hitting the wooden shutter with his feet, he slammed into it full length with a resounding thud, knocking himself out and dropping into the alley.

The other agent on the second floor of Moreau's Tavern fired into the shuttered window. There was a tremendous racket inside the house. Finn heard shouting and then he heard someone scream. Feeling helpless, he remained rooted to the spot, watching frantically for a sign of any of the terrorists. It was over almost as quickly as it had started. The front door opened and someone shouted, "Don't fire, Delaney!"

Cobra walked out alone.

"What the hell happened?" he demanded.

Finn told him. "I guess Jaguar lost his balance and swung across before you gave the word. He fell down in the alley. Probably knocked himself out."

"I hope the damn fool broke his neck," said Cobra, savagely.

"*Well? Did you get them?*"

Cobra bit his lower lip. "Taylor got away," he said.

"Oh, that's just dandy," Finn said, grimly. "How did you manage that?"

Cobra sighed. "Freytag bought him the time. He didn't need much. He must've had the plate set in advance. Freytag took out both my men before I got him."

"What about Mongoose?" Finn said.

"He's still alive," said Cobra. "He wants to see you."

Finn went into the house with Cobra. Mongoose was not a pretty sight. Fortunately for him, he had not been alone with Taylor very long. The Timekeepers had evidently intended to torture him to death. They had tied him to a chair and gagged him, then performed some delicate surgery with a laser. They had started with his face. Finn had to force himself to look at him.

"We've got to get him medical attention right away," said Cobra, "but when he found out you were here, he wouldn't let us touch him until he saw you."

Something vaguely resembling a rasping chuckle emerged from the agent's mouth as Mongoose looked at him. "Just wanted you to see this," he rasped. "Thought you might get a kick out of it."

"This isn't exactly my idea of kicks," said Finn.

Mongoose nodded, head lolling. "I really screwed it up, didn't I?"

Finn did not respond.

"I didn't go over," Mongoose said, emphatically. "I just wanted you to know that. I wanted you to understand. I thought Freytag. . . ." He shook his head. "I *wanted* him, Delaney. I wanted him all to myself. Just him and me. The best against the best. . . ."

Finn turned away. He looked at Cobra. "You got anybody at the palace?" he said.

"Sparrow should be there. But this is only her first field assignment—"

"I suggest we hotfoot it over there and fast," Delaney said.

"Delaney—" Mongoose croaked.

Finn glanced at him briefly. "I haven't got time for you," he said. "Go and get your face fixed."

Lucas listened to the news grimly. He quickly glanced back at D'Artagnan and Buckingham. Buckingham had read the letter and was engaged in an animated discussion with the Gascon.

"We haven't got much time," he said. "What happens now? Taylor could be anywhere with that plate."

"If he's clocked out to another time, we've lost him," the agent said. "But Cobra doesn't think he's given up yet."

"No, I don't think he would, from what I've heard," said Lucas. "So we just ride it out?"

The agent nodded. "Watch yourself, for God's sake. I'll look after Buckingham. We—"

They were interrupted by a shout from Buckingham and they wheeled their horses and galloped off after Villiers and D'Artagnan. They rode at full speed toward London and they did not slack their pace as they entered the city. Buckingham rode like a man possessed, running down several hapless Englishmen who did not get out of his way in time. When they arrived at Buckingham's residence, he sprang from his horse and dashed inside. Planchet stayed with the horses while they ran to keep up with Buckingham.

They ran through several elegant chambers, following the prime minister, until they came to his bedroom. Inside the bedroom was a tiny alcove and within that alcove, hidden by a tapestry, was a small door. He pulled the tapestry aside and opened the door with a little golden key he wore on a chain around his neck. Inside the door was a tiny chamber illuminated by candles in small red glasses, giving the room a sacrosanct glow. It was a shrine to Anne of Austria. A full-length portrait of the queen hung beneath a blue velvet canopy and underneath the portrait was an altar, on which rested a small golden casket, intricately worked. Buckingham lunged for this casket and opened it, pulling out a blue ribbon festooned with diamonds—the diamond studs given him by Anne.

"Thank God," said Buckingham. "They are safe. They are all here."

Lucas frowned, remembering something.

"I have only worn them once, at a ball given by the king a week ago at Windsor. The Countess de Winter—"

"Milady!" Lucas said.

"Yes," said Buckingham. "She . . . that is to say, I. . . ." He glanced up at the portrait of the queen. "Forgive me, my love."

"The Countess was *here?*" said Lucas. "She saw the diamonds?"

Buckingham nodded. "She was quite taken by them. She told me that she loved diamonds and I let her examine them. When I took them off that night, I put them back into the casket, which I left on the table by my bed. The next morning, I returned it to this chamber, but I did not open it. I later learned she was an agent of the cardinal's. When I read that letter, the first thought that sprang into my mind was that she might have . . . during the night. . . . But they are here, intact, all twelve of them, thank God." He put the studs back into the casket and handed it to D'Artagnan. "Here, take it. It was altogether too dangerous a gift."

Lucas pulled the agent out into the bedroom. "Have you got a plate here?"

The agent frowned. "Yes, but—"

"There's no time to lose. Andre and I have got to get back to Paris at once!"

"But what about D'Artagnan? You must—"

"Forget about D'Artagnan! According to Dumas, two of the studs were missing, but all twelve of them are there!"

"I still don't understand. What does that—"

"If the studs played no part in Taylor's plan, why did he come here? Why did he follow through with the original scenario, even going so far as to seduce Buckingham so that he could examine the studs more closely? According to history, Milady stole two of the studs to give to Richelieu."

"But all the studs are here," said Wolverine.

"Precisely," Lucas said. "Buckingham was supposed to have two studs made here, duplicates to make up for the ones Milady stole. *Duplicates,*" said Lucas, squeezing the agent's arm hard.

"Then if Taylor gave Richelieu two studs . . ." said the agent. His eyes widened. "Good God! Come one!"

At that moment, D'Artagnan came out of the chamber. Seeing Lucas and Andre running off with Patrick, he called out, "Where are you going?"

"An urgent matter! An agent of the cardinal!" Lucas shouted over his shoulder, improvising. "Go on, D'Artagnan, ride! We'll see you in Paris!"

They ran for "Patrick's" chambers, leaving behind them a perplexed D'Artagnan and a repentant Buckingham, kneeling before the portrait of the queen.

The timing was all wrong, but now there was no choice. Taylor hadn't planned to make his final move for several days yet. There would have been plenty of time to arrange things before D'Artagnan returned with the diamond studs, trailing all of Mongoose's agents behind him.

They would have become increasingly anxious as the journey of the musketeers progressed. They would have had to watch closely every attempt made by Richelieu's men to stop the musketeers to see if it could be a cover for a terrorist ploy. Their anxiety could easily have already triggered needless interference with the cardinal's men. That would have worked for Taylor. He knew that Mensinger's "Fate Factor" tended to compensate for the deaths of people who were historically insignificant, but in this case, such minor disruptions would only place added strain upon temporal continuity. There had simply been too many small disruptions with too inadequate compensations in too short a span of time. With the final act, the scenario would have been irreversibly disrupted and a temporal split would have been inevitable.

Milady rode in her carriage toward the palace. If the agents were sharp, and if they were right on top of D'Artagnan all the way, then they would have noticed the historical discrepancy of all twelve diamond studs still being in Buckingham's possession. Perhaps Buckingham might even have told them that Milady had "visited" with him. In such a case, the agents would have undoubtedly devised some ploy to detain D'Artagnan while they frantically examined all twelve diamond studs in order to make certain that they were nothing *but* twelve diamond studs.

Otherwise, they would follow D'Artagnan straight back to the palace, watching while he delivered the studs to the queen and all the while wondering when Taylor would make his move. An enemy on edge, nervous and ridden with anxiety, was an enemy off guard.

The ball would take place as scheduled. The agents would have undoubtedly infiltrated en masse, since with the ride of the musketeers safely and successfully completed, they would have deduced that the planned disruption would occur during the ball. They would all have been there, waiting, watching, when Richelieu gave the king the two studs that Milady had supposedly stolen from Buckingham. Richelieu would tell Louis that he doubted that the queen still possessed the diamond studs, but if she wore them, then in that case the king should count them. If the king found only ten, he was to ask her who could have stolen from her the two studs Richelieu had given him.

Taylor was to have been at Richelieu's side then. While he was with the cardinal and under his protection, the agents would have been powerless to move against him. They would have only been able to watch and wait. They would have been helpless to do anything when the queen arrived, wearing her diamond studs, and the king and Richelieu, with Milady by his side, went over to her to count the studs and to confront her with the two "missing" studs in case she had only ten of them. In that moment, when they were all together, Taylor would have pressed a tiny button.

Taylor had known for quite some time, or at least some rational part of him had known, that he was going insane. He had known that his personality was fragmenting. Before the mission had begun, he was already aware of at least two other personalities within him. Personalities that, at times, he could not control. The condition was not beyond a cure, but there was no way that he could risk obtaining therapy. He had been living underground for years and seeking help would have resulted in his almost certain apprehension. So Taylor had decided to "retire" at his peak. Quite literally, he had intended to go out with a bang. Two factors had prevented him from seeing his plan through as he had intended. There had been no way of knowing that the agents would somehow find the terrorists. He must have judged Mongoose incorrectly. Also, he had not counted on Milady. Since he had assumed her character, she had developed within him quickly. She had entirely taken over or eradicated his other personalities and she had grown very strong, indeed. Moreover, she did not want to die.

"You were a suicidal fool, Adrian," she said, as he listened somewhere, helplessly. "You never knew what you really wanted. You were clever, Adrian, but you were weak. Weak where it really mattered. Anger is not strength. Egotism is not strength. Strength lies in knowing who you are. *I* know who I am, Adrian. I am what you were always meant to be.''

She chuckled. ''You wanted to die. That doesn't surprise me. You were always self-destructive. Well, you're going to get your wish, though not quite in the manner you intended. I'm afraid that I do not share your sense of theater. You see, I intend to survive this little episode. You, on the other hand, will die. You will have made your grand and final gesture, so in a way, it will all end more or less as you had planned.''

Taylor battled his way back to the surface. Almost at once, his face became flushed with perspiration, his breath came in irregular gasps.

''Control, control,'' he said through gritted teeth. *''Don't lose it now, not yet, stay in control—''*

He was interrupted by a throaty, rippling, feminine laugh that burst forth from his lips even as the upper half of his face remained twisted in a concentrated frown, eyes staring wildly, beginning to glaze.

''No! *No!''*

''We've reached the palace, Milady,'' said the coachman, opening the door.

''Thank you, Maurice,'' she said, sweetly. ''Will you assist me?''

14 _____

As D'Artagnan started on his journey back to Paris, a trip he would make at breakneck speed in just over twelve hours, word was passed quickly among the TIA agents, with mixed efficiency. The operation which, up until that point, had gone off like clockwork began to fall apart.

The suddenly disorganized agents had to move quickly, since Taylor's hand had been forced and there was now no way of telling where he would strike or at whom. There was no time for detailed planning and coordination. There was little opportunity to check new, unsurveyed destination settings programmed hastily into the chronoplates. As a result, there was a great deal of confusion and there were several casualties.

One agent, clocked out to cover Aramis, had the misfortune to arrive in the middle of the English Channel. He also had the misfortune of not being a strong swimmer.

Another agent, assigned to Porthos, clocked in much closer to his destination than he had intended, appearing inside the musketeer's room at a tavern in Beauvais. The wounded musketeer, who had been recovering at the innkeeper's expense by consuming massive quantities of food and drink and refusing to pay for same, turned over in his bed and saw what appeared to be an armed man about to attack him in his room. Thinking that the innkeeper had hired someone to exact payment in a pound or two of flesh, Porthos grabbed his pistols off the table by his bed and shot the man to death.

Two of the men departing to look after Athos never arrived. A too hastily programmed chronoplate consigned them to the limbo that soldiers of the Temporal Corps had named "the dead zone." Trapped somewhere in nonspecific time, they would, theoretically, continue to exist, but no one could say exactly where or in what form.

Several of the agents, clocking out from different points, tried to arrive in the safehouse in the Rue Servadoni in the same place, at the same time. The agent that Cobra had stationed there watched in horror as the shapeless mass of flesh that materialized before him briefly became a writhing grotesquerie of thrashing arms and legs that flopped spastically on the floor, making a sound that no human ear should ever be subjected to. It died in seconds and was quickly clocked out to a prehistoric time, where its bones would be picked clean by reptilian scavengers.

Lucas and Andre both had a close call. They had tried for the vicinity of the palace and they materialized in the middle of the street outside the Louvre, in a spot where, scant seconds later, a carriage driven by a team of horses was to pass. No sooner had they materialized than Lucas, reacting quickly to the sound of thundering hooves almost on top of them, pushed Andre to one side and then threw himself in the opposite direction. The carriage hurtled by them and they missed being run down by inches. The coachman was a bit shaken. He had been directed to drive full speed toward the palace, not a wise thing to do in the streets of Paris at that hour, and he had been watching very carefully to avoid running anybody down. It was a mystery to him where those two people had come from. Suddenly, they were simply *there*. There had been no way to avoid them. Had they not jumped out of the way, they would surely have been seriously injured, if not killed. He would have had to stop. It would have meant disobeying the instructions of Milady, but he would have had to stop. As it was, he glanced quickly over his shoulder, saw that the two pedestrians appeared to be unharmed, hastily crossed himself, said a silent prayer of thanks, and turned into the gateway to the palace.

"Maurice," he told himself, "it's past time that you retired to the country and became a farmer."

Lucas and Andre picked themselves up and dusted themselves off.

"I will never grow accustomed to this method of travel," Andre said, taking a deep breath. "Be it magic, be it science, I care not. It is unnatural."

"That's true," said Lucas. "However, you will find that in my time, it is quite natural to live with the unnatural. We call it progress."

"Well, at any rate, we appear to have arrived safely," Andre said. "What happens now?"

"Ever break into a palace?" Lucas said.

"Not one such as this," said Andre, "and not without armor."

"This won't be quite as elaborate as a siege," said Lucas, "but we will be wearing armor, in a sense." He indicated a group of four of the cardinal's guards who had just left by the main gate. "I think that out of the four of them, we should be able to find two uniforms that we can fit into."

Andre grinned. "You think they will mind lending us their clothing?"

"Well, why don't we go ask them?" Lucas said.

Finn and Cobra, accompanied by one other agent, ran as fast as they could toward the Louvre. They had been forced to leave the luckless agent Jaguar behind them in the alley by Moreau's. His leg had broken in his fall and there was no time to waste on tending to him. Besides, Cobra was feeling far from charitable. The three of them reached a small gate at the side of the palace, in the Rue de l'Echelle. Cobra asked for Germain and, when he arrived, he said the words, "Tours and Bruxelles."

Germain nodded. "How may I serve you, Monsieur?"

"We must see Constance Bonacieux at once," said Cobra. "It is a matter of life and death."

"Say no more, Monsieur. Please follow me."

Germain took them into the palace, through a series of back corridors and several secret passages until they arrived just inside the doorway of the outermost chambers of the queen's apartments.

"Please wait here," Germain said. "And pray, be silent. There are guards stationed just outside this door."

He left them alone for a few minutes which seemed like hours and, finally, the doors on the far side of the room were opened and Constance Bonacieux, alias agent Sparrow, entered. Upon seeing Cobra, her eyes widened and she beckoned them to her urgently, holding a finger to her lips.

She admitted them into the next room, shut the door, and immediately turned to them, an expression of alarm upon her face.

"What is it? What's happened?" she said, anxiously.

"It's hit the fan," said Cobra. "We made our move, but Taylor got away. We figure he had his plate preset with the coordinates for another hideout, just in case. He wasn't taking any chances. He's probably on his way here right now, if he hasn't already arrived."

"*Here*? The palace?"

Cobra nodded. "His target's here. It could be the queen, it could be Louis, it could be Richelieu, or it could be all three."

"My God," she said. "What do you want me to do?"

"You have your laser?"

"I've got it hidden in my room," she said.

"Get it. And don't let the queen out of your sight. If you see Milady, don't even hesitate. Waste her."

She nodded. "What are you going to do?"

"We've got to get next to the king and Richelieu somehow," said Cobra. "Got any ideas?"

She thought a moment. "I've discovered a secret passageway that leads from the queen's bedchamber to the king's. It seems that there's never been much trust in royal relationships. But the queen is in her bedroom now."

"Can you get her out for a couple of minutes?"

"I'll think of something," she said. "But I have no idea how you can get to the cardinal without being challenged in the halls. There are guards stationed outside the queen's chambers."

Cobra pursed his lips, thoughtfully. "All right. Get us in that passageway and we'll just have to improvise from there. Remember, don't let the queen out of your sight, no matter what. Now think up some excuse to get Anne out of her bed-room, quickly.''

Lucas and Andre, dressed in ill-fitting uniforms of the car-dinal's guard, entered the main gate. Two of the four guards they had attacked lay tied up and unconscious in a nearby alley. The other two had both been wounded, although not fatally, and they were also bound and gagged with torn strips of clothing and ignominiously covered over with refuse. If they survived the rats, they would come out of it with nothing but their dignity impaired.

"What do we say if we are stopped?" said Andre.

"We bluff our way through," said Lucas. "I'm wearing the uniform of a captain of the guard. I don't even remotely resemble the man to whom this uniform belongs, but if we both act as though we know what we're doing, we just might get away with it."

"And if we do not?"

"Then do everything you can to avoid killing anybody. If we have to fight our way in, use the laser and aim for the ex-tremities."

"What do we do once we're inside?"

"We've got to get to Richelieu. We have to make sure that he never takes delivery of those two studs."

"Suppose he already has them?" Andre said.

"Then we'll have to find a way to get them away from him," said Lucas.

"One thing occurs to me," said Andre. "What if the two studs that the cardinal is to receive from Taylor are, in fact, genuine and it is two of the studs upon the ribbon that D'Ar-tagnan is bringing back that are the false ones?"

"I've thought of that," said Lucas. "But it would have taken too much time to examine them in London. We would have had to find some pretext to get them from D'Artagnan and he would not have parted with them easily. Besides, I think that Taylor would rather arrange things so that he can be sure that his fake studs get into the right hands. I'm betting on it. If I'm wrong, then D'Artagnan still won't be in Paris for some time yet. He'll be delivering the diamond studs to Constance, and Constance is an agent for the TIA.''

"You have thought it out quite well," said Andre.

"I sure as hell hope so," Lucas said. "But we're not out of the woods yet."

"What are these two studs that they are so dangerous?" said Andre.

"I can't be sure," Lucas said, "but I think they're something quite old-fashioned. I think that they're bombs."

There was a soft knocking at the door and Cardinal Richelieu said, "Come in."

The Count de Rochefort entered. "Milady de Winter, Your Eminence."

Richelieu smiled. "We have dispensed with secret rendez-vous, I see. I find that most convenient. Show Milady in."

"Your Eminence," de Rochefort said, inclining his head in a respectful bow and backing out the door. A moment later, Milady entered.

"Ah, Countess," Richelieu said, rising to his feet. "How good of you to come to me directly, for a change. I was growing weary of our elaborate precautions. Am I to take it that our business has been concluded successfully?"

Casually, as if it were an afterthought, the cardinal held out his hand, palm down, to Milady. She bowed low and kissed his ring.

"I no longer have need for stealth, Your Eminence," she said, "since I now possess a *carte blanche* from yourself that grants me immunity from virtually anything."

Richelieu smiled. "Yes, I can see where that would be a useful thing to have. However, take care that you do not abuse it. What was granted can just as easily be rescinded. Have you obtained those items which we spoke about?"

"I have, Your Eminence," Milady said. She handed him a small golden jewelbox.

Richelieu took the box from her and opened it. Inside, resting on a cushion of mauve velvet, were two diamond studs.

"Excellent," he said. "I trust that you were not overly inconvenienced to obtain them?"

Milady smiled her dazzling smile. "It was my pleasure, Your Eminence."

"I'm certain that it was," said Richelieu. "You have done very well, Milady." He crossed the room and opened a drawer in his desk, removing from it a weighty purse. "You have done France a great service," he said. "Please take this on account. Come back and see me again after the ball and we shall discuss this matter further."

"You are most generous, Your Eminence. I am always glad to be of service."

"The Count de Rochefort will see you to your carriage," Richelieu said.

"Oh, please, do not trouble the count, Your Eminence," said Milady. "I have found that I quite enjoy being able to go where I please these days, now that I have your official pass to grant me safe conduct."

Richelieu chuckled. "As you wish, Milady, although I think the Count de Rochefort will be sorely disappointed."

In the corridor, she flashed Richelieu's *carte blanche* at the guards and was allowed to pass without even being questioned.

"You see, Adrian, how easy it all is?" she said. She felt the little transmitter hidden in the inside pocket of her cloak. "Richelieu is as good as dead. Now all we have to do is see to the king and queen. First, Anne. Then, Richelieu goes to serve God in His own kingdom. The blast should draw everyone to that end of the palace and they won't discover Anne's body for hours, which will allow me plenty of time to attend to Louis. It will all happen very quickly and efficiently and then, Adrian, you can rest. In peace."

She turned into the corridor that led to the queen's chambers. Again, a brief display of Richelieu's signature and the added words, "An urgent message for Her Majesty," were all that was needed to get her past the guards. She knocked upon the door of the queen's outer chambers and was greeted by the queen's valet, Germain.

"I must see the queen at once," she said. "Tell Her Majesty that Countess de Winter has arrived with an urgent message from abroad."

Germain admitted her into the outer chamber, standing aside to let her pass and then closing the door behind her.

"Wait here, please, Milady. I will announce you."

The moment Germain turned his back on her, Milady leapt upon him with a knife.

They found the little peephole in the panel and looked through. They were greeted by the sight of King Louis's nude posterior. His Majesty was making preparations for the grand ball and he was surrounded by attendants, each holding up a luxurious garment for his inspection. However, at the moment, the king was not paying attention to any of the items of clothing being offered for his perusal. He was otherwise engaged. Standing regally before a full-length mirror and wearing nothing but a pair of high-heeled red velvet shoes with golden buckles and a scarlet silk garter around his left thigh, the king was examining his reflection with open admiration, turning first slightly to the left, then slightly to the right. He was as pale as a corpse and he had further exaggerated his royal pallor by liberally dusting himself with powder.

"I feel like a damn pervert," said Delaney, pulling back from the peephole to let Cobra have a look. The agent put his eye to the peephole and remained there, saying nothing.

"Look, I'll tell you what," said Finn. "One of us has got to find a way to get to Richelieu. You stay here and cover the king. I'll go back and figure out a way to get past those guards outside the queen's chambers. I'll see if I can't get Sparrow to distract them. Okay?"

Cobra did not reply, being intent upon observing Louis.

Finn nudged him. "You hear what I said?"

"Yeah," said Cobra. "I never saw anyone put a beauty mark *there* before." He looked away from the peephole. "Try to get through to the cardinal's chambers if you can. Don't kill anyone unless you absolutely have to."

"I've done this sort of thing before, you know," said Finn.

"Sorry. I guess I'm just on edge. Good luck, Delaney."

"Same to you."

Finn moved quickly back down the passageway, heading toward the queen's bedroom. Anne was seated at her writing table, with "Constance" by her side. The queen was wringing her hands and working herself up into an agitated state.

"Oh, Constance, Constance, I was such a *fool*," she was

saying, as Finn put his eye to the peephole. He saw that the queen's back was to the panel behind which he stood. If he opened it a crack, he might be able to attract Sparrow's attention and signal her to get the queen out of the way for a moment or two.

"Be strong, Your Majesty," said Sparrow. "Have faith, D'Artagnan will return with the diamond studs, I'm sure of it."

"But suppose that he does not return," the queen said, "or suppose that he does not return in time? Richelieu knows everything! Think of all the obstacles he must have set in your Gascon's path! The cardinal is out to ruin me! Oh, how I despise that man!"

Finn eased the panel open just a crack and tried to catch Sparrow's eye. The queen was only yards away from him, so he could not risk making any noise. He could only hope that the agent would glance in his direction. As he stuck his head out, the door to the queen's bedroom opened and Germain stumbled in.

"Germain!" said Constance, "how dare you enter without knocking! You know that the—"

Germain fell face down upon the floor. A dagger protruded from between his shoulder blades. Anne let out a shriek and fainted. Sparrow bolted through the door. Finn opened the panel and barreled out into the room, following hard on Sparrow's heels.

As Milady plunged the dagger into Germain's back, Taylor seized control. Furiously, Milady tried to subdue him and, for a moment, they were at an impasse, each personality struggling to dominate the other.

Germain sank to his knees, hands clawing for the dagger in his back. He could not reach it. He glanced over his shoulder and saw Milady standing there, rooted to the spot, eyes glazed over, shaking as if with St. Vitus's dance. He crawled forward on his hands and knees, trying to cry out, to call the guards, but all that would escape his lips was a strangled gasping for breath. He struggled to his feet, backing away from Milady, who stood there quivering, seemingly entranced, her fingers hooked like the talons of some predatory bird, clutching at the air. It took his last ounce of strength to reach the queen's bedroom door. As Germain opened it, he died.

Taylor stood in the center of the room, drenched in perspiration, breathing heavily. He was dizzy and his head felt as though it had been squeezed in a vice, but he had won. His hands were shaking and he fought to calm himself, to steady his frazzled nerves. He took a deep breath and reached into the pocket of his cloak for the transmitter that would trigger the tiny, but immensely powerful, explosive charges hidden within the synthetic diamond studs now in the cardinal's possession. It wasn't even necessary for them to be on his person. The blast would take out the entire wing of—

The door flew open and a young woman burst into the room, holding a laser in her hand. As she fired, Taylor threw himself to one side. The tiny transmitter fell to the floor. As she fired a second time, Taylor rolled and pulled out his own laser and shot Sparrow, who never had a chance to fire a third time. Finn threw open the door. Taylor raised his weapon and fired again, but Finn ducked back out of the way in the nick of time and the deadly beam passed by him. Sparrow crawled forward, reaching for the transmitter. Her hand closed around it.

"Guards!" shouted Taylor, getting quickly to his feet. *"Guards!"*

The two men stationed outside the queen's chambers responded immediately and rushed in. As Finn glanced out from behind the door, hoping to get off a shot, Taylor quickly pointed at him and said, "An assassin! Save the queen!"

The guards drew their rapiers and ran forward as Delaney slammed the door, cursing. As the guards pounded at the door, Taylor moved toward Sparrow, who had died clutching the transmitter in her hand. As he started to bend over, he felt Milady surfacing within him once again. He froze, doubled over, trying to force her down, to stay in control.

"Run, Adrian," she said. *"Run, save yourself!"*

"*No!*"

"Run, I said!"

The door flew open and one of the guards was knocked off his feet as Delaney engaged the other with his rapier, still holding his laser in his other hand and trying to get off a shot at Taylor.

Milady ran.

Finn fired, but missed Taylor and got the guard who was getting back up off the floor. The other guard froze at the sight of the laser beam and Finn took advantage of his astonishment to smash the handguard of his rapier into the man's face. The guard crumpled to the floor.

He ran to Sparrow's side, saw that she was dead, then noticed the tiny box she clutched in her hand. He pried her fingers away from it and carefully put it in his pocket, then ran after Taylor.

As she ran down the corridor, Milady kept glancing over her shoulder. She was almost to the end of the corridor when she looked back and saw Delaney coming after her. She stopped, raised her weapon, and fired wildly. Delaney dropped to the floor and rolled, but as he raised his own weapon, Milady turned the corner—

—and ran right into Lucas Priest. They both fell to the floor and Milady lost her grip upon her laser. Seeing her drop the weapon, Andre was on her in an instant. For a moment, they rolled around, thrashing like wrestlers as Milady screamed hysterically, raking Andre's face with her fingernails, going for the eyes. Andre grabbed a fistful of her hair and slammed her head against the floor, once, twice, three times. Milady went limp and Andre quickly patted her down, searching for other weapons.

Finn arrived upon the scene to see Lucas standing over Andre, holding both his and Milady's weapons as Andre searched her.

"Dead?" he said.

"Alive," said Lucas, "but out cold. Were we in time?"

Finn took a deep breath. "Just barely," he said. He looked up. "We've got company."

Guards were running toward them from both ends of the hall, rapiers drawn.

"I left one guard dead back there and one unconscious. If

he comes to, we're going to be in a lot of trouble.''

"Perhaps not," said Andre, rising to her feet. She held a piece of paper in her hand.

As the cardinal's guards ran up, Lucas quickly hid the lasers and drew his rapier. "We're going to have to bluff our way through," he said.

"What is this? What's going on?" said a lieutenant in the cardinal's guard, arriving at the head of a group of five men. They were joined at once by six other guards who had come running from the opposite end of the hall. They were surrounded. The lieutenant glanced at Lucas, frowning. "Captain?" he said. "Do I know—"

"It's all right," said Andre, approaching him. "These men are with me."

Finn and Lucas exchanged quick, uneasy glances.

"And who are you? What have you done with this woman? Speak and be quick about it!"

"This woman is an English spy," said Andre. "This man," she indicated Finn, "is an agent of the cardinal who has been working with us to unmask her. This will explain," she said, handing the paper to the officer.

The lieutenant opened the paper and read aloud, "It is by my order that the bearer of this paper has done what has been done. Richelieu."

Finn quickly picked up his cue. "These two officers had arrested this spy and were conducting her to the Bastille when she tried to escape. As you can see by this man's face," he indicated Andre's scratches, "she became very violent and had to be subdued."

"We will take charge of her now, Lieutenant," Lucas said. "You and your men are to be commended for being so alert and responding so quickly. I will be sure to tell the cardinal. What is your name?"

"Lieutenant Bernajoux."

"Good work, Bernajoux. I will include your name in my report to the cardinal. This could mean a promotion for you."

"Thank you, Captain! Thank you very much, indeed!"

"Don't mention it. You're a good man. And now that you and your men have helped us to get things under control, we can go about our business with our prisoner and you can return to your posts."

"Yes, sir!" The lieutenant looked around at the other guards. "Well? You heard the captain. We've got matters well in hand. Go back to your posts!"

The lieutenant saluted Lucas, turned smartly on his heel, and marched off with the other guards.

"That was pretty quick thinking," Finn said to Andre.

She grinned. "With you two, one learns to think quickly." She tapped the paper that Bernajoux had handed back to her. "This helped a great deal. I will never regret having learned to read and I am thankful that Reese Hunter took so much trouble in furthering my education to prepare me for this time. I will miss him."

"So will we," said Lucas, remembering how Hunter had saved their lives on their last mission. And now, through Andre, he had helped them once again.

Finn picked up the unconscious Milady. "I think we'd better get while the going is good," he said.

"I'm with you," said Lucas. "Let's head back to the safe-house. We can commandeer a carriage."

As they started walking down the hall, Finn, carrying Taylor in his arms, chuckled.

"I just remembered something," he said. "I left Cobra in a secret passageway, watching the king preen bareass before his mirror."

"Getting him out might prove to be a problem," Lucas said.

"Yeah, his problem," said Delaney. "I think we'll just let him sweat it out."

EPILOGUE ═══════════

It felt good to be back in the comfortable green transit fatigues and relaxing in the First Division lounge at TAC-HQ. Major Forrester was buying, but he did not insist upon their drinking Red Eye, so Finn and Lucas were sipping Irish whiskey and Andre was having her first taste of unblended Scotch. She was still numb from future shock and she couldn't tear her eyes away from the huge window that looked out over the Departure Station. Everything that she had seen so far exceeded her wildest expectations. She felt very small and insignificant.

"Cobra got out that night," Finn was saying. "Fortunately, he still had a comset on him, so they were able to contact him from the safehouse and tell him that it was all over; otherwise, who knows how long he might've been there." Delaney chuckled. "He waited until Anne was asleep. After seeing what had happened to Germain, the poor woman was up half the night. The palace must have been a regular circus after we left. Anyway, Cobra waited until the queen fell asleep, and then he snuck out and stole some of her clothes, bundled himself up in one of her traveling cloaks, and got out of the palace passing as a lady in waiting." Finn laughed. "He's got initiative, I'll say that much for him."

"What happened to Taylor?" said Forrester.

"Sad case," said Lucas. "When he came to, or rather,

when *she* came to, she denied knowing anything about anyone named Adrian Taylor. We didn't believe it at first, but it wasn't long before it became obvious that Taylor had completely lost his . . . *her* mind. She really believed that she was the Countess de Winter.''

"Which gave Cobra the idea to dispense some Draconian justice," Finn said. "When D'Artagnan made it back in time to deliver the diamond studs to the queen so that she could wear them to the ball, Richelieu was forced to make a gesture and give her Taylor's two synthetic studs as a present, in addition to the twelve studs she already owned. Those explosives might have been harmless without the transmitter to trigger them, but Cobra sent a female agent in to join the queen's handmaidens and steal them. Probably a good thing, they would have made a hell of a bang if they ever went off.

"Sparrow was dead, of course, and unfortunately that meant that the TIA had to kill the real Constance Bonacieux, who would have been murdered by the real Milady in any case. Cobra said that she died painlessly while unconscious, but just the same, it was a messy business." Finn sighed and took a long drink. "In a way, Cobra followed the original scenario. He had us turn Milady over to the musketeers."

"They took her to Lille," said Lucas, "where Athos had been the Count de la Fère before he joined the musketeers and the real Milady, Charlotte Backson, had once been his countess. We took part in her trial, for the murder of Constance Bonacieux, among other things, and she was predictably found guilty. Athos turned her over to the executioner of Lille and had her beheaded. She believed she was Milady right up to the very end."

"After that," said Finn, "all that remained was to tie up some loose ends, not the least of which was clocking ahead a few years and altering the memoirs of M. D'Artagnan to make certain changes and delete any references to a couple of soldiers of fortune named Francois D'Laine and Alexandre Dumas. In a way, I'm sorry about that. I wonder how Dumas would have felt if he had seen his own name mentioned in D'Artagnan's memoirs?"

Forrester nodded. "Well, it was a close call," he said, "but you pulled it off. There will have to be some ongoing adjustment monitoring, but you've done your job. I think you can expect another promotion, Priest, and as for you, Delaney, I'm sure you'll be happy to know that the review board took your performance on the mission into consideration and they dropped the charges against you. The officer concerned lodged a formal protest which will go on your record, I'm afraid, but then, considering what your record looks like, I don't think that one more breach of discipline will make much difference. Congratulations."

"Thank you, sir."

"What is to become of me?" said Andre, hesitantly.

Forrester glanced at her and smiled. "Well, I understand you desire an implant. Under the circumstances, I think that's a good idea. You've held up pretty well, considering, but you're liable to break down from sensory overload if we don't do something about it fast. However, implant education is very expensive."

Andre licked her lips and looked from Forrester to Lucas, to Finn and back to Forrester. "I have no money," she said, softly.

Forrester grinned. "That's okay. Soldiers get them free. Welcome to the Temporal Corps."

MORE SCIENCE FICTION!

ADVENTURE